KILLING TIME
IN
BUFFALO

NOVELS BY DEIDRE S. LAIKEN

Death Among Strangers
Killing Time in Buffalo

———

NONFICTION BY DEIDRE S. LAIKEN
Daughters of Divorce
Listen to Me, I'm Angry
Lovestrong
(coauthor: Dorothy Greenbaum, M.D.)

KILLING TIME IN BUFFALO

A Novel by

DEIDRE S. LAIKEN

LITTLE, BROWN AND COMPANY

Boston   Toronto   London

Library of Congress Cataloging-in-Publication Data

Laiken, Deidre S.
    Killing time in Buffalo: a novel / by Deidre S. Laiken.—1st ed.
        p.   cm.
    ISBN 0-316-51223-0
    I. Title.
PS3562.A335K5 1990
813'.54—dc20
                                                    89-49358
                                                    CIP

10 9 8 7 6 5 4 3 2

FG

*Published simultaneously in Canada
by Little, Brown & Company (Canada) Limited*
Printed in the United States of America

For Stuart and for J.T.

———

KILLING TIME
IN
BUFFALO

ONE

I was late. Fran was waiting downstairs. Strung out, my last flash of energy flickering hesitantly, I moved like a record on the wrong speed. I'd been awake now for almost twenty-four hours and without the aid of artificial stimulation, it was a struggle to maintain balance. Fran, on the other hand, was in her glory. She was a speeding bullet, sharp and clear, ready to probe into every corner, to leave no mystery unsolved.

She was determined to find Barry.

That night we'd searched everywhere, combing the streets of Buffalo, making surprise visits to the Rathskeller, Held's all-night bakery, Freddie's Donuts and the little place on Hertle Avenue where you could buy a real New York–style egg cream.

Barry was nowhere to be seen.

*　　*　　*

3

We hadn't found a trace. What we *did* find, were two guys from Tonawanda who'd just returned from the first Grey Line tour of Haight-Ashbury. We followed them back to their place on Elmwood and they told us incredible stories: how the Haight had been transformed into one mind-blowing, psychedelic paradise; how even the bus driver had been stoned on purple sunshine.

This is the perfect place for me. The perfect time. At last I fit in. No one knows about the green house and what happened there. It doesn't matter that I'm different. It doesn't matter that I have no home to return to.
We are all orphans and outlaws here.

We stayed there all night, listening to the Grateful Dead and watching the eerie glow of the single red bulb that burned through the ribbons of marijuana smoke. I tried not to think about September when I'd have to return to the grind of classes and my part time job in the bookstore. This was the Summer of Love. Fran and I had saved just enough money to pay the rent and sustain ourselves. Sure, we'd rather be in San Francisco wearing flowers in our hair or backpacking across Europe. But it just hadn't worked out that way for us. Maybe it wasn't so bad. At least we weren't in school taking multiple-choice tests and writing papers. We weren't living at home under the oppressive weight of parental thumbs and we had liberated ourselves from the necessity of brain-numbing jobs.

It was 1967 and we were on the loose — wild, free, waiting for adventure. Something big was going to happen. Something important. Fran said it was in the stars. We were preparing ourselves, getting ready. Fran believed in fate. I believed in action. Either way, it was clear we were doing a lot more than simply killing time in Buffalo.

■

When I got home there was blood on the door knob.

It was pretty much the same story as the last time. Nothing ghoulish, no dripping globs of red, just a subtle smudge, a fingerprint. I noticed when I tried to open the door that my thumb and the bloody print were a close match. That's when I got the unsettling feeling that whoever had left the print knew something about me.

An image, half-forgotten, flashes behind my eyes. I will not go back there. I will not remember.

Slipping the key into the lock, I pushed the door open with my foot. I cleared my throat. I rattled my keys. If there *was* someone there, I was hoping he'd have the sense to crawl out the bathroom window and down the metal fire escape.

I never knew what to expect these days: the sound of footsteps running through the hall, creaking bedsprings, weirdos lurking in the shadows. Anything was possible. I don't think it would be an exaggeration to say that my life had taken an unpredictable turn.

I sniffed first. It was one of those crazy inexplicable habits. I guess I believed that if there had been an intruder, I'd smell him. Maybe I was just stalling for time.

I hated doing this.

I checked the usual spots. There were no notes. Nothing was dramatically out of place. But when I walked past the bathroom, something made me stop: an inkling, a suspicion, a fuzzy glimpse of a small detail not-quite-right.

That's when I saw the splotches of red on the mirror. Like the fingerprint, they were subtle, barely there.

She is smoothing down the long auburn hair. She is putting on the rouge and the lipstick. But something is wrong. Blood. There is blood on the walls and the windows. Blood dripping from the sink. When she turns to look at me, I see the places on her arms and her legs, the gouges in her skin that she has cut with the knife. She smiles. I look away. This is not supposed to be happening. I am not supposed to be here. I close the door and hide in my bedroom.

Examining the marks, I caught a reflection of myself framed by the blood.

It was me all right; completely unkempt, my hair a wild mass of untamed frizz, my eyes shot with red and slightly dilated; a trace of something sticky clinging unattractively to my chin. This was a far cry from the girl who only months before had been steadfastly ironing her hair into submission, who had never once missed an opportunity to cleanse, moisturize and tone, who had been a soldier, unquestioned in her dedication to the pursuit of eternal beauty and daily good grooming. I was horrified. I was, as my mother so often warned on her good days, "letting myself go."

It was time to pull myself together, to do the thing. I closed my eyes and imagined my brother, Leon. This was my technique, the one that had always worked for me in the past. Sometimes I held my breath and counted backward; other times I just thought about the green house on Long Island where we'd grown up; where Leon and I had tapped out messages on the thin wall that separated our bedrooms, and where we'd shared the secret that shaped our lives. It happened instantaneously. There he was: his sallow complexion, his blue-black hair. Next came the face. Not a smiling face. Nothing as ordinary as that. The image that floated around in the murky depths of my mind was of my brother wearing a familiar expression, something midway between concentration and disdain. I guess most people would call it a smirk. I called it the lemon-look.

I began to breathe like Leon: short, asthmatic breaths, until I felt another me was breathing. Being Leon was safe, rational, in total and unquestionable control. Not being me was a relief. It would make everything easier to figure out.

I do this alone in the bedroom, after I see her hide things and talk to the people who are not there. Leon is not home yet. He is still in school. The sun is very bright. There are no shadows to crawl into. The fear knots in my stomach. I can run or I can stay. But no one will believe my story. I am only a child. She is the adult. I breathe while I wait for Leon.

When I opened my eyes, I saw the murderer's thumbs. Mine. They were gripping the edge of the sink.

Leon was the one who discovered that's what they were called. When we were still kids, he came upon it in some medical journal or one of the obtuse science magazines he got in the mail. I remember him reading it out loud to my mother in the yellow kitchen.

"A broad, short thumb and nail with a blunted tip," he'd said as he grabbed my hand and held it up to the light. "A genetic trait."

I was marked for life. Only one other person in my family had murderer's thumbs. My uncle Sidney, and he was dead. Leon liked to speculate what twist of genetic fate gave me the thumbs and not him, which only made me more self-conscious. In high school it got so bad that I'd hide them inside my palms until the pins and needles turned into cramps that shot down my wrists.

I thought I was all over that. But here I was doing it again, letting Leon get the better of me, conjuring up all sorts of primitive, superstitious magic, scrambling to reestablish the connections I was hoping I no longer needed.

I promise Leon I will never tell anyone again. They never believe us. They say we are lying, that we imagine things. That we are bad seeds.

Leon wipes up the blood in the bathroom with a paper towel. She covers the cuts with loose trousers and long sleeves.

She smiles when she answers the telephone.

I reached down beneath the sink for a sponge. Looking away from my disheveled reflection, I cleaned the blood from the mirror. I wasn't going to let any of this get the better of me. I wasn't going to regress, to become Leon's pathetic, helpless little sister. We are grown-ups now. He is in Chicago. I am in Buffalo. We no longer live in the green house. I am finally free. It is all over. Nothing, no one, can ever terrify me again.

■

"Renee, can't you hurry up? We'll miss prime time." Fran's voice had a cutting edge, a hint of irritation. She was ready to leave. The motor was running.

I put on the beige raincoat with the epaulets on the shoulders and smoothed my hair back in a ponytail clipped with a barrette. This was the style Fran insisted worked best. She called it "toning down my look."

By the time I reached the first landing, she was already tapping her fingernails against the wall. I composed myself. There was no sense telling her about the blood now. There'd be plenty of time when we were finished.

I am used to not telling. I am used to secrets. I pretend to be funny. I crack jokes. People laugh. I am the class clown. The wise guy. A scream. It is my disguise. But the terror is always there. If they only looked they would see it. Beneath my skin. Pushing up through my smile. No one looks. Leon is right. People close their eyes on our nightmare.

"Let's not screw this one up," she said. "I'm really psyched."

She was wearing a navy cape that stood out from her torso like a wool umbrella. Gold earrings glittered in her pale ears. Her hand grasped a leather bag that we both knew was deceptively slim.

We inspected each other carefully, tilting and turning, checking for the ever-present loose thread, or telltale slip. Fran opened a bobby pin with her teeth and slipped it over my stray hairs. She stood back, an artist admiring her work. This was all part of our ritual. Part of the transformation.

"How do I look?" I asked.

"Like a matron."

We both smiled. It was one of Fran's words. Matron, as in the bourgeois, lifeless, robots who'd been hammered into stupefying dullness by the three M's: monogamy, mortgages, and maternity. It was everything we'd sworn not to be, yet everything we desperately tried to emulate in our present, meticulously arranged costumes.

■

We never talked on the way. Anticipation could be dangerous, and planning was a definite jinx.

I pressed my head against the window and watched as the dreariness of Buffalo flickered past us. Rows of Victorian homes gave way to endless highways spotted with flat, concrete malls: cement chicken coops peopled with consumers feathered in duck down and fur.

The sky had become an iridescent splash of gray. It was as close to a sunny day as we were likely to get. This was, after all, Buffalo. Gray was the official color of the sky, the air, the skin of anyone crazy enough to live here for more than six months. Fran, of course, fit the bill. Her parents were transplanted midwesterners, but she'd been born in Millard Fillmore Hospital. A native Buffalonian, she understood the appeal of the regional specialties: over-cooked roast beef on salty Kimmelwick buns and bony chicken wings slathered in hot sauce. And although she loathed the practice, she could flatten her A's with the best of them.

It was different for me. I was in my third year at the university, and I still disliked the place. I was here by default. Buffalo certainly hadn't topped my list of colleges. It had been my "safety." Then things got dangerous. My alternatives dwindled, until I was left with only one offer. Like a bride at a shotgun wedding, I simply had no choice. It was this, or nothing; this university or some mind-cramping, provincial junior college where I could major in secretarial skills or home economics. Besides, I couldn't live at home. I had to get as far away from her — from the two of them — as I possibly could.

Fran disapproved of my attitude toward her native city. She found it tedious, predictable. It would be simplistic to say that Fran merely loved Buffalo. It was more than that. She was enthralled, captured, mystified by it. "You don't understand," she'd explain when I complained about the long tunnel-like winters and the air that smelled like a rotten tooth.

"It's atmosphere. It's character."

Then, as if to prove her point, she'd tell me the story of the anarchist's handkerchief.

It had happened more than half a century ago. McKinley was president. The Pan-American Exposition was in full swing. Standing confidently on an unguarded receiving line, President McKinley shook hands with his public. Then, from the shadow of a towering elm, the anarchist approached. In his hand he held a white linen handkerchief, beneath which was secreted a loaded pistol. He fired several shots. McKinley didn't die right away. He lingered for two weeks, during which time Buffalo became the capital of the United States.

During her summer internship at the historical society, Fran had been chosen to place both the gun and the handkerchief in the glass exhibition case. It was then that she'd felt the electricity, "the vibrations" as she called them.

"At that moment, when I touched the gun, I knew," she'd whisper in a breathy half sigh, "that my fate and McKinley's, this city and my life were all intertwined in some mystical way."

Not normally swayed by psychic premonitions, the paranormal or anything remotely spiritual, I found myself chilled to the bone. This was all part of Fran's allure, her attraction. Our friendship wasn't based on anything as predictable as shared interests or common experiences. No way. We were in this for the adventure, the high, the promise that together we would elevate ourselves from the ordinary, push past our own inhibitions, and free our lives from the dreaded possibility of matronhood — forever.

■

"Let's synchronize watches," Fran said as she pulled up the emergency brake and fit the car neatly between the white lines. We had arrived at our destination, a mall: bland, complacent, a sitting target.

She checked the gold watch with the brown suede band. It was a quarter to twelve. Prime time because lunch breaks were just beginning. Distracted by the sounds of their own hunger, salesgirls paid less attention to us than they did to the institutional clocks which told them when to leave for their lunch breaks.

We checked each other one last time. Straight. Normal. We could be anyone.

"Let's think of THE NOW," Fran said.

I nodded my head and tried to imagine white clouds drifting through a blue sky. It was a yoga thing we always did first. It made us better. But this time I kept seeing the fingerprint, and how my thumb had naturally curled into the trace of red. I wondered if that was an omen, a bad vibe.

"Ready?" Fran asked. She had that clear, serene look.

"Don't forget why we're here."

I didn't answer because it was something we never actually said out loud. We didn't have to. We both knew the reason.

We were here to steal.

TWO

The perspiration stops as soon as I press my fingers against the glass door. Miraculously, I'm calm. My face is a plaster mask, every grimace frozen, the slightest twitch or telltale blink purposefully monitored.

I'm moving through the store. Fluorescent lights illumine racks of clothing. Glass cases containing jewelry, handbags and perfume are arranged in neat L's. I watch as Fran's hip disappears behind a metal rack. We never watch each other. Once inside, we operate individually, except for times when we might need help removing an especially large or awkward object.

My hands run across wool, cotton and cashmere. The contrast of sensations against my skin is a mock foreplay, a stimulation essential for what will follow. Beneath the mask I'm watching, checking, making mental notes. I know the position of every salesgirl — the location of every dressing room.

Fastened to each garment with a tether of white plastic

14

is a tag which I pretend to study, but the blue ink is confusing. Prices and sizes become a jumble, a secret code stamped across perforated white paper. I know by habit where to look first. Anything under fifty dollars is forbidden. Anything not of the very best quality is discarded, thrown into the trash as is, to be discovered by an incredulous garbageman or a curious passerby.

Today I'm taking my time. We have two and a half hours. I don't want to make any mistakes. I savor every second that my bag is empty and I'm innocent. With smug self-righteousness, I watch as a suburban matron compares price tags and tugs at her girdle. Two teenagers rummage through the sales merchandise. They immediately attract the attention of a wary, gray-haired saleswoman who pushes toward them, asking if she can be "of any help." If anyone asks me if I need assistance I never answer "just looking." Sometimes I simply say, "No thank you," an attempt to be firm, yet polite. Other times, I request a specific item, sending the saleswoman shuffling back and forth on fruitless missions.

I pass a display of summer coverups and my first temptation is to whisk two or three off the rack and try them on. But I remember that light-weight merchandise should be chosen last, it's easier to pack and can be rolled into tiny balls and wedged in among heavier articles.

Everything here is very white, very clean. Beams of light dance off the corners of display cases. When I get close to them, the highly polished metal racks reflect distorted images of my lips and teeth.

I pace the aisles silently, concentrating on my feet as they move over the black and white commercial flooring. Anything I want can be mine. The power swells until I'm almost dizzy. A childhood dream. To be let loose in a toy store, to be locked in Macy's overnight. I remember staring at the pink and white dolls in the organdy dresses: perfect dreams encased in glass and locked away from my touch. There were so many things I wanted then: baby dolls and white boots, souvenirs and plastic pinwheels. Leon and I always knew growing up would be better. We saw through the lie that childhood was the best time. Being grown-up, without forgetting the old dreams, that was the secret — the way to have it all.

With Fran's help, there are no locks, no cases and no doors I can't open.

I'm clutching several linen suits and making my way toward the curtained area, behind which the dressing rooms are arranged like impersonal office cubicles. Head erect, imperious, I sail past the clerk who forgets to hand me the colored plastic hook with the holes indicating how many garments I'm holding. Fran's right about prime time. The fluorescent lights and the dreariness cause hunger to take precedence over diligence. No matter, I've come prepared for everything. In the outside pocket of my tan bag, arranged carefully, is a series of red and green plastic hooks. If the need arises, I can substitute one of mine for one of theirs.

In the poorly lit cubicle, the curtain makes a squeaking sound as I move it across the metal bar. Broken garment hooks and a chipped stool intrude upon the emptiness. When I'm undressed, the light directly over the mirror shines down on my skin, giving it a disturbing bumpy look. Fran and I have classified this decor "early cellulite." Thinking of it now, I smile to myself and slip easily out of my one-piece shift.

Caught in the frenzy of the act, I rarely have time to examine the articles I try on, quickly buttoning up, pulling over, checking to make sure the size is right. Much later, when I'm miles away from the mirrored cell with the hook and the stool, I can see the errors of my haste: dresses that cling to my backside, pants that dig unattractively into my thighs, blouses that pull across the back. New things quickly become old as they're piled into shopping bags and discarded like ancient rubbish. Sometimes Fran and I wear curly wigs and return our mistakes. She, claiming they were gifts for a wedding shower or an anniversary, me, crinkling my forehead and explaining in earnest that my mother still doesn't know my proper size. Occasionally, we receive cash refunds. These are of no use to us. Neither Fran nor I like money. We hate the sound of the cash register as it rings up a sales and we're unaccustomed to waiting for slow-witted cashiers to wrap articles in tissue paper and hand us our legal purchases. We prefer credits. Then we can exchange in a manner that bypasses the use of money altogether. A barter system that conforms to our secret rules.

Nothing I have in this batch fits right. The suits are too tight and the string sweater reveals the outline of my bra underneath. A shame. I sigh, hoping the lethargic clerk is still slumped in the vinyl chair, uninterested in my comings and goings.

As I swish boldly out of the dressing area, garments held an arm's length away, I notice Fran moving stealthily through sportswear. Her satchel is still innocently slim, so I know we're both on the same schedule. She's sorting through the size twelves. I approach her on the way to the eights. "Any luck?" I whisper.

"I'm ready for a trip," she answers. I nod and move away. Fran needs room. I avert my eyes as she heads for the changing rooms.

Wearily, I poke at some pastel slacks. Everything here is beginning to look like a nurse's uniform. The approaching summer means pink, blue and yellow: colors that belong on china dolls in glass cases and the girls in high school with Peter Pan collars and circle pins — both untouchable — both forbidden.

I finger the hem of a black-and-white mididress. The new length. I choose three from the rack. In my mind, I fold and roll them up in the tan bag. A neat fit.

This time the clerk is busy talking to a customer and chewing a soft wad of pink gum that pokes in and out of her teeth as she speaks. I lower my gaze and walk by.

Two of the dresses fit. I don't try on the third. In the next cubicle, I hear Fran as she scrapes the stool against the floor. Quickly and deftly, I roll up the two mididresses and place them compactly in the bag. Zipped up, it still holds its shape. There's no telltale bulge. Nothing sloppy here. I hang the two extra hangers inside the third dress, and holding them securely, make my way out of the curtained area.

I walk back to the dresses and place the garment with the two hidden hangers back in its exact spot. No one will check as long as everything appears in order. I tarry at the dresses, pretending to look things over carefully. But I'm unable to see anything clearly now. I can feel the rush of my own blood and the throbbing of the vein in the left side of my neck. My eyes peer out from behind the mask. No one is beside or behind me. I begin to walk slowly. Always slowly. Not toward the door, but directly to the cosmetics counter. There, I look inquisitively at boxed moisturizers and lipsticks. The polished chrome easily reflects anyone who might be lingering, following, suspecting. I tap my fingers against the countertop, feigning impatience. Letting out a planned, frustrated sigh, I turn on my heel and walk reluctantly through the swinging door.

An imaginary arm grips my shoulder. I catch my breath in dread. Dry lips. Shaking hands. I whirl through the door and move quickly across the parking lot. With the tiny silver key, I unlock the trunk of the car. The cartons on the left side are empty. They're mine. The ones on the right are filled with crumpled garments, a leather belt and a designer scarf. As usual, Fran is way ahead of me. All the boxes must be filled before we can leave. My bag is now empty of all incriminating evidence. I could stop now, quit while I'm ahead. But that's impossible. I'm in this all the way. Rebel, outlaw, nemesis of the mall, saboteur of the Capitalist State, I smooth my untamed hair, hum a line of "Good Vibrations," and dutifully return to the store to fill my quota.

THREE

The highway flashed gray and yellow. Fran's mouth was a twist of red reflected in the car mirror.

No one followed us. There was no moment of breathtaking fear, no high-speed chase, no whirring red lights or grinding engines. The disguises had worked. We'd pulled it off without a hitch.

Leaning my elbow on the open window, I pretended to be someone else: a homebound commuter, a God-fearing, law-abiding citizen, a housewife who baked bundt cakes topped with swirls of homemade frosting. Fran and I could be anyone we imagined. The merchandise that bulged and swelled the cartons in the trunk were not frivolous items. They were disguises that enabled us to acquire still more disguises. We were losing ourselves in layers.

I want to disappear when it happens. I want to make myself small and dissolve into the television. To be a doll

in a doll house. A character in a family sitcom. Leon says
that this is dangerous. I must be careful. Today she is
talking on the telephone. She is using the other voice.
Leon makes me pick up the extension. I hear a dial tone
and the voice. There is no one on the other end. See, Leon
says. It's coming. Get ready.

Fran liked to talk as she drove back. It relaxed her.
Unfortunately, it also distracted her. Red lights, stop
signs, speed limits, became inconveniences, annoying re-
strictions which inhibited her train of thought. More than
once, I thought about driving, but the Saab had a stick
shift. My mechanical abilities, limited to activities such
as plugging in major appliances and pushing down toast-
ers, did not stretch far enough to include shifting, braking,
clutching and steering simultaneously. I was Fran's pris-
oner. Trapped in a vehicle which whizzed like a red bat-
mobile through the narrow streets of Buffalo, my only
remaining option was to listen to her stream of consciousness and pray we didn't hit a pedestrian.

This afternoon's topic was her younger sister, Anna.
Fran worried that Anna would marry the Polish mortician
she'd been dating. I closed my eyes and saw a tall, heavy-
ish man with a too-small hat. No good. I couldn't even
remember Anna's face.

Fran's family was exotic in its plainness. Her father
wore a green mechanic's suit with his name embroidered
in red just under the left pocket. Her mother, outfitted in
a checkered apron, seemed perpetually suspended in the
fragrant air over the electric range. She'd glued a picture
of a poodle with rhinestone eyes on the inside cover of

their toilet seat, and chosen a shiny blue rug with President Kennedy's face as the centerpiece of their paneled living room.

That's the sort of parents Fran had. I'd never known anyone like them. They were a combination of the Cleavers, the Nelsons and the Beverly Hillbillies. Fran liked to say they were pushed out from a pastry tube.

Now she was talking dangerously fast. The speedometer was quivering. She ran a red light on a four-way intersection. I warned her about being more careful. She ignored me.

"Does Anna really think that marrying this guy with the funeral parlor right under his apartment will make her happy?"

I shook my head in disbelief. Marriage was a goof. Death was an ugly rumor, yet to be proven real.

I knew, despite Fran's concerns, there was no possibility we could save Anna. She was a matron-in-the-making, destined for a paneled living room and a rhinestone-studded toilet seat cover all her own. Sometimes we gave her things we took in the hope that their magic would rub off, that in some way they would transform her. Fran thought they might pique her curiosity, make her startled, suspicious. But Anna only took our gifts and stared out from dull eyes. She arranged Peter Max dishes and the zebra-striped sheets, the psychedelic paperweights and the tie-dyed nightgowns in the maple hope chest and wordlessly smiled in oblivious appreciation. It was hard for me to believe that Anna was Fran's sister. "Oh, but it's true," Fran said when I first told her that. She emphasized the word true, holding on to it, drawing it out. "We're not as normal as you think."

Normal is a word I am forbidden to use. Like "crazy" it is a measurement reserved for other people. She is not crazy. She is not normal. She has episodes. That's what we call them. They are moments when time stops, when the past and the present merge and our lives are twisted into hers.

I laughed. Fran only knew that my father was a shirt salesman who traveled constantly and that my mother was an invalid. It was easy not to talk about them, easy because families were boring, and besides Leon was her real interest.

"How much would you give me for Leon?" I'd ask.

My brother, and her lack of one, was a real sore spot between us.

"Three Annas and a hundred Mel and Evelyns," she answered.

"You say that now. You don't know what it's like to be tormented by your big brother."

"No one's ever satisfied with what they've got. Don't you agree?"

You cannot have it, Leon says as he pries the turtle from my hand. It is still moving, turning its tiny head toward the light. He flushes it down the toilet. I watch the brown shell swirl around in the moving water. I had already given it a name. It was my friend. Leon forbids me to cry. *I should be happy. At least he hasn't crushed it. Stomped on it and made me see what can happen. I fight back the tears. If he sees them he will tell me about the fish. It is a story I can not bear to hear. He is sorry about the fish. Sorry he didn't force me to look, didn't hold my face and make me see. To learn a lesson, he says. For my own good.*

The ride was almost over. The excited, twitchy feeling was gone now. I watched as the lights changed on Delaware Avenue and the gloomy Victoriana loomed from behind the oak trees.

Fran slowed down too. This was how it always was. We had returned to our other world, the one where we hid the disguises in the back of our closets and never told anyone what we did when we drove out to the malls and came home damp and drained.

Cautiously, the Saab rounded the corner. Fran pulled up the emergency brake. We scurried back to the trunk and piled up our cartons.

I let her walk ahead of me. I enjoyed playing with the idea of how we looked together. Where I was round and full, Fran was flat and narrow; where I was dark and frizzy, she was blond and smooth. Sometimes I thought that Fran was me upside down.

We parked directly in front of 72 Days Park. Which sounded a lot better than it actually was, since there was nothing even remotely green or pastoral about it. Days Park was a circular dead end on the edge of a section of downtown called Allentown. It was surrounded by hideous brick buildings, all crying out for rehabilitation. The "park" was a shapeless lump of hard ground that barely sprouted a blade of grass. It always seemed darker here than anywhere else, and that was no small feat, since most of Buffalo was the Land of the Midnight Sun until some time in late May.

In keeping with her mystic connection to the city of her birth, Fran thought our location was perfect. "Picturesquely desperate," was how she described it. Furthermore, she believed Days Park was more than a random choice dictated by poverty and its proximity to Elmwood Avenue, the hub of student life. No, she insisted. We were fated to live here. Nothing was accidental.

I wasn't so sure about the fate part. I'd moved here in my sophomore year. It had been Barry's place. No one lives in the dorms anymore, he'd said. Of course he was right. Dorms had curfews and singsong rules like "mandatory open door, when a boy comes to visit, two feet on the floor." Dorms were for sorority girls, hopeless suburban throwbacks, ex-cheerleaders, professional virgins, members of the student council and editors of the yearbook. The goal was to get away, to live on our own. Sex, pot and politics were all forbidden in the dorms. Sex, pot and politics were what we craved. Of course our obsession with the first two severely limited our energy for the third.

Days Park was walking distance from the college and a quick ride from the stellar attractions of the city: the movie theaters and the burlesque house. It was the center of Buffalo's large Indian population and was flanked on one side by a bar that was smoke-filled and crammed with very large, very drunk men who wore flannel shirts and soiled caps. Most of them were Iroquois who'd left reservations close to the city and in nearby Ontario. They certainly didn't look like the Indians I'd watched chasing cowboys on TV. These men had none of that lean, proud look. Most were fleshy and slow and indescribably sad. One of them, a guy named Duane, occupied the basement room in our building.

On the other side of Days Park was a towering brick tenement with rickety wooden fire escapes that looked very close to collapse. The bar and the tenement were both owned by our landlord, Ken McCullum.

The hallways of Days Park were all painted institutional green. Fran called it "McCullum green" since Ken painted every hallway and every apartment the identical color. Fran and I painted our own apartments. Hers was white. Mine was a shade of yellow, which at the moment of purchase had seemed cheery enough, but when actually applied to the walls turned sickeningly harsh. "Hmmm," Fran had said when she first came up to look, "being here is like a bad day at the beach."

Probably because we rebelled against the green and rejected McCullum's clumsy and unsubtle propositions, he made the mistake on the buzzers. It was almost certainly a pathetic act of revenge, but we turned it to our advantage.

When he installed bells and mailboxes in the dingy downstairs hallway (a city ordinance he had long ignored) he wrote "Renee Johnsten" on my buzzer and "Fran Weiss" on hers. My immediate impulse, when I saw the mistake, was to correct it.

"Wait a minute," said Fran. "I kind of like it. It's got possibilities."

I wasn't exactly sure what she meant, but I agreed to leave things as they were. After all, everyone who knew us already knew our real names. It didn't seem likely that a total stranger would wander into the gloomy, mildewed halls of 72 Days Park.

Fran dragged her carton across the threshold of #2. I continued up another flight and pushed open the door to #3. Apartment #1 was occupied by Frank Vitale, who was the perfect neighbor for Fran, since he was a codeine addict and rarely stirred before midnight. Vitale was small and dark with deep rings beneath his eyes. Fran thought he was a creep, but I liked his mouth. He had enormous pink lips that moved like fat rubber erasers when he talked. But what was really special about Vitale, what set him apart from the nameless, faceless progression of long-haired weirdos that populated our world, was his drums. Bongo drums. The kind every kid bought in the sixties because it was cool, but no one ever learned to play. For some reason Vitale had taken the time, or had simply had the talent. He could play just about anything on those drums, my personal favorite being his Belafonte-type rendition of the Banana Boat Song, to which Fran and I sang the words in a wild frenzy of teenage nostalgia.

Upstairs next to me, and directly over Fran in #4, was Marshal Sherman. Sherman was Buffalo's leading drug dealer. He talked so fast, and moved so quickly, that Fran and I called him "the flash." He was skinny as a rail and wore pointy leather ankle boots that made a racket as he clip-clopped along the floor (which was Fran's ceiling) during his many sleepless nights.

"I'm going to kill him," Fran would say through

clenched teeth, as she listened to his staccato walk at 2 A.M. "Can't he sit down and take off those goddamn boots?" Inevitably, when we'd go upstairs to complain, Sherman would answer the door in his jockey underpants and ankle boots, offer us everything from black beauties, to meth crystal, to hash, and we'd wind up listening to him talk endlessly right through the next morning.

Fran and I liked living in Days Park. It suited us. But, like many things in our lives, we wanted to change it just a little. We thought it should be renamed "Daze Park."

FOUR

As I gripped the doorknob, I noted that the bloody finger-print had all but disappeared, no doubt I'd wiped it away with my own thumb. Entering the apartment, I made my usual clatter. All clear.

I never go to the purple room without knocking. I never open doors or enter any place without listening first. I might see things. I have learned to be careful.

I breathed a sigh of relief and eased into the worn red armchair in the center of the living room. The loot from my cartons cascaded gracelessly onto the floor. I had no idea where I was going to store all this stuff. My closets were filled to capacity. The only available space was the metal rod in the bathroom. It hung over the defunct tub McCullum had promised to replace. After several months of futile negotiations, I simply gave up and resigned myself to quick showers in the small bathroom at the end of the railroad-type hallway.

I avoided the room with the tub and even took to keeping the door closed. I had an excellent reason. Barry had hung his clothing on that rod. He'd used the tub to store his phenomenology books and the old jazz albums he no longer played.

I hadn't touched a thing since the day he disappeared, except of course to see if he'd taken anything with him. He hadn't.

I poked at the clothes littering the floor. It was doubtful I'd ever wear any of them: a gray gabardine jumpsuit, a stylish black and white checked mididress, a felt vest decorated with peacock feathers. My taste had become wildly eclectic. Not that I *had* any particular taste. Where the concept of quality and style might have once flourished, quantity and compactness now reigned supreme. I took just about anything that simultaneously fit both in my purse and on my body. Need had nothing to do with it. Fran and I agreed we should pay for needs. It was the extras that were free.

We were breaking all the rules and so far we hadn't come close to getting caught. This gave me the heady, omnipotent feeling that I could just keep going — that nothing, not even Leon's stern warnings, could cramp my style. If there was such a thing as a guilty conscience, a vigilant, ever-watchful superego, I guess mine took the form of my brother's voice. It was inescapable, relentless. True, it didn't stop me, but it did slow me down, plague me with doubts, torture me with retribution. Fran tried to counter what she called my "suburban angst," with astrological predictions, tarot card readings and psychic wisdom.

I was torn. Leon didn't believe in magic or sentimen-

tality — only science. And I had grown up under his tu-
telage. Once firmly in the grip of his vise-like control,
there was no getting loose.

*I am nine and he is eleven. Something is changing. I
don't understand. My father is on the road most of the
time. We get shiny postcards: Chicago, Kansas City, Los
Angeles. He is rarely home.*

*But it is my mother who is taking the journeys. Some-
times for a few unexplained hours in the afternoon. Sometimes for an entire day. Watch her, Renee, Leon tells me.
Listen for the lies. I tell Leon I don't hear any lies. He
invites me into his room and lets me look through his
microscope. He adjusts the eye piece so I can see the tiny
amoeba he has stained purple under the lens. His hand
feels hot — burning on my sleeve.*

That's how you observe things, he says.

I am still a child and I don't know what he means.

I always knew there was something special about my
brother. He had an indescribable magic. It was almost as
if Leon could rise above his own childhood. I remember
this most clearly when we played Indian Poker. It was
before things began to change. My mother was still happy.
She laughed a lot, went to her art classes and painted
bright canvases in thick layers of oil. It was the year she
taught me how to cross stitch and how to tweeze my eye-
brows.

Indian Poker was a silly card game my father, who
came home almost every weekend, taught us one Sunday
when the TV lost its vertical hold.

*   *   *

Everyone got one card and held it up against their fore-head. The point was, you could see the other cards but not your own.

We'd all sit around the yellow, simulated-marble, For-mica table, arranging ourselves randomly around Leon, who always took the corner chair closest to the counter. Then the game began. Leon would place a card on his forehead with a flourish, and stare straight ahead as if he was in some sort of trance. It didn't seem the least bit scientific, but it worked every time. I always had this feeling that even when he lost, he'd planned it that way. But losing was rare for Leon. He won nearly every time. It drove my father crazy. My mother smiled at Leon. It was an odd smile, although I didn't realize it then.

I was sure my brother had something up his sleeve. The lemon-look that fluttered across his face confirmed it.

I probably would never have found him out if it wasn't for my alien theory. At about this time, I guess I was feeling out of sync with other kids my age. No doubt a direct result of Leon's premonitions and mysterious hints about what was to come.

Anyway, I developed this nutty concept that I was the only surviving earthling left on a planet in the farthest reaches of the galaxy, and the places I inhabited — my house, the school — were really only plastic sets arranged so the aliens could observe me. It was my one slip into the world of the paranormal and it resulted in the develop-ment of The Thing — the technique of becoming Leon.

One afternoon when I was thinking that maybe I wasn't the only earthling, maybe my whole family was being observed, I passed by the very spot where Leon always sat during Indian Poker. Easing into his chair, I closed my eyes and pretended to be my brother. I guess I figured if I *was* an alien, I could project myself into someone else's body. This was the perfect opportunity for my experiment. No one was home. The door to Leon's room was open. A square mirror hung over his dresser. I remember putting my hand to my forehead as if there was a card there. When I opened my eyes, I saw myself. I unraveled the mystery. I understood how Leon did it. It was the reflection. He had cleverly positioned his chair in a way that he could see himself during the game, leaving the rest of us, quite literally, blind to his antics.

It was a triumph of sorts. But, like most of my victories over Leon, it filled me with dread: I realized I was glimpsing something that had always been there, but was never intended for me to see. I felt frightened at that moment. It was as if Leon had deliberately given me a quick look into a dark room — a room where we would spend the rest of our childhood.

I never told anyone this story until I met Fran. I rarely talked about my life before Buffalo. It was something I'd come here to forget. But, with her psychic leanings, her love for the strange, the unusual, the utterly weird, I knew she'd appreciate it. Of course I was right. Fran doted on my Leon stories. She was insatiable. Sometimes I thought that I was responsible, that my complicated connections to Leon were what got her to concoct the unlikely notion that she too had a brother, someone who had been a product of a very hush-hush liaison between her father and a mysterious stranger. Initially, I dismissed this as one of Fran's more absurd ventures into fantasy, but after a while she began to sound convincing. Finding her long-lost brother became a cause for her, a sacred quest, or as she put it: "my *raison d'être*."

I guess someone more stable would say that Fran was always looking for trouble, that she was never content to leave well enough alone. I didn't see it that way. In this gloomy city of endless winters, Fran was a breath of fresh air, a mad, exciting adventuress. She was always looking for dangerous things to do. She was like a magnet pulling me closer with a force I didn't completely understand.

Fran believed we were charmed, that we could get away with anything. She was ready to expand, to go for the "big time." She called it "The Caper."

"Come on, Renee," she'd say, "let's plan a caper."

Ordinarily, I'd be about two steps behind her, but since Barry's disappearance, I had, admittedly, grown just the tiniest bit cautious. Not Fran. She liked the mystery of it. She wanted to sleuth.

"We can sleuth this one out for ourselves," she told me. "It's a challenge."

That's why we never called the cops.

When I got the first calls, strange breathers with no one speaking, she was thrilled. Later, the notes, in that cramped semifamiliar handwriting, only made her more determined. Then, of course, there were the blood smears. Fran pooh-poohed my fears.

"It's not like anyone's been murdered," she said. "It's just Barry and he's essentially harmless. He's out there," she assured me, "and we'll find him."

I wasn't so sure. Not that the calls and the notes, mostly incomprehensible gibberish with my first name misspelled, scared me. Not exactly. The way my life was now, without all the old rules and limits, I felt as if I was on one long breathless free fall, tumbling wildly through the atmosphere with no direction and nothing anchoring me to earth. Fear wasn't the word. Sometimes, I experienced an odd tingling sensation in my wrists. It was the same feeling I'd had as a child when I stood at the edge of a balcony and looked straight down.

We are on the roof of the aunt's apartment building. We have come up here to escape. She is downstairs in the living room smiling the fake smile. She is eating cake and staring at old photographs of Uncle Sidney. Leon leads me to the edge of the building. I can see the sidewalk, a stretch of gray. The cars move in obedient rows. I pull back. I am vibrating with terror. Leon grips my hand. He wants me to look down. My wrists are throbbing. He moves behind me. I feel his palm push against my back. I close my eyes. I am going to die. I see myself falling through space — torn open, a smash of bloody viscera splattered hideously on the gray sidewalk.

When I open my eyes I am still on the roof. Leon is beside me. His mouth is a grim, unsmiling line. Good, he says. You are doing better.

I don't want to remember, but something triggers that moment. Now I get that weird wrist feeling on level ground. I'll be sitting in a chair or walking down the street and it ripples through me.

I haven't told Fran, but the same two words do it every time.

Sleuth and caper.

FIVE

Ned stood at my door. He was giving me the peace sign and feeling no pain. Spontaneity and surprise were not part of Ned's rather limited repertoire. I knew almost everything that was going to happen next. For one thing, he was still holding Fran's orange coffee mug. This, and the sleepy look in his eyes, told me for sure that he'd just finished brushing her hair.

So far, Ned was the only stranger who had knowingly wandered into 72 Days Park. He'd been looking for someone named Johnsten whose father could give him a deal on body work for his recently dented, but otherwise brand-new, 1967 Saab.

When he came upstairs to me, I reluctantly explained the mix-up on the bells and sent him to Fran. Wasting no time, I promptly called her and previewed what was coming. A man with a chest. And arms. A man who was neither emaciated nor stoned out of his mind; a man whose libido had not yet been overloaded, impaired or destroyed completely. A definite candidate for sex.

The two of them didn't leave the apartment for twenty-four hours.

"Delightful," was how Fran described it. Then she gave him to me.

Individual ownership was, as Fran said, "contrary to the goals of an enlightened society." No running dogs of the Establishment, we decided to make Ned a communal venture. In all truth, our decision wasn't completely political. Sexually speaking, Ned fell short in several areas.

Since he wasn't what you'd call deep, he accepted the arrangement without question. Of course, we never actually explained that we'd planned the whole thing. Fran simply asked him to brush her hair and then told him to go upstairs and borrow a book from me. He lingered in the doorway, gorgeous, blond and completely unruffled. I smiled, unbuttoned the top button of my blouse, offered him a glass of wine, and nature took its predictable course.

Fran said she liked the idea of being someone else's foreplay.

Ned became another adventure, a giddy diversion, for Fran and me. When he wasn't around, we dissected him mercilessly, imitating everything from his flat, Buffalo accent, to his sexual athletics. Once in a while I actually felt a little guilty.

"No one feels guilt anymore," Fran said, when I told her this. "It's a bourgeois emotion. Besides, we're only doing to him what guys have done to us for years. Remember high school? Doesn't it feel better to be on this side of the fence?"

It did feel better. But sometimes it just didn't feel as good as Fran made it sound.

*   *   *

Ned and I slept together for two months. In all that time I never once had an orgasm. But I enjoyed watching. Ned was on the swim team at the university, the only person I knew who was still involved in organized sports. His body was hard and chiseled; his stomach was divided into small, square muscles. He considered intercourse a gymnastic event. I didn't move as much as I was moved on. It was not an unpleasant sensation, but even more pleasant was the thought that Fran and I were sharing a man, even though we were doing it in an odd way — sequentially rather than simultaneously. But more and more, I was having to work myself up psychologically before I slept with him. In this case, desire was three-quarters fantasy. The reality, I could live without.

"Wanna hang out?" Ned was now asking. It was as close as he came to saying I was the object of his desires.

"Wait right here." I pointed to the hall, then made a hasty retreat into my apartment where I pushed the carton of stolen clothing under the bed. Ned was used to secrets. Fran and I certainly had an abundance of them.

"You can come in now."

"Got anything to eat?"

I led Ned to my frost-encrusted refrigerator which held little more than a bowl of brown rice, some vegetables and a container of milk.

"Fran's ordering a pizza, want any?"

Fran had an unnerving way of eating during times of stress, excitement or imminent danger. There was no way I'd be eating for hours. My guts were still in an uproar over our recent heist, Fran's wild drive through the streets of Buffalo and the memory of the bloody fingerprint that continued to linger in the back of my mind.

Ned pulled a fat, yellow joint from his back pocket. "Gotta match?"

I handed him a matchbook with a curled-up cover. While he inhaled, I noticed two things: how his cheeks filled with air like a blowfish, and the name of a bar on the cover of the matchbook. "The Aragon Lounge."

"Have you ever been inside this place?"

Ned's cheeks deflated like a punched-in beach ball. He squinted as he read the name.

"Isn't that the Indian bar on the corner?"

"Yeah, and I'd never step foot in there."

"Don't look at me," Ned said. "I wouldn't go in there if my life depended on it."

He pronounced "on" more like "aan," once more reminding me that despite my hopes for his eventual improvement, Ned would always remain, sadly, a "townie."

"Then how'd it get here?"

"Who knows? Vitale sometimes hangs out with that Indian guy in the basement. Maybe he left it here."

The Indian guy was Duane, and I hadn't seen him or Vitale for weeks.

"What's the big deal anyway?" Ned asked. His eyes were dilating. I knew his coherent moments were fast slipping away.

"Nothing. Forget it. I'm just being paranoid."

I couldn't exactly explain it, but the matchbook made me uneasy. It was a discordant note, something that didn't belong. White people avoided the Aragon. It was just one

of those places we all understood was off-limits. Especially after the night we'd witnessed the assault. Fran and
I, Sherman and Vitale had stood huddled around the window in Sherman's apartment and looked down on the
street as four huge Tactical Patrol Unit cops made a circle
around a drunken Indian and mercilessly pummeled him
with their nightsticks.

"We should do something," I had said.

"Yeah, like what? Call the cops?" Sherman warned us
against messing with the TPU. He'd been on a couple of
civil rights marches in the early sixties, "being in the
belly of the pig," he'd called it. He'd been hosed and
tear-gassed. He figured he'd had enough political activity.
Now he sold dope.

Although we talked about it, we never did anything.
Neither did any of the Indians who'd seen the beating. It
was just another quiet moment of brutality, an example of
bloody justice meted out on a dark, dead-end street.

I slipped the matchbook under a chair cushion. Ned was
staring vacantly up at the ceiling. "White Rabbit" was
playing on the stereo. For a second, I thought I felt
that tingly feeling in my wrists, but then it just went
away.

Ned and I made love. While we were doing it, I tried to
think of other things. Better things.

"Let yourself go," he whispered as he moved slowly
up and down inside me.

But I wasn't going anywhere. The grass, the music and
Ned's considerable talent for sexual endurance, all failed
to stimulate me.

I dredged up my best fantasies, to no avail. My body seemed frozen from the neck down. I was numb, inert, a plastic Barbie doll copulating with her Ken. I wondered if maybe I was ovulating. Fran said that no one ovulated anymore. Everyone we knew was on the Pill. Our bodies were being regulated by a conspiracy of gynecologists with headlights, speculums and rubber gloves.

"I'm coming," Ned whispered.

Since my body was controlled by chemicals, I figured it wasn't really me who answered, "Hurry up."

I don't remember too much of what happened next. There was a pleasant moment when I watched Ned walk naked down the hall toward the bathroom. His ass looked like it was carved out of marble.

Then I heard the scream.

It sounded like a woman's scream, sort of high-pitched and twittery. It was Ned. I ran to the bathroom at the end of the hall. Wrong. The screams were coming from the room with the defunct tub. The door was wide open.

Ned was standing with his hands over his mouth, pointing to something hanging over the curtain rod. At first I only noticed one of my bras swinging oddly between a leather jacket and a pair of Levi's. Ned's finger jabbed at the air. Then I got the message.

My name was written, scrawled, in what looked like drops of black blood over a picture of some sort. It was supposed to be a face, me maybe, with a noose around the neck and hair standing up like one of those magnetic Wooly Willies I used to play with as a child. Beneath my name was the word *die*.

I pulled the note down from the metal rod. It had been sloppily taped up with the bra.

I touched my fingers to the paper and then brought them to my mouth (something I'd once seen Mike Hammer do on TV).

"This isn't blood. It's probably magic marker."

"It says 'Rene Die.' Who would do that?"

If I didn't know better, I'd have thought Ned was actually shaking.

"It must be Barry."

Now he WAS shaking.

"Barry's dead."

"What? Where'd you get that idea?" I was shouting. My voice echoed off the tiled walls.

Ned recoiled. He rolled into himself like a furry blond ball.

"Noplace. He just disappeared and I thought, and Fran said."

"Listen, Ned. Barry *is not* dead. He's around somewhere and this isn't the first thing like this he's done."

"You mean he did this before?"

"Not exactly. Nothing this extreme. He's left silly notes and called and breathed a lot." I decided not to mention the real blood.

"How'd you know it was him?"

"I just know. It's his idea of a joke or something."

I wasn't entirely sure of any of this, but it seemed like a calming thing to say. What I did know was that Barry could get into my apartment any time he wanted. There seemed to be no stopping him. Why he wished to torment me remained a mystery.

"I can't believe Barry would do something like this."

Ned was pacing the floor. His eyes were clear, glowing as if some internal fog had lifted. "He sure has a warped mind."

I stared at the drawing. My name was misspelled again. For the first time since we'd met, I had to agree that Ned was actually right about something. Funny thing about Barry's mind. It hadn't seemed warped when I married him.

■

It wasn't until much later, after Ned had smoked himself to sleep, that I saw the knife. It was the long one that Barry had used to cut hard blocks of hash. He would heat the knife in the flames of the gas stove and slice through the dark, compressed squares as if they were butter. The knife was always sharp and it was always in the kitchen drawer. I'd returned to the bathroom the way a detective returns to the scene of a crime, just to see if there was anything else, any clue. And there it was, lying on the bottom of the white tub. A bead of blood clung to its tip. I stood there in the garish light expecting the knife to move or blood to gush from the tub. It seemed too staged, too artificially theatrical to be real, but when I reached down to touch the knife, I suddenly felt dizzy, like someone was pushing me closer to an invisible edge.

I am afraid of spiders. They horrify me. I imagine their spindly legs on my flesh, their tiny brown heads moving inside the orifices of my body.

I am naked in the bathroom when I see it. I start screaming. A daddy longlegs is moving slowly along the

white porcelain bathtub. There is another one on the fau-
cet of the sink. I shout for Leon. I hear the bathroom door
close. I push against it. Someone is holding it. Locking me
in. Please, I scream. My voice is raw, desperate. Please.
The spiders are moving slowly, making their way over the
ceramic tiles. Everything goes black. When I open my
eyes the door is ajar. Leon is looking down at me. You
cannot be afraid, he tells me. You cannot afford to be
afraid. She isn't home. You were lucky this time.

I promise him I will never be frightened of anything as
silly as a spider ever again.

But that night, when it is dark in my room, I wake up,
sure I feel the creepy legs moving inside my pajamas. I
cannot tell if I am dreaming or if what I see is real. Spi-
ders everywhere. On my arms, my legs, creeping into my
nostrils, my vagina. I thrash at them with the covers. Then
I look up and she is there. Smiling in the doorway. Watch-
ing my terror.

I swallow my scream.

I steadied myself on the side of the tub. This blood
hadn't been there before. Or maybe it had. Ned had distracted me. It was just possible I'd overlooked it. I put my
finger to my mouth. This blood was real. Was it my imagination, or did it seem warm? Then I got this crazy idea.
Maybe whoever was doing this was right here all the time,
a silent shadow, who could actually be in my apartment
without me sensing him. Someone who could duplicate
my every move, who could breathe when I breathed, making himself totally invisible to me. I knew this theory was
probably as weird as the one I'd had about being the only
earthling on an alien planet, but just to be sure I pulled a

KILLING TIME IN BUFFALO   45

few hairs from my head. I moistened the hairs and placed them across all the doors and all the thresholds of my apartment.

Leon teaches me this. It is the only way we can know before we enter our rooms. There are no locks on any doors. Locks are forbidden. So we use the hairs. When I see they are gone, I know she has been there. The rule is that I wait for Leon. I remember about the fish. I tremble when I think of it. The hairs are good. They protect me. Sometimes I am afraid she will see them. But Leon says no. He is more clever. He is always one step ahead, the master of the game. I have no choice but to believe him.

In the morning I checked and all the hairs were right where I'd left them. The knife was still in the bathtub, but the blood had dried into a small, nearly invisible brown dot.

SIX

"It's too hot to be grilled."

It was the next day in Fran's living room. I'd spent the entire night tossing and turning, wrestling with my demons, both real and imagined, while I listened to Ned breathing and Sherman pacing the floors. Now Fran was interrogating me.

"Come on, Renee. Think. You must remember something else."

"Like what?"

"Look. We know he disappeared. We know he didn't take anything with him. Now he's leaving all these macabre little messages. This obviously means something. We've just got to put our heads together."

This was what Fran called sleuthing.

"I have no idea. Can you open a window or something?"

It was unusually hot for the first week of June. An unexpected weather front had floated into Buffalo and now we were having what Leon and I used to call "science fiction weather," a surprising change of climate that made me feel like I was moving around in a black-and-white episode of *The Twilight Zone.*

"It's not that hot. You're just uptight."

I stared at the drawing that now lay on Fran's floor. In the morning light the picture looked more threatening than it had the night before.

"Sort of like Sluggo in the Nancy and Sluggo cartoons," Fran had said when she first saw it. "Nothing like you at all."

That had been her first reaction. Now she was sure Barry was hatching some sinister plot.

I watched as she clicked around the living room in her Dr. Scholl's sandals. It was so hot, I just wanted to close my eyes and drift off.

"Snap outta it!" She spoke in an exaggerated, Brooklyn accent, one of her many impersonations.

"None of this makes sense. Barry was a perfectly normal person."

"Perfectly normal people don't send other people death threats."

Fran's words rotated in the air like crystals.

"I never thought of it like that."

"How did you think of it?"

I didn't want to admit that I wasn't thinking about any of this. I was just sort of going with it, "riding the wave," as Barry himself used to say. The expression reminded me of the day we had gone on a picnic to Goat Island. Barry had been transfixed by the rapids. He'd actually leaned over the railing and said he wondered what it might be like to throw his shirt or his shoe into the foaming water. I encouraged him to do it, sure it was one of those things he'd just said off the top of his head. I never believed he'd have the guts. Right then and there he pulled off his left shoe and flung it into the rapids. It was an impulsive, nonthinking moment. The shoe didn't go down right away. It bobbed up and down on the blue foam: a wild, unpiloted boat, a captainless ship desperately trying not to succumb.

We ran alongside the railing trying to catch glimpses of it before it disappeared beneath the water. For a long time, we stared at the place where the shoe finally went down. Later, Barry walked back to the car carrying his other shoe.

"Why don't you throw that one in too?" I'd asked.

He'd answered that he wanted to save it, to remember. He said it gave him ideas.

"What kind of ideas?"

Then he told me: "Do you realize that a person could completely disappear here? You could throw a body over the rail and they could never find it in a million years."

Even then, I thought it was an odd thing to say. I still remember looking at Barry as he carried his one shoe and stared up at the sky as if he'd just seen a vision.

Fran knew all this. I had told her about it in a moment of weakness shortly after Barry disappeared. She had insisted that we drive out to Goat Island.

"Maybe we'll find his car there, or a note."

"That's ridiculous. Where would he leave a note? It's a public park."

"Well if we find the car, there just might be a note inside."

I knew it was pointless, but Fran drove us out there anyway. It was a freezing cold afternoon in mid-March,

icicles hung from the rocks, puddles hardened into min-
iature skating rinks. I'd forgotten my gloves. Fran stopped
off at a gift shop and slipped a pair of fuzzy lamb's wool
mittens into her pocket. It was against the rules, but Fran
explained it as an unexpected emergency.

We never found Barry's pink Rambler, which was the
only thing that he seemed to take with him, so there was
no note and no clue. I still had the mittens in the top
drawer of my dresser.

"Let me see that matchbook again?"

I slipped the curled cardboard into Fran's open palm.

She studied it the way Leon had studied bugs under a
microscope.

"Have any idea why this is curled up?"

I shook my head.

"Someone probably used it to smoke a roach. Someone
broke into your apartment, smoked a joint and left you a
death threat."

"You mean it wasn't Barry?"

"It had to be him. All we've got to do is figure out why
he went to the Aragon first and where he's been all this
time."

"How about why he'd want to kill me?"

"Yeah, and that too."

For some reason, I could sense Fran losing interest. Her
gaze wandered around the apartment.

Anna was standing in the doorway. She was wearing a
short-sleeved, white cotton blouse with a Peter Pan collar
and a red and white polka-dot miniskirt. She bore an eerie
resemblance to Fran. Everyone in the Johnsten family
looked oddly like one another, enough to make you look
twice. I was doing that now.

"Hi," Anna said. "I hope I'm not interrupting anything."

Fran was on her feet in a flash.

I knew they wanted to talk, but I was in no hurry to leave. Being alone in my apartment was beginning to make me edgy. I had no intention of taking part in this conversation, which I was sure had to do with Anna's plans to marry the Polish mortician.

I eased back into my chair and tried to remember some detail that would explain the drawing. The only thing that came to mind was an image, a half-remembered moment, something beyond words.

It was the night before the wedding. Barry was asleep. He was lying on his back with his mouth open. A triangle of light had settled on his face. He looked inhuman, like one of the startled fish I used to flop into the bottom of the wooden rowboat at Camp Winoway. I touched his face and pressed my cheek against his. He didn't move. I whispered his name, and moved my hand through the irregular patch of light, hoping he would wake up. For a moment his eyelids quivered, but he remained motionless. I stared at the tiny pores in his face. Each one was filled with a black stub that would be a full-fledged hair by morning. Barry had shaved off his beard and trimmed his hair in response to his mother's hysterical pleading. Without the beard, it looked as if someone had walked away with the lower half of his face. I remembered thinking how easy it would have been to call the whole thing off, to have tiptoed out the door and never come back. Instead, I spent the rest of the night sorting through my childhood photographs, wondering if Leon was right, if I really would feel different after the wedding.

Remembering, beads of sweat rolled down my neck. For the first time since all this began, I thought that maybe it was partially my fault. Maybe the near-violent events of the last few weeks hadn't really come upon me without warning. Perhaps I had unconsciously put myself in a dangerous position. Maybe there was something I knew, something I'd seen or overheard accidentally.

I will always be different. I cannot be like the other girls. I will never be a cheerleader. Go to pep rallies. Drink egg creams in the candy store after school, have sleepover dates. Things are changing in the green house. Some days are like the TV shows. She greets me at the door in an apron. She bakes lumpy oatmeal cookies. She kisses me and I feel her warm tears against my cheek. Please, I want to say, Stay like this. Please. Mommy.

On those days I believe I can finally be like the other girls, that it is all over. A mistake. A bad dream. But then something happens. Something small. A twist at her mouth. An odd echo in her voice. I know it is coming. I admit it. There is no way I can live through this and be like other people. I am marked. The fear rules my life. It hides in the bottom of the drawers, in the back of the closet, in the purple room. It makes me strange. This secret. This nightmare. It sets me apart from the girls at school. So I hate them. Their pajama parties and their fluffy prom dresses. I am defiant. Odd. Wild. They think I choose to be this way. But it was never my choice. I am trapped in a spiderweb of memories and fear. It is a dan-

ger that won't go away. A danger that follows me. This is how my life will always be.

I closed my eyes and saw the brown shoe bobbing up and down on the white foam.

Anna and Fran were talking. Their heads were very close together. I half-tried to hear what they were saying, but their voices were drowned out by the sound of rushing water.

SEVEN

I had just left Fran's apartment and was lingering in the dank coolness of the hallway, when I saw two men come rushing up the stairs. One was plump with close-cropped hair and the other was very fat and wore a white short-sleeved shirt. I knew instantly they didn't belong — over thirty, overweight and straight. Maybe they were cops. But they didn't have that look. They pushed right past me as if I wasn't there. I flattened myself into the wall and watched as they pounded on Sherman's door. When he opened it, he was wearing his usual jockey shorts, T-shirt and black boots. They jostled him as they shouldered their way inside. Definitely uninvited guests. I crept up the stairs, more curious than frightened. The door was partially open. And that's when I saw it. At first I thought it was a silver flashlight, the kind I once used for hunting frogs in the darkness of summer nights. Why would anyone hold a flashlight against Sherman's neck in the middle of the afternoon? Of course, when I looked again, I saw that it was a gun. Sherman was white as a sheet. Then they slammed the door. Hard.

I ran back down to Fran's. I was nearly breathless.

"There's a guy with a gun upstairs."

"In your apartment? Barry?"

I was shaking my head like one of those hula dolls in the back of my father's 1958 Dodge.

"Sherman. These big guys. They've got him with a gun."

"Renee, are you sure?"

My voice came out dry and cracked. "I'm sure."

Fran motioned with her thumb toward her sister Anna.

"Don't let her hear you, she'd freak," she whispered.

Anna was sitting all folded up on the couch. With her pert little polka-dot skirt and white shoes, she reminded me of Minnie Mouse. It was an odd feeling, to be staring at Minnie Mouse while two thugs were holding a revolver against Sherman's neck.

"Do you think they're narcs?"

Fran was probably wondering if we should all flush our stashes while there was still time.

"I don't think cops just push in like that without a warrant."

"Right."

I glanced upstairs. It was so quiet, you could hear a pin drop. If they were planning to blow Sherman's brains out, they hadn't done it yet. There was still time. To do what?

"Listen," Fran said. "I'll make up some excuse to get Anna out of here. Go next door to Vitale's. He hangs out with that Indian guy Duane. They've all got guns and shit like that."

"Fran, are you crazy? This isn't a shoot-out. Maybe we should call the police."

Fran made a face. I knew as soon as I'd said it, it was a dumb idea. Sherman was a dope dealer. This was not a job for the law.

She turned me around and put her hands on my shoulders. "GO! NOW!"

Vitale gave me a wide smile when he opened the door. The bongo drums were nestled in the crook of his arm. I could see Duane sitting on a torn blue couch in the corner of the room. They'd been listening to Olatunjii's "Drums of Passion." Books were strewn all over the place. An orange dog was curled up in a matted heap in the corner. The apartment smelled like stale milk.

"There's two guys with guns in Sherman's apartment." I didn't bother with small talk. There wasn't time.

Vitale's smile just sort of froze there. Staring at his stained teeth and his gums, which were the color of a cherry Popsicle, I wondered if he was going to scream. He never had the chance. Duane shot up like a second-grader whose name had just been called by the principal. He was tall with acne-pitted skin and a long, black ponytail held back in an elastic. His eyes settled on my breasts. A definite warmth moved through the lower part of my body. I couldn't believe I was feeling sexy at a time like this.

"Narcs?" Vitale asked.

I went into my head-shaking routine again.

Duane paced the floor like a caged animal.

Just then we heard a door slam. I slipped into Vitale's apartment and peeked into the hallway. The two guys were walking down the stairs. I couldn't be sure, but I thought I saw a bulge in the fat guy's shirt. The gun. But we hadn't heard any shots.

Within seconds, all of us, me, Fran, Vitale and Duane, were upstairs. Sherman was leaning against the living room wall. Behind him, posters of Che Guevara, Allen Ginsberg and Mama Cass were taped over the peeling green plaster.

"Jesus. Shit. Jesus." He just kept saying that over and over again.

"I've never been so fuckin' scared in my life." He added that when we pressed him for information.

Vitale lit up a joint and we all sat down while Sherman talked.

"Those were Mafia guys. Shit. I don't believe it. They told me I was dealing too big. Do you believe it? They held that gun to my head the whole time. I nearly crapped in my pants."

Fran let out a hoot and Duane smiled. Considering the fact that I'd just been the target of a gruesome death threat myself, the humor of the moment escaped me.

"Sherman, you've gotta get a gun," Fran said. "For protection."

Fran always had a flair for the dramatic.

Vitale inhaled and spoke at the same time. "You know, that's probably not a bad idea."

"Where the hell am I supposed to get a gun?"

Everyone looked at Duane. He was leaning back against the worn couch. From this angle, I could see that he really did have high Indian cheekbones. Maybe that's what saved his face from being ugly. There was something about him that made me tremendously uncomfortable. He glanced at my breasts while he passed the joint to Fran.

"Hey man, what makes you think I got a gun?"

"Come on," Vitale said, "you guys always have guns and knives and shit like that."

By "you guys" we all knew Vitale meant Indians. Duane didn't seem to object to this racial stereotyping. Maybe he liked the idea of being the only nonwhite in the room, or maybe he was secretly laughing at us in some deep Indian way.

He pulled a switchblade from his back pocket. The knife flipped open like magic. He swished it through the air, making a wide gash in the lingering smoke.

Sherman shuddered. Fran's eyes were gleaming. I was beginning to suspect that this whole thing: last night's death threat, today's visit by the mob, Duane's knife, turned her on.

"I'll look around," he said. "If you've got bread, you can get anything."

Vitale nodded. Sherman closed his eyes. I started to pick at the flesh around my thumbnail.

"Anybody for pizza?" Fran asked.

Thank God no one was hungry. We all just sat there listening to Simon and Garfunkel sing "The 59th Street Bridge Song," and letting the events of the day sink in.

The Mafia had actually been here in Marshal Sherman's apartment. I had seen it with my own eyes.

"How soon can you get the gun?" Fran asked.

Duane smoothed his hand down the long ponytail. I noticed how his knuckles were thick and swollen from labor. Vitale had told me that Duane worked at the steel plant in

Lackawanna. I'd been there once. A seething, belching monument to pollution, it was an industrial nightmare that made Days Park look like a garden paradise.

"I'll have to look around. Check it out," was all he said.

I wondered if Duane had ever used the switchblade.

" 'Cause I was thinking," Fran said, "none of us really knows how to shoot a gun."

Now it was us. Suddenly, this was my problem too. Vitale started talking about how easy it was to learn and how we could all go out to a field somewhere and shoot holes in beer cans. It sounded like something out of a Wild West movie. Vitale grew up in the Bronx. I knew for a fact he had graduated in the top quarter of his class at De Witt Clinton High School. Where on earth did he get the idea we could just acquire a gun, drive out to some dusty field, prop a couple of cans on a log and become sharp-shooters?

"That sounds logical," Fran said. Sherman nodded. Obviously, I was outnumbered.

■

It was well past midnight when I stumbled back into my apartment. The phone was ringing. I walked down the long hallway to the kitchen.

It has a smell. Horror. Like something half dead. Rotting. Bad breath. Something hideous coming from the inside. Always the inside. Not something you can see.

I am still a child when I learn to sense it. Smell it.

Don't come in here! Leon shouts.

He has found her again. There is always a warning.

As soon as I picked up the receiver, I knew I'd made a mistake. There was that old familiar smell. Someone was breathing. Heavy, raspy breaths.

"What do you want?" I was careful not to shout.

I heard something that sounded like air rushing through an empty seashell. The voice was barely audible, as though it were coming from someplace far away. I wasn't even sure of what it said, but it sounded very much like "Renee die."

EIGHT

The surprise heat wave settled in, turning stale and old. I sat by my window fan and stared at the swirls in the rug. Next door, I could hear Sherman's relentless pacing. He hadn't left the building since the gun had been pressed against his neck. Fran said he'd been traumatized. We all knew it was serious when he sold his tickets for the Monterey Pop Festival. Vitale said there were just too many bad vibes to travel. I figured it had to do with the weather. After so much cold and impossible grayness, the sudden warmth made us all unsure, suspicious. It was hard to believe that, like a vampire from the grave, winter wouldn't suddenly resurrect itself, rendering us pale and bloodless.

June was hard to trust. It wasn't until July that I could really relax and have faith that summer was real.

Summer calmed me, made me nostalgic for things like Duncan yo-yos, paddle balls and orange-flavored ice pops that melted before they could be completely consumed. It also made me miss Leon. Summers were our best times together. That's when he'd take me along as he trekked through the woods behind our suburban house looking for samples of mold, or drops of pond water.

Sometimes I thought Leon was born with a microscope attached to his face. Nothing escaped his glass slides and his dissecting kit. If he paid me, I consented to giving him samples of my blood or scrapings from the inside of my cheek. He'd stain my bodily contributions with a bit of purple dye and peer at them for hours through the lens of his microscope. Then, of course, he'd charge me for a look and we were evenly exploited.

Leon wanted to show me the world stripped bare and explained, and I fought him all the way. I guess I had to, because Leon's world was a place to be probed and studied and diagrammed.

I remember the time my father came home from a long business trip and brought us gifts: little burlap sacks filled with Mexican jumping beans. The first time I held one of the small brown jumping beans in my hand and it responded the way those beans do, I wanted to believe the thing really had a life of its own; a life different from mine and Leon's, one that only came into being in the warmth of my palm. But right away Leon got that lemon-look and told me there was a black worm trapped inside that jerked in reaction to the heat from my hand. It was a horrible thought. Just to imagine a factory somewhere in Mexico where they sealed worms up in capsules was enough to make me sick. I challenged Leon.

"If that's true," I said, "how do they stay alive in there?"

In an instant, he whipped out his dissecting kit (he had made it himself from toothpicks and straight pins) and began working on the bean. I escaped into the den where my father was watching a football game and filling the room with cigar smoke.

Much later, when I was curled up in bed, Leon came in and told me how multiplication worked and how to make a crystal radio. That was his way of saying he was sorry. In the morning he never even mentioned the worm or told me what he'd found when he opened the bean.

There are some things Leon will not tell me. Things I am too afraid to know. These are the things Leon searches for so he can stay one step ahead.

For your own good, Renee. For your own good.

Whenever I talked about Leon, Fran would start conjuring up images of her own lost brother. She felt that in some way, this brother, this ghost, was the enigma that haunted her unconscious. He was like a missing limb, a severed arm or leg that despite its separation from the body continued to throb with feeling. Finding her brother, she said, would complete her, would help her understand the part of herself she believed was missing. He was alive, she was sure of it. It was just a matter of routing him out. She told me that although she had absolutely no proof, she believed her father had been married before and had had a son. "I can feel it, like a brother vibration," was how she put it. Naturally, I was skeptical, but Fran insisted. She hated the idea that something so important had been kept from her all her life. Finally, she was ready to search for genuine documentation of her phantom sibling. This project fell under the joint category of "sleuthing" and "caper."

*   *   *

I watched as a sliver of sunlight flashed through the fan blades. Outside, people were sitting on the tufts of grass that pushed through the hard soil of Days Park. Someone was playing a guitar. If I closed my eyes, I could imagine the scene: girls with long hair parted down the middle, tall, skinny boys with dirty hands and love beads knotted around their necks and wrists.

My brother thought the sixties was a government plot to preoccupy a whole generation, to keep us from dealing with what was really important. He subscribed to the leftist *National Guardian,* wore mostly black clothes, sprouted a straggly goatee and took pleasure in disagreeing with everything anyone said.

It was Leon who warned me that marrying Barry would ruin my life. But Leon had been warning me about everything since the moment I was old enough to listen. He was the one who first pointed out that the ground beneath the rotting logs in the woods behind our house contained a universe of insects; building, hunting, reproducing. One afternoon, as I walked aimlessly beside him, picking up stones and flinging them into the darkness between the trees, he rolled over a log scarred by beetle holes and covered with mosses, and showed me a whole world I never would have believed existed. Then after he talked, pointing out the bark bugs, wood lice and the tiny winged digger wasps, he carefully rolled the log back into place. It was as if he was sharing this special secret with me and wanted to leave no trace of our trespass. That's how it always was with us. Leon told me things and I listened.

On an astonishing day in 1955, he came home from

school with a small 45 rpm record. It was shiny and black
and he slipped it over the thick spindle of our hi-fi. Behind him, in our paneled den, his beloved tank of black
mollies and angelfish hummed complacently.

"I want you to hear something," he said. "It's called
rock and roll."

The song was "Rock Around the Clock" by Bill Haley
and His Comets.

After that, I was convinced my brother single-handedly
discovered the music that would change the world. Years
later, when he told me the Beatles sounded like a bunch
of babies crying in a crib, I only felt a little betrayed. By
then he had discovered Ornett Coleman, John Coltrane
and Miles Davis.

I desperately wanted to believe that Leon wasn't always right, that his smug, self-righteous attitude, his
strong opinions about everything would someday be
proven wrong. So when my brother told me not to marry
Barry, it was, in a way, my first real chance to actually
rebel.

It's not as though I didn't believe I truly loved Barry,
because it's important for me to remember that I did.
When I first met him (at a beer blast for the fraternally
disaffected on the grounds of the university), he seemed
sensitive and distracted enough to make me think he had
some deep, sad secret. He was small and dark with wild,
thick hair that sprouted from his head like corkscrews. He
drove a 1957 pink Rambler that he started up early in the
morning so the engine would be warm and humming by
the time he got behind the wheel. There was something
else about Barry. He whistled in candy stores. It was one
of those quirky Bronx-type things, and it reminded me so

much of my father (about whom there wasn't that much to remember), I decided right then and there I was madly in love. I had to. It was all part of why I had come to Buffalo in the first place. To forget. To run away.

I want to belong to someone, to have a new name, a new identity. I want to escape from both of them. Her and Leon. I want to be married. To be a wife. Not a child. Not a sister. I want to start all over again. To erase the lingering nightmare of the green house and what I saw.

Barry wasn't what you'd call "dependable." He'd be sitting in a chair next to me, and the next minute he'd get up to talk to someone and wouldn't reappear for hours. When we moved in together, he'd get up in the middle of the night and drive away in the pink Rambler, returning some time late the next day. When I questioned him about these unreported disappearances, he'd look at me as if I'd lost my mind. "I got hung up," was all he'd ever offer in the way of an explanation. Sometimes I found him talking on the phone late at night. He'd called Vitale and gotten into "a rap," or had a sudden desire to speak to his older sister Carole (who looked remarkably like him, except for her chemically straightened hair).

His totally guileless manner, the way he looked surprised and sad when I told him how all this got me crazy with worry, made him even more endearing (although it had no marked effect on his behavior).

But none of this had anything to do with getting married.

We did that strictly for money.

Barry had an idea about going to Mexico, buying large quantities of marijuana, stuffing them into a tire of the Rambler and rolling happily over the border. He'd done this once before with Marshal Sherman and it had worked like a charm. But now he needed capital. The money would come from our wedding presents. We'd drive down to Acapulco, bathe in the ocean, eat peyote buttons with the peasants and come home tanned and wealthy. The way he described it sounded almost poetic: the ocean, the sand, the brown wrinkled hands of the hill people who would share their mushrooms and their wisdom with us. We'd sit together in Days Park, watching a solid mass of gray winter clouds cluster outside our window, and dream we were baking beneath the scorching Acapulco sun. Barry would pass me a joint and we'd slip off our clothes and make love on the worn rug with the swirls. More and more, reality seemed to drift away. Leon's voice became less convincing.

Barry and I were married at his uncle Hymie's apartment somewhere in the Bronx. It was a hastily thrown together affair. There were a lot of old men wearing felt hats, whining children and relatives (his) with gold teeth in the front. My father stood in one corner, while my mother, heavily sedated, fought to stay awake. Leon, wearing an ugly black suit that looked as though he bought it at a rabbinical supply shop, sulked sourly against a wall. Barry's mother, Harriet, passed sponge cake through the crowd and offered everyone scotch in paper cups. Carole was the only one who cried. What began as a few picturesque tear drops soon became a flood of uncontrollable sobbing. Finally, an elderly aunt whose nylon stockings were rolled into neat balls beneath the hem of her dress had the good sense to bundle her off to a bathroom somewhere.

Nothing much was said in English, which was probably a good thing, since Barry and I had shared a pipe of hash just before the ceremony. I swear, I never remember saying anything even remotely like "I do." But I knew it was all real and legal by the way Leon squinted when he signed his name as witness on the license.

Afterward, we drove away in the pink Rambler. The daisies I had held under the wedding canopy lay wilted in the back seat. Barry stopped at the first gas station we passed. He opened the window and asked the attendant to "fill her up." That's when, inexplicably, he began to stutter. I had to finish the sentence for him. Then he forgot where we were going. I took out the map with the Holiday Inn circled in blue. He nodded while he rubbed the side of his face, lightly at first, but soon he rubbed so hard there was a purple streak all along one side of his nose.

When we got to the hotel there was a green carpet on the steps. Plastic flowers poked out from plaster wall sconces. A sign outside read, "Happy Birthday Susan Welch." Barry was buttoning and unbuttoning his shirt. His hands moved along the fabric like pale spiders. By the time we reached the room, his shirt was buttoned up the wrong way and he had forgotten to tip the bellhop.

As soon as the door closed, we sat on the king-sized bed, sorting through the envelopes. The bedspread was an odd sort of purple material flecked with orange and red. The white paper rectangles looked like clouds in a tweed sky.

"We've got almost fifteen hundred dollars in cash and

checks." Barry's voice shook when he spoke. He stuttered again when he said my name. I reached out to touch him and he pulled away, rubbing the side of his nose.

We didn't make love that night. Barry couldn't get an erection. I told him it was nothing to worry about. He laughed and said he had been freaked out by all his relatives. Then he touched my cheek and curled up into a ball on his side of the bed.

Nothing in my life will be like the TV shows or the glossy magazines. Even my wedding night is twisted, freakish.

I will never be like the other girls. I will always be different no matter how hard I try.

When I got up the next morning he wasn't beside me.

He was completely dressed and sitting very business-like at the small Formica desk. During the night, he had made a list. He wrote each relative's name in one column; next to the name was the amount of money we'd received. It was the first time I'd ever seen his handwriting. But when I looked down again, the list had been pushed aside. Barry spread his hands out on the blue ink blotter. His fingers were even and small. On his left hand was a plain gold band, identical to mine.

"They look just like my father's hands," Barry said. He stuttered when he spoke.

We ate a quick breakfast in the coffee shop downstairs. I had to order, since Barry could barely speak.

As we left the Holiday Inn, I made up some excuse, and ran back to the room. I opened my suitcase and stuffed the purple tweed bedspread inside.

*   *   *

When I told her the story, Fran tilted her head to one side and looked very thoughtful.

"I've noticed that Barry is talking less and less," she said.

Then she admitted to actually hearing an occasional stutter and seeing him button and unbutton his shirt and rub the side of his nose.

"It could just be some nervous habits. Temporary ones," I said, hopefully.

"Hmmm," she said. "Or maybe it's something else."

"Like what?"

"Like maybe marriage really changes people."

I wanted to kill her. Those had been Leon's exact words.

NINE

Allen Street, after which Allentown was named, was a narrow strip of shops that ran in a perpendicular angle to Days Park. The tallest and most prominent building was the Allendale Theater. Once an elite "art cinema" it was now *the* porno palace of Buffalo. The names of the films were listed boldly in black letters on the white marquee. The day I first held the gun, *Thigh Spy* was the featured film. The words floated eerily over the worn sidewalks as Duane pressed the revolver into my hand.

On certain days, just after a rain, or when the snow was melting into muddy brown pools, Allentown smelled like a stack of old newspapers. Wet ones, that had been left out by the garbage and forgotten. That's what I remember most about the first time I held the gun. That smell was everywhere.

"It's a Smith and Wesson .38 special. Single action," he said. Of course I had no idea what any of that meant.

There was no sense faking it. I could tell that Duane knew, which made me feel very uncool, very suburban. His peregrine eyes darted back and forth as he moved his hands lovingly over the barrel. I had forgotten all that stuff about men and guns. But I felt it as Duane flipped the cylinder open and showed me where the five bullets were loaded. Slugs, he called them. He moved with complete assurance. Pure power. Pure sex. I was mesmerized. The way he talked about notches, sights and ejection ports, the accuracy of single action as opposed to double action, made me wonder just how many times he'd actually fired a gun. The switchblade had been impressive, but this was something else. The real thing.

The gun felt warm. Duane showed me how to line up the groove in the back with the blade in the front. Front and rear sights he called them. It reminded me of the shooting games Leon and I used to play in Rockaway Playland. I was pretty good, eventually accumulating a stack of prizes, all identical straw Chinese finger puzzles.

But this wasn't a game. I could tell the way Duane pointed to the lead slugs on the kitchen table.

"Can you really kill someone with this?" I asked.

"Blow their head off at a hundred yards."

I didn't want to say that I had no need to blow anyone's head off at any distance. Instead I asked where the safety latch was.

"S and W's don't have no safety latch."

A double negative. I hated that. But Duane was rising above his grammar. He knew more about raw violence than anyone I'd ever met.

"Here," I said, "take it back."

"Go on, hold it. Get the feel. It's got a little kick."

He slammed his palm into the barrel as a demonstration.

It was almost as if he were inviting me, daring me. The gun was a messenger from another place. It was an object none of us could have acquired ourselves. Duane wouldn't say where or how he got it. I could picture him passing a roll of bills under the table in the Aragon Lounge and waiting until he felt a slap of steel in his open hand. It had no serial number; he was careful to tell us that, as if any of us cared. Sherman was never going to use the gun. It was the idea of it that excited him, excited all of us. It was a taste of a world about which we knew very little. And the way Duane looked at me made it clear he understood. We were all hungry for something more.

Vitale told us about an empty field behind an abandoned farmhouse in a small town not far from Buffalo, called Cuba. Fran liked the sound of that. She said it made it seem more romantic, more dangerous. She was already dressed for the part; a suede fringed vest with a thin T-shirt underneath. The effect was very Wild West. "What are you — Annie Oakley?" Sherman had said when he saw her. Fran ignored him. Costumes were her thing. More and more she had been talking about wearing disguises when we went out to steal. Not just wigs and straight-looking raincoats, but uniforms and her personal favorite, a nun's habit. She had an elaborate scenario about that. She'd be a French-speaking nun (she also did accents) and I'd be a schoolgirl in knee socks and a parochial-school uniform. The idea didn't have great appeal to me, since the closest I'd ever been to a nun was Julie Andrews in *The Sound of Music.*

"We could take everything in sight. TVs. Stereos. No one would dare stop a nun." She had something there. I wondered how many nuns had ever been questioned for carting major appliances out of department stores.

"I love this," Fran whispered to me as she held the gun in both hands. Her fingers curled around the trigger like flesh-colored snakes. "It has such great possibilities. Can you imagine holding up the lingerie department in Hengerer's?"

"Yeah. Give me all your negligees or else."

"Hand over those nightgowns or we'll blow you away."

I laughed, but I felt that sensation move through my wrists. I remembered the story of the anarchist's handkerchief. Fran and a gun. Not a safe combination.

■

Duane had collected a dozen empty Genesee Beer cans. The plan was simple: we'd drive out to the farmhouse, set up the beer cans and practice shooting until we all felt comfortable with the gun.

"You never know. These guys could come back anytime," was how Vitale put it.

I knew the idea was ridiculous, but I was anxious to get away from both the smell of Allentown and the foreboding feeling I'd had since my last breathy death threat.

Vitale was driving. He was the only one with a van, a square black Volkswagen bus with peace symbols painted on both sides. Holding his precious drums in one hand, he led his dog Nickel Bag into the front seat. Nickel Bag was a rangy orange-colored mutt who survived on a diet of marijuana and Malomars. I sort of liked him. He was friendly in a slobbering kind of way. Fran called him "The Beast."

"You're not going to bring that beast along?" she asked as Vitale settled him down on the floor next to Duane. "If he pukes on me, I'll shoot him." It was true that Nickel Bag found his unusual diet hard to keep inside his digestive tract.

"He needs a day in the country," Vitale whined as he ran his scrubby hands over the dog's back.

"Aim for him," Fran whispered. She pointed from Nickel Bag to the gun Duane had jammed into the waistband of his pants. I wondered why he would put a loaded weapon (I assumed it was loaded) with no safety catch so close to his genitals, but Duane wasn't the sort of person you could ask questions like that.

Fran invited Ned. He showed up just as we were settling into the van. No one seemed to mind, and I knew Fran liked the idea of having him along. The two of us, our mutual lover, three other men, a dog and a gun. There was a symmetry there only Fran could appreciate.

The back of the van smelled of hashish. It was littered with anti-Vietnam fliers, a few old gas masks, clusters of dried cigarette butts and empty bottles of Robitussin. The engine sputtered as we lurched out of Days Park. I only hoped we wouldn't break down on the way to Cuba. How could we explain ourselves? With the gas masks and the gun it wouldn't be easy.

*   *   *

The field was exactly as Vitale had described it, which surprised me, since he was hardly a reliable source of information. Nickel Bag bounded out of the van as if he'd been imprisoned his entire life. He rolled in the grass, scratched himself and vomited at the base of a huge elm tree.

The sun was hot and the air had turned thick with humidity. My hair sprung into frizzy corkscrews while Fran's hung lank against her pale face. Ned looked dazed as he walked aimlessly around the rock Sherman had chosen for target practice. It was one of those gray granite slabs that protruded from the ground as if it had once been attached to something important. Vitale busied himself arranging the cans, carefully spacing them a few inches apart. Duane watched us. He stood with his legs apart, the grip of the gun protruding from his waistband. He ran his hand along his black ponytail. With the sun burning over his shoulder, the gun and his tight black jeans, he looked almost attractive, in a sinister way.

Sherman was the first to shoot. Duane showed him how to load the cylinder and take aim.

It wasn't like TV. The sound was violent, deafening. It shattered the thick, still air like a rock thrown through a plate-glass window. And it didn't go away. Afterward, it just hung there, resonating through the field in a smoky cloud of dust.

I hadn't expected it to sound so real. Fran clamped her hands over her ears. Ned watched dumbfounded. Nickel Bag climbed into Vitale's lap.

Sherman missed every time. Bullets flew wildly, gnawing into trees, ricocheting off rocks, burrowing into the ground. The revolver held only five bullets. Sherman reloaded. This time he dented one can and sent another flying.

By the time my turn came, I was used to the noise. Duane stood beside me as I flipped the side latch, opened the cylinder and loaded five rounds. I aligned the sights and pretended I was back in Playland with Leon. Bingo. I hit two cans and made one shake with the impact.

"Not bad," Duane said. There was no mistaking it; he was definitely looking at my breasts. I was tough, cool, an unflappable outlaw, a woman to be reckoned with. I placed the gun in his open palm.

"Thanks."

Fran was hopeless. Despite the vest, this was one part she just couldn't play. Duane tried to steady her hand, but the slight kick of the .38 sent her reeling. Finally, after two rounds, she gave up and passed the gun to Ned.

Fran and I sat silently, side by side, listening to the gun shots. They seemed far away now and not nearly so menacing.

I watched as tiny black ants scurried back and forth from their hill. When I held my hand over the ground, making the slightest shadow, they raced, suspecting danger. That's when I remembered the game.

The game always begins the same way. We fill the iridescent pink, plastic water guns at the kitchen sink. It is hot and the sun burns at my back. We go outside together. Leon crouches down on the slate walk and watches the ants as they move busily to and from the little mounds of sand they have built between the cracks.

Then he chooses one ant at random. It has to be an ant that wandered away from the others. When the slate is hot and dry from the August sun and the ant is in position, Leon squirts out a large circle of water from the gun. He surrounds the ant with an impenetrable wall of liquid. Gradually and methodically, Leon makes the circle smaller and smaller. We both watch in silence as the ant maneuvers frantically, hitting the wall with every movement. As I crouch next to Leon, I feel the sun blaze against my arms. I wonder at just what moment the ant realizes that its world has become a deadly circle.

Eventually, Leon makes the circle of water so small that the ant can only sit motionless in the center, resigned to its fate. Sometimes, Leon stares at the ant for several minutes. Then, because I am the one with the murderer's thumbs, he hands me the gun. I squirt at the black speck until its body floats up in a bubble of water.

"Look," Fran said. She pointed to a lone ant crawling slowly toward her foot. She lifted her leg, casting a long shadow. The ant began to run in circles.

"Do you think they can sense these things?"

"I'm not sure. Maybe they can."

"Ants," she said, as she squeezed the squirming black speck between her fingers. She moved into a rectangular patch of shade and dropped it on the ground. Ned's shots echoed into the dusty air. We both looked down, but it was too dark to see the body.

TEN

We stayed in the field, getting high and eating Malomars as we watched the sun set. And we made all the promises we always made: we'd never be like the straight people, never live in the suburbs, never play golf, never be our parents. Fran swore she'd never go to a beauty parlor and Ned told us he'd never go to Vietnam. There was no doubt in our minds, we were changing the world irrevocably and for the best. The Establishment was on its knees. We were the rising tide of the Age of Aquarius, the generation who warned ominously that the times were a changin'. It was mind-blowing, inconceivable, that everyone didn't recognize it. There were still straight people left. They lived in places like Kenmore and Cheektowaga, places where families gathered innocently around kitchen tables, saying grace and eating three square meals a day; places where teenage throwbacks joined fraternities, went to proms and signed up for the draft.

We'd all but denounced that anachronistic world of mainstream values, thrown in our lot with the Indians,

Che, Ho Chi Minh, the coal miners. But there was still one sticking point, one little detail we hadn't completely ironed out. Money. About money, we were divided. Sherman and Vitale were into it. They knew they couldn't deal forever (especially after the last incident), so they talked about moving to L.A. and managing rock groups. Fran and I figured we could steal everything we'd ever want. Money wasn't a burning issue. We'd practically forgotten what it was for. Only Duane was silent. He sat staring into the woods as if none of us existed. The gun was still jammed into his pants.

It was Sherman who asked about Barry.

"Where is he? How long has it been now?"

"Nearly six weeks," Fran answered for me.

"Shit. That's really weird. It's like he disappeared into thin air."

"Not exactly," Fran said.

I knew she couldn't keep it to herself any longer, so I told Sherman and Vitale and Duane (who I didn't think was listening) about the calls and the notes.

Vitale shook his head. "That just doesn't sound like Barry. He's not into stuff like that. He's a pacifist. Remember when he told us all that bad stuff about eating red meat? Someone who won't eat meat could never be violent."

"He's spiritual," Sherman added.

In a little while they'd make him sound like Mahatma Gandhi.

"Well maybe something happened. Maybe he freaked out, had some bad acid. It happens," Ned said.

*   *   *

I watched Duane's eyes. Was he laughing at us? I couldn't be sure. His face was expressionless. The information about Barry had piqued his interest. I was sure of that, because he was no longer staring vacantly into the woods. His hand caressed the grip of the gun.

We'd gone through two boxes of bullets. One hundred shots, most of which had hit trees and dirt. The target practice had been fun. But now the old feelings of dread were returning. In their own crazy way, Vitale and Sherman were right. Barry wasn't the violent type. None of this fit. Maybe something horrible *had* happened to him. A mood-altering drug. A bad trip. I didn't want to go over every event in our brief life together. Not again. But I knew if we didn't get off the subject soon, I'd start obsessing. I couldn't help myself.

The madness just begins one day. I am sure of it. No reason. You're wrong, Leon says. It started when we were babies. You just did not see. I am watching. Always. You are not careful, Renee. You will make this mistake again.

"I'm starving," Fran said. "Let's eat."

It was late but we knew Freddie's Donuts on Main Street would still be open. All-night bakeries sustained us. I couldn't remember the last time I'd had a meal that consisted of four food groups. "Carbohydrates are the staff of life," was how Fran phrased it.

I admit we must have looked ominous as we entered Freddie's. A ragtag band of counterculture types — hippies under the spell of mind-altering substances, madmen, gun-toting criminals. Fran in her fringed vest, Vitale toting his worn and filthy bongo drums. Sherman with bloodshot eyes, contracted to specks. Ned looking like a fraternity boy who'd slipped into depravity, me holding Nickel Bag by a rope attached to his collar, and Duane with the grip of a gun peeking out from his waistband.

Freddie's was a vast open space. The store, only a small glass-enclosed counter with Freddie's limited selection displayed proudly, was the retail outlet for the factory that whirred and buzzed in the back. The place was empty except for a pimple-faced clerk wearing a white paper hat and leaning against the wall behind the counter.

I'll never know what the clerk noticed first. All we wanted were some deep-fried Freddie's Famous Peanut Sticks. But I'm sure he never heard us order. His face got all loose and shaky, like unmolded Jell-O. He had these little white hands with bitten nails and he threw them up in the air as if he wanted to shake them off.

"The money's in the drawer. It's all I got."

The fringes on Fran's vest vibrated in the silence. Nickel Bag curled back his lip and growled. I felt Duane press himself against me. He stepped up close to the boy, who was now visibly trembling. "That's cool, man," he said. He made a peace sign with two fingers, then looked directly at us. We were ready for anything, Duane was our leader. Mere proles, soldiers, robots, we awaited his command. He jerked his thumb toward the door. "Okay, let's go." He turned on his heel and we followed him out to the street. Then we began to run. Only no one was chasing us.

We never touched the money. And we left without the peanut sticks.

By the time Vitale started the van, it hit us. We'd almost held up a store. And we didn't have to do a thing.

"It was so easy," Fran said.

I looked back at Freddie's bakery, growing smaller and smaller as we sped down Main Street.

"What if he reports us?"

"To who? What did we do? It was all in his head. All we wanted were peanut sticks."

"That was unbelievable," Ned said. "We could have gotten killed."

But then I remembered we were the ones with the gun.

"Do you think he saw it?" I asked.

Fran looked at the revolver in Duane's pants. "You can hardly notice it. I think he sensed something about us. Vibrations. A certain outlaw élan."

Only Fran could put it quite like that. Make it sound like the name of perfume, make us seem like poetic bandits.

"How much do you think he had in that drawer?" Vitale asked.

Ned was finally sweating. "All I saw was ones."

"Ones are always on top," Duane said. "Especially at the end of the day."

Information. More and more, I was beginning to believe that Duane had actually used a gun, and now I suspected this wasn't his first holdup (or near holdup).

"How do you know that?" Fran asked.

"Just do." Duane looked at me when he talked to Fran, which was pretty unnerving, since I was sure there was a message there that I wasn't completely ready to receive.

*   *   *

We rode the rest of the way in silence. Fran got all glassy-eyed the way she did when she drifted into one of her fantasy scenarios. I guess this one qualified as a real caper. I worried what my relatives would say, what Leon would think. I wrote imaginary headlines. Things like: "Band of dough nuts terrorize Freddie's clerk" or "Gang pulls peanut stickup."

I knew nothing had happened. Not really. But we'd come so close. It was more like a movie than real life. Fran and I were wandering farther and farther from the ordinary. Tonight someone had seen something about us, sensed a danger we hadn't felt.

She is standing in front of the school. The sun is moving behind a cloud. She calls my name. I run to her. Then I realize it is the middle of the day. There are kids all around. She shouldn't be here. The smell. Look, she says. She shows me a small black mark on her forehead. Someone shot me in the head.

I look down at the cracks in the sidewalk. Tiny veins feeding into an invisible heart. There is a tearing pain in my chest. The kids move away from me, an ocean receding. I am alone in the sun on the sidewalk. I wonder if it shows. I wonder if they can smell it.

I thought again about Leon and the ants. And for the first time, although it only lasted a second, I was truly terrified.

ELEVEN

"My advice to you" (Leon really talked that way) "is to find some new, so-called friends and to disassociate yourself from these people. Obviously they're abnormal."

I knew it had been a mistake to call him. There was no way Leon could understand my life now. Not that I told him everything. But even the slightest hint of anything out of the ordinary alarmed him. It was always like that.

I am sitting at the kitchen counter. Everything is yellow. I pick at the cheese that oozes from between the white bread. I feel him look at me. Watch me. That's how she eats, he says. He moves away. I am suffocating in the yellow. Be careful, Renee, he says. I know what he thinks. That I am becoming. I want to scream, to rip myself open and show him. But that will only make things worse. I pick up a knife and fork. I cut the sandwich in half like he does. See Leon. I am not like her. See.

It took me three weeks of stalling until I revealed that Barry had disappeared. His advice had been typical. "Call the police. Call his parents. Get an annulment. I sensed from the very start those people were abnormal."

My brother meant well. But at an impressionable age, he'd read the Modern Library edition of *The Basic Works of Sigmund Freud*. That was all he knew about human behavior, and according to him, all anyone ever needed to know. The world was an easy place to live if you were Leon. There were microscopes and people. Microscopes were either powerful or weak and people were either normal or abnormal.

"I suggest" — there was no stopping him now — "that you concentrate on what you're in Buffalo for. You're a student. In my opinion, you're allowing yourself to be deluded by the bankrupt culture in which we live. Drugs are a trap. Opium is the opiate of the masses."

Did I mention that my brother was also a Marxist?

I let Leon go on, and he did (since we always charged our calls to our parents, whom we only called on Sundays, birthdays and selected holidays).

It was nice to hear his voice, stable and self-righteous, and completely convinced of every word. But something was lost on the telephone. I needed to see his face. I could imagine the expressions that corresponded to just about everything he said, but it wasn't the same. During a pause, I forced myself to interrupt.

"Leon, do you remember the game we used to play with the water gun and the ants?"

"What game?"

"The one where you shot water out in a circle and surrounded the ant until it couldn't move anymore, and then I finished it off."

"Renee, I think you're making this up."

I hated when he did that. Leon had the memory of record. If he couldn't recall a particular event or person, then it never existed. Of course I hadn't made that up. It was too real. And it was just the sort of thing Leon would invent. Maybe if I mentioned the thing about the murderer's thumbs he'd remember, but most probably he'd still deny it. Leon hated talking about our childhood. I knew he wanted to forget things too. But sometimes his denial made me feel more isolated and alone than I had back then.

It is the day before my birthday. There is snow on the ground. I come home from school late. I use my key. There is an odd silence. I call for him. There is no answer. I walk through the rooms. Quiet. Something bad. The air vibrates. I am standing in the den. He is bent over the fish tank. He is using the net. The mollies and angelfish are piled high on top of one another. Dead. The tank looks different. The water. It is stained. I walk closer. He bristles. Get away, he says. I look. He is draining the tank in the sink behind the bar. But I see it anyway. Blood. The dead fish.

He smashes the tank against the floor. The glass breaks into thousands of deadly shards. Then he looks at me. The curtain moves behind his eyes. Like the iron curtain I hear about on the radio. This never happened, he says.

I run through the house. The smell is everywhere. I find her in the purple room. She is combing her hair, putting rouge on her cheeks. She holds the gold-framed mirror up to the light.

There is blood on her hands.

It's not that I was angry at Leon, or that he purposely meant to be cruel to me. That's just the way he was. Unusual. Eccentric. He had to be. There were reasons. I understood that, and I loved him. He was my mainstay, my friend, my mentor. And he could make me smile in my darkest moments. I remember how he'd come into my room when I was down with a virus, or recuperating from a teenage crush, and draw hilarious caricatures of our teachers, relatives and neighbors until I screamed with laughter. When everyone else, from my father to my algebra teacher, had given up and called me hopeless, he'd take me into his room, look at my math homework and painstakingly explain the reasoning behind things like multiplication, square roots and negative numbers. He had the patience to wait it out, teach me until I understood. Leon never called me stupid. He never made me feel ugly or awkward. He even liked my poetry. He was the first person who totally and completely believed in me. It's just that we were so different. Where Leon was all science and reason, I was a muddle of emotion and impulse. Sometimes I wondered how we could have both grown in the same womb, been shaped from the same gene pool.

Leon left for college two years before I did and he rarely came home to visit. Those last two years, I was largely on my own. Even after my mother went away, my father continued to travel. The aunt came to live in the green house. But by then I was sixteen and could take care of myself. I flew to Chicago twice to visit Leon at the university. The visits were awkward for both of us. He showed me around the campus and introduced me to his friends. He acted formal, almost courtly. I guess it had something to do with the fact that he was putting his childhood behind him. I wondered if I was part of that.

We ended our conversation the way we always did.

"I'm going to send you some literature from the *Guardian* and some technical reports about genetic damage from the use of LSD."

It didn't matter that I'd only taken acid once. Leon was convinced I was destroying myself and my future prospects for child-bearing.

I promised I'd get back to him on what I'd read. There was already a stack of clippings piling up to unreadable proportions beside my bed.

After speaking to Leon, I wanted to break out, to do something really bad. The trouble was, I couldn't think of anything I hadn't already done. "Everything's relative," that's how Barry dealt with thorny issues like right and wrong, good and bad. Fran and I liked to believe that bad still existed. "Otherwise what's the point? Where's the thrill?" was how she put it.

Fran and I weren't interested in mean or cruel, just bad in the sense of forbidden, bad in the way grown-ups used to say, "That's not for you."

That's the kind of bad I was looking for when I caught a glimpse of Duane sauntering down Allen Street. I watched him from the window in the corner of the living room, the one that gave me the best view of the street. He was standing beneath the Allendale marquee. He glanced up at the title: *There's a Whip in My Valise*. I saw him smile. And I wondered what he would be like in bed.

Fran had never had an Indian lover. Once she'd been attracted to someone named Rick, a full-blooded Canandaigua, whom she described as "fierce and implacable with a head that melted into his neck." Not my type. But obviously hers. The problem was, Rick was married. When his wife confronted Fran at the Laundromat and threatened her with bodily injury if she didn't back off, Fran got the message.

"Keep away from those guys," she warned me. "They have their own rules."

She referred to the incident with Rick as her "Indian Drama."

When I remembered how Duane had looked with the gun, I got all warm inside. It was just the sort of bad I craved. Nothing evil, just something out of the ordinary.

I realized I needed an excuse. Without some sort of reason, there was no way I could approach Duane, who, when I stretched my imagination, was sort of fierce and implacable himself. Then it hit me. Of course. I went to my dresser drawer and dug out the matchbook cover from the Aragon Lounge. Perfect. It might even prove helpful. Either way, I wouldn't lose face. Not completely.

I waited awhile, until I heard the front door of the building slam shut. Then I walked slowly down the stairs. I liked the idea that Duane lived in the basement. The perfect setting for my own Indian Drama.

He opened the door before I knocked, as if he'd been expecting me all along. It wasn't dark, as I'd imagined. A watery light poured in through the basement window.

Duane stared right through me. His skin, when I looked closely, wasn't really acne-pitted: it was acne-scarred. Almost as if someone had planed it down nice and smooth, but had left enough marks to remind him it had never really been good, soft, white man's skin.

His eyes were burning. Black, like two shining onyx stones.

I walked inside. The room was small and very clean. There was no furniture, just a few orange crates and an expensive-looking stereo. Procol Harum was singing "A Whiter Shade of Pale."

I sat on an orange crate; Duane eased himself onto the floor. I was beginning to feel dizzy, I knew I had to say something soon.

"Look, I'd just like to ask you a question."

"Shoot."

It was hard for me to breathe. My chest felt tight. I had this weird, floating feeling.

"You remember Barry, the guy who used to live upstairs with me?" I just couldn't say the word *husband*. I couldn't ask him if he remembered my husband.

"Yeah, I remember him."

"Well, you know he's sort of disappeared and I have reason to believe he might have been hanging out in the Aragon Lounge. Have you ever seen him there?"

I was aware that, just by asking, I was admitting I was too white to go to the Aragon. Too white and too afraid.

Duane stood up. His long black ponytail bounced against his back. I couldn't help noticing how tight his jeans were, how they molded to his body.

"Wanna beer?"

"No thanks."

He walked back toward the rear of the apartment. I heard him open the refrigerator and punch two holes in a beer can. I changed my mind. Maybe a beer might be a good idea. Too late. I couldn't ask him now. It would make it sound as though I wanted to stay.

He sat down very close to me. I could feel his breath, sweet and warm from the beer.

Then it just happened. He didn't ask. There was no elaborate discussion. He just reached up and touched my breast. I felt damp everywhere. The room got all soft and blurry.

He didn't say a word. His hands moved beneath my blouse. In a second, he had unclasped my bra and had his mouth against my flesh. I watched his hands move along my skin. I wanted him to touch me everywhere at the same time.

He never took my clothes off. He unbuttoned my jeans and pushed them down around my ankles. When I went to slip my underpants off, he stopped me. There was an insistence in the way he moved. He wanted to be in control. He pushed the crotch of my underpants over to one side and touched me until I was moist. I reached out for him. His penis was hard and thick in my hand. I wanted him to slow everything down, to make it last. But he couldn't wait for that. He covered my mouth with his lips. The light seemed to disappear. Even with my eyes open, I was suspended in an odd sort of darkness. Then he entered me, moving up and down in a steady rhythm. I couldn't have enough of him. I wanted him deeper, faster, more violently. I never wanted this to end.

The orgasm came slowly, working its way up my body, until the sensations were almost painful. I held him, still hard, inside me after it was over. Neither of us spoke. Then, as if by mutual agreement, we fell apart from each other.

I moved my hand over his arm. The skin on his body was smooth and hairless. His chest was hard and muscular. Lying on his back like this, with his long hair splayed out like a dark fan beneath him, he looked exotic, almost handsome.

I was afraid to say anything. When he turned and looked at me, those eyes still burning, I thought my voice would break the spell, make it all real and ordinary.

He stood up and zipped his pants. I felt ashamed. Physically, I was exhausted, but I wanted more. I think at that moment, I realized this was different from just having sex, making love or simply fucking. This was passion, lust. It was something beyond my control — beyond my desire to control.

He lit a cigarette and handed it to me. We watched as a drift of yellow smoke hung in the air, mixing with the scent of beer and sex.

"In answer to your question, no I never seen Barry over at the Aragon."

I sat up, buttoning my blouse and straightening my pants. I hated hearing Barry's name now. My original question seemed silly, a transparent excuse for what I had really wanted.

"Are you sure?"

"Yeah, I'm sure."

I honestly didn't know what to do next. I didn't want to leave, but I didn't want to talk either. If it had been possible, I would have stayed there with him, silently watching the light from the basement window turn from yellow to purple, until darkness came and went. I wanted him to make love to me again. The neediness made me uncomfortable. I knew, that given the time, I would start talking — jabbering nonstop. I didn't want Duane to see that side of me.

I walked toward the door. He made no effort to stop me.

"Listen, if you do see him, or hear that he's been around, will you let me know?"

"Sure."

Duane didn't ask any questions. He didn't mention what had just happened between us. Like a jerk, I was already wondering if he cared.

He opened the door. Just as I was about to leave, I felt his hand flutter to my shoulder. He's going to kiss me, I thought. I turned my face up toward the light. But he was talking. I couldn't make out the words.

"Could you say that again?"

"I said, I never seen Barry there, but I seen your girlfriend from upstairs. I knew it was her. She was dressed in man's clothes."

TWELVE

Most people only wait for the big things. That's all they know about. Big things, like falling in love, getting married, becoming famous. They don't watch out for the little details. Leon explained this to me on a field trip at Camp Winoway.

There we were, tramping through the woods. Everyone was looking for the big things: deer, rabbit, wild turkey. Leon let them all walk ahead. We listened as their heavy boots made loud thumping sounds through the earth. He told me to take off my shoes. We walked like the Indians, our feet silently slipping through the thick grasses. And we always looked down, watching for the little things. I found a patch of tiny, wild strawberries, bright flecks of red poking through the green. And Leon found the egg. It had already been hatched, a jagged, desperate hole torn along one side. But it was still, miraculously, intact. Thin, translucent, like the finest porcelain. And blue. Robin's egg blue.

Leon let me carry the egg back to my bunk. I placed it

on the cedar chest alongside my bed. In the morning it was shattered, bits of blue shell crushed against the wooden floorboards. Someone had accidentally brushed against it, someone in too much of a hurry to notice the delicate miracle.

I thought about the egg for a long time. It was one of Leon's lessons that stayed with me. It was the image that constantly reappeared to me that night as I paced the floors of my apartment. It was only a little thing. But the big things had become overwhelming, rolling in one right after another, without a moment's pause. There was no time to stop and examine the details.

I was doing that now, trying to understand just what had happened between Duane and me, trying to understand what he had told me. But it seemed as if there was just too much to unravel.

I looked out on Allen Street. It was almost dark now. Dusk was what we called it those summers at Camp Winoway. But dusk didn't seem like a city word. Dusk was when the light got all golden and mists floated in from behind the mountains. It was the best time to spot deer running in herds through the meadows, the time to pitch tents and start camp fires.

Summer just didn't seem right in the city. Buffalo was made for winter. Everything looked wrong here now. Shabby. Overbuilt. Dangerous.

I heard a door slam and saw Fran emerge from the building. She was wearing her famous denim miniskirt, the one she'd worn when she emceed the folk festival at the university. Tonight her hair hung long and freshly combed down her back. It was smooth, like a straight blond curtain. From the back, in the bluish light of evening, she looked like Mary Travers of Peter, Paul and Mary. I'd told Fran that not long after we'd first met. I remember how she'd smiled in spite of herself. It was a comparison she approved of.

I was totally in awe of her then. Maybe because she was a year older and she moved with an elegance that was completely unexpected. But probably it was because of the suicide attempt.

They had just coaxed her off the roof when I saw her for the first time. She was sitting dry-eyed and composed on Sherman's couch. And she was wearing this cloche. It was black and soft with a bell-like brim that cast dramatic shadows across her face. I'd always wanted a hat like that. But hats made me feel self-conscious, short, fat, ridiculously pretentious.

She looked great for someone who only moments earlier had threatened to fling herself from the roof of a three-story building. It was all for love, or the lack of it. Her then boyfriend, whom she simply called Silver, had abandoned her for a dark-skinned beauty in his Robert Creely poetry seminar. I remember how she'd sat silently on the couch while Sherman offered her every drug in his arsenal. She shook her head and stared at the worn carpet. Finally, Vitale brought her a cup of herbal tea and asked her to throw the I Ching. He pressed three small brown coins into her hand and she sat down with him on the floor and began making strange predictions about all our lives.

After almost an hour, she finally noticed me, and

flashed a conspiratorial grin that seemed to indicate she was reveling in all the attention.

Fran never talked about the suicide again. Afterward, I think we filled a certain void in each other's lives. Men couldn't come between us. We never actually said it, but it was understood. Even after I married Barry, Fran was my real soul mate.

That's why none of this made sense, until I began to look for the little things. Duane couldn't know about Fran's penchant for disguise. There was no way he could have made up something like that. And dressing like a man was something Fran had done before. She had done it with Silver when he took her to McSorley's, the all-male bar in Manhattan. They'd made a bet. He didn't believe she'd have the guts. "The balls, you mean," she'd said. She taped her breasts, and pasted a thin mustache over her lip. She wore a tight-fitting wool cap, jeans and combat boots. After chugging three drafts in her best boy style, she gleefully collected one hundred dollars from a completely astonished Silver.

But she had told me about that. Just like she told me about everything. Like the fact that despite all her sexual adventures, she'd never, not even once, had an orgasm.

"Tell me how you do it," she'd asked.

I explained how I closed my eyes and drifted into a fantasy, thought of something that turned me on.

"I haven't got any fantasies," she'd explained. "I live them all. There's nothing left to imagine."

I had tried to explain about erotic fantasies, how they were different from the scenarios we planned together.

But Fran drew a blank on that one. It was her only flaw; her only regret.

When I thought about all this, I felt sad and confused. I realized that Duane would be my first secret; an erotic adventure, an "Indian Drama" I couldn't share with Fran. I wasn't exactly sure why, but something told me what had happened between us was too charged, too powerful to talk about. And of course there was that other thing. That big thing that I wasn't ready to accept, if it was true at all. That Fran had been in the Aragon. The disguise didn't matter. She'd been there and she'd never breathed a word. I couldn't help it, but the thought of keeping secrets from one another conjured up visions of the two of us dashing around in trench coats like the "Spy vs. Spy" cartoons from *Mad* magazine.

Maybe it was all a joke, a misunderstanding. Duane could be wrong. I knew there were some little things going on here, little things that would link up neatly to one another until the truth of the big thing would be revealed. Like the way the hole in the robin's egg told us that after a desperate struggle, a living thing had been born and had flown off into the air.

But this wasn't Leon's world. It was mine. It wasn't as easy as putting my ear to the earth and listening for the silence, I couldn't slip off my shoes and find riches beneath my feet.

Watch her, Renee. Look for the lies. The fake voice. The twisted smile. Don't let her see your weaknesses. She can hurt you. Leon holds the photograph of my dead Un-

cle Sidney up to the light. *This is a clue, Renee, he says.*
This means something.

I watched as Fran walked quickly down Allen Street.
She seemed to be headed somewhere. Then I remembered
about the movie. Something called *Bonnie and Clyde* that
was playing downtown. Fran had heard it was shocking,
violent. She was meeting Ned in front of the theater.

I stared until her silhouette faded into the darkness. That's
when I realized I was alone in the forest. Lost, without a
guide, without someone to lead me into a safe, bright
place where I could find my way by tracking the little
things.

THIRTEEN

I try to imagine the scene; a smoke-filled bar, thick men with grime-encrusted hands gripping beer mugs and wiping sweat from the insides of their caps, barmaids with teased hair and tattoos. Fran enters from a side door. She's wearing the boy disguise: breasts taped tightly beneath a heavy cotton shirt, a woolen cap catching all her hair. Maybe she's painted on a thin, brown mustache. She nods to the bartender and silently points to the bottle of Southern Comfort behind the bar. She downs a shot, careful not to shake her long hair loose. Then she moves invisibly to the back room. There's a pool table and a broken pinball machine. In the darkest corner she finds the phone booth, the old-fashioned wooden kind, with a well-worn seat. Names are carved into the wood. She takes out a penknife and digs the sharp point into a blank space. "Joe," she writes, or "Bill." I think about the name Fran would choose. It would be a simple masculine name, John, maybe. Then she gets into character, I've seen her do this

100

before. She does the breathing thing, visualizing herself as the mythical boy. Then she dials my number. Pressing her hand over the receiver, she creates the raspy wind sound. "Renee. Die."

■

I was trying to be Fran, just as I'd tried to be Leon, but it wasn't working. I couldn't picture the Aragon, I could only imagine something I might have seen once on TV. And the images of Fran frightened me. It was as if she had another self, someone I didn't know. Something struck me then about Fran, something ancient, a moment that would last forever.

She goes away in the blue car. She holds me close. I feel her breath on my cheek. I'll be home soon, my baby, she says. She smiles and waves. But then it gets dark. I wait by the window aching to see the tip of the car turn the corner, aching to feel her arms around me. It hurts too much to love her so. Leon scowls. He presses a pin into the wing of a butterfly he is mounting on a board. Don't wait for her, he says. I pretend to go to sleep. It is pitch-black when I hear her car in the driveway. I tiptoe past Leon's room. I stand by the door, just wanting to breathe her in. Mommy.

But she is different now. Her eyes are glassy. Her movements quick and jerky. There is a twist in the corner of her mouth. Sidney, go to sleep, she says. I am not Sidney. I am Renee. Sidney is her dead brother. He died of a fever when they were teenagers. I am alive. I am her child. I do not move. I say nothing. She is lost to me now. Lost in that place where there is no time, where memory and terror are intertwined, leaving only madness.

In the morning we find her. There is a trail of blood that leads to the purple room. The cuts are not deep. She only hurts herself. For now, Leon says. Just wait.

It was 2 A.M. I walked to the window and stared out at the street. Even in the semidarkness, I could see a group of people sitting on the scrubby dirt of Days Park, passing a joint and staring up at the sky. If I opened the window and craned my neck, I could see a corner of the Aragon. Maybe I could catch a glimpse of the other Fran.

I knew as I dressed, throwing on the Levi's I used to wear in high school and the gauzy white Indian top, that I was doing something crazy. I tried to think of it as dreamwalking. I used to dreamwalk as a child. It was different from sleepwalking, because from what I could figure out I never actually left the bed.

The dream was always the same; I'd get up, walk past Leon's room, through the yellow kitchen, and out the door. Then I'd run down the empty suburban streets, swinging on the neighbors' jungle gyms, rummaging in garages, peering into windows. I was a ghost, a vision, a nocturnal thief who defied detection. After the dream walk, I always woke up with the same apprehensive feeling: Had it really happened? Had I really left? That's when I began some of the rituals: the nearly invisible strand of hair placed across the threshold of my room, along the front door, inside the crack in the slate walk — the row of objects arranged in random order to block my path. Some mornings the hairs would still be where I'd left them, other times they were gone, blown away perhaps. The objects were usually where they'd been the night before, but I could never be absolutely certain.

That's how it felt being out on the street, a dream commingling with reality.

The park was illuminated by a single streetlight. A sweet cloud of marijuana smoke wafted toward me. Somewhere in the distance I could hear Jim Morrison singing "Light My Fire."

I walked across to the Aragon. The place had a distinct odor, a heady combination of booze and cigars and those dried pork things that looked like dog treats. I couldn't see very much. Big, broad-shouldered men clustered around the dark bar. The Aragon wasn't the sort of place a woman could casually saunter into and not be noticed. Like a cub scout den or a postgame locker room, it was strictly "off limits." No girls allowed. Maybe, I reasoned, that's how it had happened with Fran. Maybe she just wanted to get a glimpse of the inside, so she dressed like a man. Why not? She'd done it before. Fran and I had talked a lot about how much easier it was to go places as a male: bars, garages, restaurants. It was the ultimate costume, the most complete transformation. Maybe when she was inside, she got carried away, felt she actually *was* a man. But that's where my theory hit a dead end. Why would Fran, even as a man, want to threaten me? No. It just didn't work. Duane had to have been mistaken, or maybe I wasn't being careful. Maybe I was missing the little things. I heard Leon's voice:

Be careful, Renee. Don't make the same mistake again.
Watch. Listen.

I heard a car door slam in the distance. As if on cue, laughing voices rippled through the stillness. When I turned to look back at the Aragon, there he was. Duane. He was leaning against the bar, and in the electric twilight of Days Park, I could easily make out his profile.

It was like watching something intimate, something I shouldn't be seeing at all. He held a thick glass mug in one hand and gestured toward the bartender with the other. I could almost smell him, that unmistakable male aphrodisiac: smoke, beer, sweat.

There was a man standing next to him. A tall Indian wearing a floppy suede hat. He rubbed his hand along Duane's back in a reassuring, brotherly way. Duane laughed. When he threw his head back, his ponytail swung onto his shoulder. I concentrated on his hands. It made me feel off balance to think of that now. Duane wasn't like Barry or Ned, or the other nice, safe boys I had known. He wasn't a boy at all. He was what every mother warns her daughter about and what every daughter eagerly, hungrily anticipates from that first bloody moment of puberty. A man.

I wondered what Fran would think, what Leon would think. Duane was someone outside our world. Someone who hadn't grown up with "the advantages": a private home, a backyard, an English racer, parents who shelled out for an orthodontist. Maybe that was the attraction. Duane was tough. Hard. Blue collar all the way. An excellent choice for my first man. I smiled to myself when I thought of the expression "Sex, hard and fast." It was something Fran and I had talked about on one of those nights when we sat and smoked grass in front of the Laundromat. "No one," she had said, "is really into sex any-more. Not like the boys in high school who wanted you so bad, they made you feel good to want them back. Those were the days when we had sex, hard and fast."

I hadn't answered because I was too timid to admit what Fran probably knew anyway: I'd been a virgin in high school.

Fran was one of those girls most mothers would have labeled "off limits." She'd tried sex early. Like me, she never went in for the rah-rah all-American image. She'd wanted to be a beatnik, to wear her hair unteased and parted down the middle, to read poetry by Ferlinghetti and Ginsberg, to travel "on the road," and use words like *cool* and *man*. Sex was part of the image, "de rigueur," as Fran put it. But where Fran had thrown herself with total abandon, I had held back, unable to go all the way, I was a virgin beatnik, a halfhearted, fully intact, angry young woman. It was too embarrassingly square to admit it, but Barry had actually been my first lover.

Ironically, with all her varied experiences, everything from middle-aged stunt men to pubescent choirboys, Fran now found sex boring, as casual and as automatic as a friendly hug. I half agreed with her.

Then there was Duane. I was afraid, as I watched his face become a discolored blur in the darkness, that what had happened between us would change things between Fran and me. It was a passion that couldn't be shared. Duane wasn't Ned. He wasn't our sex toy, our experiment in communal copulation, someone we could mock as we passed him back and forth. I was experiencing something different now, an intensity, a lust, a sexual secret that was deliciously private.

I narrowed my eyes, hoping to catch one last glimpse of Duane in the hazy interior of the Aragon. But he'd moved away, perhaps to some dark back room where he talked about football and engines and the things that occupy men's minds.

I walked across the park. The circle of star gazers sitting on the grass had widened. Someone was playing a recorder. Two women sang in thin, strained voices. A bearded boy with beads woven through his hair flashed me the peace symbol. Wesley. He believed he was a warlock, someone who could heal the sick and cast spells. Fran had slept with him once and he'd been impotent. It was the sort of story that made her reel with laughter. Imagine, a warlock, a magician who couldn't perform the ultimate trick.

He waved me toward the circle. I walked slowly, enjoying what was left of the summer night.

"Renee, want some Purple Sunshine?" Wesley held up a stained sugar cube. "Acid. Great stuff." Remembering Leon's warnings, I shook my head. Wesley rolled his eyes and pointed to the sky. "We're part of the great cosmos. Have you ever seen infinity?"

Wesley smelled of LSD. Barry believed when you dropped acid, the chemicals were released through the pores. He only took natural drugs: mushrooms, grass, things that grew from the soil. He didn't believe in manmade highs. I guess he was a purist that way.

I sat down beside Wesley and, declining the Purple Sunshine, took a deep toke of a joint that was passing around the circle. "Acapulco Gold," I heard someone say. "Far out."

Almost without warning, the park darkened, whirling

and dipping like a carnival ride. Wesley's voice grew louder and more intense. He pointed to the stars and talked about a cosmic consciousness, a new cycle, a positive karma. One of the women began chanting. A second one, with skeletal arms and a pinched face, joined her. They swayed together like some dreamy liquid apparition. I couldn't make out the words of their song although I strained to listen. Wesley placed another sugar cube under his tongue.

Suddenly I didn't want to be there. The once friendly circle became threatening. From where I was sitting, I could see the light I had left on in my apartment. It glowed yellow and welcoming as I walked home.

Standing in front of the door to my building, I glanced back at Wesley and his group. They seemed to be moving closer, a black ring of bodies swaying to an eerie rhythm. Like ants, they clustered greedily around a square of sugar, milling, humming. Engrossed in their activities, they were totally unaware of anything beyond themselves. That's when I thought of other summer days.

I am holding the gun in my hand. Kill him, Leon orders. The ant is frantic, running against the ever-tightening wall of water, looking desperately for escape. Like me, I think. Trapped. I feel Leon's hand on my arm. Kill him! I close my eyes and pull the trigger.

I am at once the murderer and the victim.

There was no one beside me when the phone rang, no one to verify what I heard. My walk in the park might have been a dream, and I might too have imagined the call as well. I couldn't be sure about anything that evening.

The voice had that same raspy, furtive texture, as if someone was placing a hand over the receiver. I closed my eyes, and pressed the phone against my cheek, hoping this was part of the dream, hoping the voice would fade into the blackness. He said only four words:

"Tonight death will come."

FOURTEEN

"They knew they were going to die. It was inevitable. But it didn't stop them."

Fran was standing beside my bed waving her arms like windmills in a hurricane. She was excited. I'd been up half the night, tormented with fears, unable to escape that anonymous voice breathing through the telephone. Finally, I remembered where Barry kept the Seconals, a vial of slim orange bullets he saved for emergency LSD rescues. His "safeties," he called them.

I was still feeling pretty drugged, only partially emerged from that hazy torpor Leon and I called the "crusty state."

"What are you talking about?" I asked, wondering how Fran could have known about the death threats. Suspicion made me suddenly alert.

"*Bonnie and Clyde.* The movie Ned and I saw last night. It was amazing. It blew my mind. He was completely impotent, but she loved him anyway. Then they finally made it and they died."

*   *   *

"From sex?" I tried to remember if it was salmon or praying mantises or both who died immediately following copulation.

"No. The cops caught them. Their bodies were riddled with bullets."

None of this was very clear to me. I assumed Fran was leaving out major elements of the plot.

"You've got to see this movie. It's revolutionary. For the first time, the criminals become the heroes."

"But I thought they got killed at the end."

"What do you expect? This is still America."

At this moment, I noticed the knife resting against Fran's bare thigh.

"What's that doing there?"

"I found it in your bathtub."

For an instant I thought about the hair I'd carefully placed against the door. It was probably gone now and there'd be no way of knowing if it had been Fran or someone else who'd dislodged it.

"What was a knife doing in the bathroom? Didn't this belong to Barry? I seem to remember him cutting hash with it. Does this mean he's been back?"

"I don't know. I saw it after Ned went to sleep. It was just lying there with a tiny drop of blood on the tip."

"I didn't see any blood," Fran said.

"You really had to look carefully. It was almost a speck."

Fran glanced at me doubtfully. *Gaslight*, I thought. It was an old movie where Charles Boyer tried to drive Ingrid Bergman crazy by putting things one place, then moving them and denying he'd ever seen them. Leon and I had seen it three times.

"*Believe me*, there *was* blood."

Fran sidled over to the window. She was wearing a gray knit minidress covered with tiny white peace symbols. I had stolen it on a whim.

"Ned's gone," she said. Just like that. Like people vanished every day.

"What do you mean, 'gone'?"

"Weird shit. We talked about the movie all night. It was incredible. Then we went to Held's bakery and scarfed a dozen of those pink and white cookies, drove back here and nodded out. When I woke up, no Ned. That's not like him, usually he sleeps till noon."

"God, I hate that. Barry did that all the time. I'd wake up and reach over to his side of the bed and it was empty. No note. Nothing."

"Men can be real shits," Fran said.

My mood took a further dip. First Barry, now Ned. Maybe there was a man-eating vortex, an invisible configuration of paranormal quicksand, a Bermuda Triangle located somewhere in the environs of Buffalo into which both Barry and Ned had fallen. It was an interesting theory, something that were it not for the raspy calls, blood smears and onerous notes, might have neatly explained everything.

I was thinking that maybe, instead of fatally disappearing into the hole, Barry and Ned were pulled down by some unknown force. Then, once captive, they became something else — the undead, perhaps — when Fran called my attention to the window.

The morning was shrouded in the usual comforting

gloom. One sickly, halfhearted ray of sunshine quivered through the streaked glass.

"Something's going on out there." Fran pointed from my window down to the street. Her nails clicked against the glass like ten eager little Indians. "Look."

I dragged myself from the rumpled bed, reluctant to abandon my innovative theories concerning first Barry's, now Ned's disappearance.

Downstairs on the littered street, a crowd of tie-dyed, love-beaded, and decidedly bleary-eyed Allentown residents had formed. Red lights flashed. An ambulance pulled away.

Fran lunged for the door.

"Wait for me to get dressed," I shouted.

But Fran, half running, half floating, was way ahead of me. The peace symbols on her dress became a wild pattern of frenzied motion. I pulled on my jeans and followed, hurtling down the stairs like a bowling ball headed for the gutter.

The instant my sandaled feet touched the sidewalk in front of Days Park I knew something was wrong. It was like one of those picture quizzes I used to take in elementary school, the ones with the drawing of a happy family sitting beneath a tree sharing a picnic lunch, and there in the foreground was, inexplicably, a tractor wheel or a bedroom lamp. "What's wrong with this picture?" the prune-faced teacher would ask. Now I knew why I'd been submitted to those tests. Preparation for this moment. My eyes scanned the crowd. A sorry collection of anti-establishment misfits gathered around a spot on the pavement, pointing to nothing in particular. That was it. The nothing in particular. This was a play with no protagonist. An accident with no victim. I breathed a sigh of relief. For some unfathomable reason, I'd experienced a moment of dread, a premonition that this scene and my life had some horrible connection.

It is a danger that won't go away. This is how my life will always be.

Then I saw Ned's car. It was just there, parked alongside the curb. The door was open. It hung ominously from one corner. That's when the moment became a De Chirico painting, the kind where nothing bloody or gory is actually visible, but you feel as if you just missed it all, which is even worse, because your imagination begins to create demonic scenes of unmentionable horror.

Something dark and turbulent was tugging at my insides. A voice was calling out to me. It was Sherman. He was pulling at my arm. His mouth was moving. The words were coming out in giant comic-book bubbles that floated into the dreary sky.

"He never saw it coming. Hit from behind. Didn't feel a thing." Sherman pointed to a spot on the sidewalk. There wasn't any blood. Nothing. Not even a scrap of cloth. I wondered if they'd taken everything away. Fran was crying. Big gulping sobs that contorted her face until she looked like an ugly clown.

A cop moved through the crowd taking notes on a little pad. He was an enormous blue presence, a messenger of doom from another world.

I stood next to Fran. The peace symbols had realigned themselves in restive, orderly rows.

"Ned," she cried. "He was getting into his car. I told you he got up and left. It was a hit and run. There were no witnesses."

The world was suddenly strange. Somewhere in the distance a chorus of "Twist and Shout" drifted from an open window. A dog barked. Two birds twittered in a rotting elm.

I picked at the skin around my thumb until a thin trickle of blood made its way down my wrist.

"But there's nothing here," I said. I wanted proof: spilled guts, mashed brains, cords of twisted disemboweled innards. I wanted the full horror of it, not this pale, silent, bloodless imitation.

Sherman shrugged his shoulders. His face was molded into an ambiguous scowl. So it wasn't real. Ned was hurt, that was all. The hellish scene I'd imagined was a figment of my own warped mind. It was all finally catching up with me: the junk food, the repeated X rays in the Buster Brown shoe store, the hours spent watching television, the masturbatory ecstasy in the pink bathroom. Okay. I was sorry. I was ready to change my ways. I turned to Sherman, an anticipatory smile on my lips.

His expression was grim. "They didn't think he was breathing when they took him away."

I wasn't ready to surrender. Not yet. Not when I hadn't seen the body, not before I knew the details.

"How come we didn't hear anything?" I looked accusingly at Fran.

"No one was there. I guess there wasn't anything to hear. Maybe he never even screamed," Sherman answered.

I tried to picture Ned floating in a hollow of air above the green Saab. Maybe at precisely the moment Fran had told me about Bonnie and Clyde being riddled with bullets, Ned was pinned helplessly against the car door.

"It happened a few hours ago. We were all sleeping," Sherman said.

"But I just saw the ambulance leave."

"That was for Wesley, you know, the warlock. He flipped out on some bad acid and they took him to Millard Fillmore to come down."

"Is he dead?"

"I doubt it."

"I mean Ned."

Fran began sobbing hysterically. Watching her mouth twist into a rubbery pretzel, I realized that before today I'd never seen her cry.

There was a static feeling in the air, a scent of stale cigarettes and dust. I was an actor in a movie, any minute someone was going to shout, "Cut!" and all the characters milling about would relax. Wesley would hop up out of the ambulance and Ned would saunter around a corner looking blond and perfect as ever. It was all a joke, an hallucination, one of those trippy fantasies that seemed real but wasn't. I got this crazy, desperate idea that if I could only remember Ned's face, if I could recreate him in my mind, then I could make him alive. Undead. It was like imagining a key or a book I'd lost, picturing it until I remembered where I'd lost it. But when I tried to retrieve his image, it flickered and dimmed, dissolving into a murky composite of male features. Maybe that meant that Ned was dead, that his essence was being erased from my mind.

No one saw me walk away. The crowd was growing

restless. Someone said something about calling the hospital. I drifted from the scene like a dry leaf on a windy autumn day. Checking my back, I tiptoed up the stairs to my apartment. That's when the voice returned. If I listened closely, I could hear it blowing through the air, floating in the pearl-colored light. It didn't matter what the voice had said. It was there, its presence was undeniable. Someone would die, it had said. And as I looked out on the street, I could almost imagine that it was me down there; that I had been the one who had been hit. Then the bitter taste in my mouth dissolved, leaving a chalky texture of gray dust and bones.

■

Beside my bed, on a table with the telephone, was a photograph the aunt had taken of Leon and me just before he left for college. I stared at the photograph before I picked up the phone. It had been late September and the trees were just beginning to yellow. Leon was wearing a pair of brown cotton slacks and a short-sleeved shirt. I had on a white cotton minidress. There was a space between us. Not a large space, just a few inches, enough to reveal a sliver of luminous sky. I remember the instant the photograph was taken. The aunt had wanted us to pose with our arms entwined. Brother and sister. But at the last minute, I had arched forward, creating the separation. I couldn't stand to touch Leon. It was as if he was surrounded by a physical force field, a barrier that emitted an energy which made contact dangerous.

I don't know why, but now I found myself thinking back to that day and how I'd pulled away from him.

I saw what you did, Leon. I saw you in the purple room.

I dialed his number. It rang five times. The voice that answered was not Leon's. It was his roommate, Stevie Green.

"Leon's not here," he said, groggy from sleep. "He's on a date."

A date. I tried to picture it. Leon on a date. It's not that he never went out with girls, but being on a date conjured up images of soda pops and malteds with two straws and all the things Leon despised.

"What do you mean, a date?"

"He's with Ruth. His girlfriend."

I felt as though I had pushed through something. The force field. The impenetrable barrier surrounding my brother. What girlfriend? Leon had never mentioned dating. I had never heard him say the name Ruth.

That was when I got the panicky feeling.

The images are closing in on me. I see reflections. I am remembering. Leon. I saw you do it. I was watching. No. This will pull me down. A black vortex. It will drain me until there is nothing left.

Again, I reached for the Seconals. I only took two, just enough for the sounds and the visions to dissolve into an opaque blaze.

■

I slept for a long time. A deep dreamless sleep. When I awoke Fran was sitting beside me. A square lozenge of light rested on her face, framing it like a pale mask.

She sipped tea from a blue china mug. Her hands were steady, but there was a quivery movement beneath her eyelids. I wanted to hear her say the words. This time the voice had to have a source, I had to see it shape itself from sound to meaning.

She was still wearing the gray dress. If I reached out I could touch one of the tiny white peace symbols. But I didn't move. I knew what was coming. I'd had advance warning. That's why it was easy to breathe, why I barely flinched as Fran spoke.

"Renee," she said, "Ned died two hours ago, while you were sleeping."

FIFTEEN

This time I was sure. I knew he'd been there. I checked the closets. His clothes were gone: the battered leather jacket and the paisley shirts, the jeans and the turtlenecks. The drawers had been emptied too. But there was no note, nothing ominous or threatening. Barry had been here. He was alive. I touched the sides of the worn red armchair, hoping to feel any vibrations he might have left behind. I ran my hand across the wooden knobs of the dresser drawers, expecting to experience some warmth, some last residual sense of him.

Barry took only what he needed. He'd been neat and orderly and careful not to touch anything that wasn't completely his. He'd left the cardboard box with our wedding pictures behind.

He must have come while we were in the field. Fran had planned a memorial service for Ned. We'd driven out in Vitale's van and watched the sun set over the abandoned meadows. Fran lit sticks of incense and we'd formed a circle and tried to make contact with Ned's aura.

It wasn't easy, but Wesley, who'd recently been released from the hospital, told us he'd had a vision of Ned floating serenely through the cosmos, his blond hair trailing a web of seashells and stars.

We sat in the meadow for hours waiting to feel something. Everyone wore white, the color, Fran said, that symbolized positive spiritual karma. I'm not sure how it happened, maybe it was the purple sunset and the nostalgia of the moment, but instead of talking about Ned, we talked about ourselves, about all the safe, sure things we remembered: high school and cars and TV shows. We sat in our ghostly circle, a ring of white shirts talking in quiet voices. Sherman told us how he'd grown up on TV and comic books, watching shows like *Andy's Gang* and *Queen for a Day* while he read every "Archie" and "Little LuLu" comic he could get his hands on. It was easy to imagine Marshal Sherman somewhere in New Jersey in a house with aluminum siding and a pale green, 1955 Dodge parked in the blacktopped driveway. It was easy, because we'd all grown up in much the same way, surrounded by TV and comic books, baseball cards and Ginny dolls. We were charmed, packed like fragile dolls in cotton and cardboard.

And that's how we'd left it. Bits and pieces of our memories, scattered like ashes over the meadow. I never did get in touch with Ned's aura, but Fran said we'd touched his spirit in some profound way.

■

I wondered as I walked through my apartment, checking here and there for some clue Barry might have left behind, if he'd been spying on me all this time, skulking in the shadows, sidling up to door frames, peering into keyholes. Maybe, and the thought just crossed my mind for an instant, Barry had known about Ned and me and Fran and our less than torrid, but hardly ordinary, sexual arrangement. Maybe *he'd* been the one to warn me. Maybe it had been jealousy that had pushed him over the edge. But I knew that couldn't be true. For someone else, but not for Barry. Barry was perpetually, almost unendurably cool. He was a devotee of jazz and pot and the beat generation. He'd never let himself get angry or jealous, or at least he'd never shown it. Sometimes I even wondered if he'd really loved me at all, or if our marriage was just a counterculture capitalist venture.

I decided to go about things in a neat, orderly way, a scientific way. I made a list of everything Barry had taken. There was a chance that what he took as well as what he left behind might give me some sense of where he'd gone and what he needed there. What the hell? It was something to keep me occupied while I repressed frightening possibilities.

He'd taken his clothes and three record albums: The Lovin' Spoonful, Doors and Jefferson Airplane. His hash pipe was gone and so were the phenomenology books. Wherever Barry was, he was still doing the same things he always did. He hadn't been kidnapped or murdered, that much was clear.

When I ran my hand against the bottom of his dresser drawer I found a photograph I'd never seen before. It was of him and some girl. The girl seemed familiar, and when I looked closer, I saw that it was his sister, Carole. Their arms were intertwined and their faces seemed almost joined around the jaw line. In the background, I could make out the indistinct shape of the gray stone apartment building in the Bronx where they'd grown up. It was hard to be sure, but I figured Barry must have been about fifteen and Carole seventeen when the picture was taken. It was odd, that picture. I couldn't put my finger on it, but it made me uneasy.

I tried to remember the last time I'd seen Carole. It had been at her wedding. Come to think of it, that had been odd too. Two months after Barry and I had married, Carole announced, to everyone's astonishment, that she'd met "the one." He was as unlikely a match for her as anyone I could have ever imagined. An offensively straight and overly polite guy with short hair and horn-rimmed glasses named Noel Willinger — a throwback to a time when cars had tail fins, Mom teased her hair and all the really cool guys wore crew cuts. In short, he was a creep.

Barry claimed she was marrying him on the rebound since her heart had been broken by someone he only referred to as "that bastard."

The wedding was garish, vulgar and formal. In a time when getting married barefoot on a hilltop while various long-haired friends in altered states of consciousness played flutes and assorted string instruments was all the rage, this wedding was a painful anachronism.

Barry's parents huddled at a little table in the corner and tried not to appear wildly out of place. His relatives were dark spots, refugees sinking into a sea of glowing blond hair and perfect white teeth. But it wasn't the food, the guests or the band (some sad leftover quintet from a stale New Year's Eve, circa 1953) that I remember most vividly. It was my dress.

Fran and I had copped it a week earlier at a place called The Bride's Shoppe. A chirpy gray-haired sales-woman complete with cat's eyeglasses hanging on a silver cord around her neck urged me to stand on a round ped-estal in a mirrored dressing room decorated with hearts and ribbons. While she carried in all sorts of fluffy pink creations, Fran expertly slipped a long yellow cotton gown into her purse.

The dress looked adequate when I tried it on in Fran's apartment. But there were these pert little bows on the shoulder straps that I just wasn't sure of. "They're not me," I complained to Fran. Pert wasn't my thing. The last time I'd worn a bow it had been Scotch-taped to my hair for a less than minor part in the chorus at Camp Winoway. I just wasn't a flouncy, ruffled type of girl. "Leave them," she said. "It's one of those straight, Protestant weddings — everyone will have ruffles and flounces and organdy bows. You'll fit right in."

Now that wasn't Fran. Standing out was more her style. Making a statement, she called it. I had no idea what sort of statement I was making in my stolen gown with the shoulder bows, but it was something I didn't want to hear. The bows had to go. Admittedly, I put it off. This was not exactly an occasion I was looking forward to. Let's just say it was easy to forget.

So there I was on the actual night of the wedding, staring at myself in a pink incandescent glow that glinted ever so softly off several life-sized mirrors in an oversized ladies room. A rotund black woman, her hostility barely concealed, sulked in a pink upholstered chair and handed me a white terry cloth face towel I hadn't asked for. Cigarettes were stuffed into gleaming china cups like cancerous still lives. The counter was scattered with satin-covered matchbooks engraved with the names "Carole and Noel." It was embarrassing. Didn't anyone here know what year it was?

In the pinkish glow of the well-appointed bathroom, the bows became the object of my dissatisfaction, my rage, my urgent, unrelenting need to express my individual angst. They had come to represent everything that was wrong with the world: rococo ornamentation, bourgeois vulgarity. They were dead butterflies pinned to my shoulders. Without a thought, I ripped them off.

What I couldn't have known was that beneath the bows the straps were not a seamless expanse of fabric. No. Someone had taken a short cut. The straps were joined with thick strips of white elastic. The kind of elastic used on the waistbands and leg holes of underwear; the kind of elastic that is found at the back of a brassiere; the kind of elastic that should never, ever see the light of day.

Instantaneously transformed, I was no longer the sister-in-law of the bride. I was a weirdo in a dress that looked like a long bathing suit; a ragamuffin remnant from some schlock wholesale house on the Lower East Side. A Rebel without a Cause. A fashion statement that ended with a question mark. There was no way to remedy the damage. The black attendant stirred in her nylon uniform. I was sure I heard her laugh discreetly. What the hell? I'd make the best of it. Fran had an expression. *Épater les bourgeois.* It had something to do with shocking the middle class. Well so be it. No one would notice anyway. If I stood back a little, who would see the tops of my shoulders?

I was wrong. Noel Willinger was 6'2".

At some point between the band's saccharine rendition of "Three Coins in a Fountain" and "Misty," Barry cut in on Carole and Noel. He whisked her across the polished dance floor, leaving Noel, arms outstretched, ready to receive me. Then, as the organdy set twirled by in a whiff of perfume and talc, he saw the exposed elastic. His head snapped back as if he'd been stung by a speeding spitball. He concentrated on the table of hot hors d'oeuvres, the limpid band, the lurid flower arrangements. His hand folded into fleshy fans by his side. There was no way he was going to dance with someone who resembled a rubber mermaid.

Even in my righteous, disdainful state, I didn't take rejection well. Not well at all. I'm not the vindictive type, but right then I remember clearly hating Noel Willinger. Hating his tall, haughty frame, his vulgar, social-climbing family, his arrogant, humorless self. I think it was at that moment that I got an inkling, or maybe it was just a magical wish, that someday, sometime I'd get even. Horribly, diabolically even.

In the meantime I did what any self-respecting flower child trapped in an unbearable situation with a prep school throwback for a brother-in-law would do.

I gave Noel Willinger the finger.

Barry and Carole danced a long time. She pressed her face against his and from time to time they whispered in one another's ear. I drifted over to the warm hors d'oeuvres and helped myself to a plate of Swedish meatballs, which were smothered in a spicy gravy that spattered on impact, creating a random, pointillist pattern of brown flecks on my dress.

Let's just say, it was not the most glorious night of my life.

■

Now as I stared at the photograph, I realized that the way Barry and Carole were positioned, with their faces almost touching, was the way they'd appeared as they'd danced at the wedding. It was an unusual closeness. But then, thinking back about how Leon and I were so physically uncomfortable with one another, I envied them. Just a little.

That's when I felt the ache. A slow, dull throb that moved from my belly up to my chest. I hadn't spoken to Leon since the day Ned had died. I tried not to think about the date, about the girlfriend named Ruth and about the life Leon had apart from mine. If I closed my eyes, I could still transport myself back to the house with the yellow kitchen, and the den with paneled walls and humming fish tanks. I could see Leon as I liked to remember him, his whole body bent in an intense arch over the black eyepiece of his microscope; his long fingers, graceful, almost evil, as they expertly dissected insects, frogs and mice.

It was one of those rare, light-filled moments when all at once things take on a special clarity. I felt I was very close to something. There was a danger, real and palpable.

Barry had vanished, someone was leaving messages, warnings. Ned had been killed. There were connections. Secrets. Things I was just beginning to sense; things I could almost touch before they slipped quietly beneath the surface, leaving a ripple, a wave, a subtle current that I knew would carry me closer to the truth.

A voice was taking shape inside my head. The voice wasn't Fran's and it wasn't Leon's. It was only a whisper but it was urging me to follow the danger, to trust my fears. I no longer had a choice. There was no safe place left. I had to follow.

SIXTEEN

I wondered why these things always happened when I was alone and there was no one to tell, no one who could see.

I was sitting in George's Ice Cream Parlor on Allen Street, the one with the real marble counter and the wrought-iron chairs. It was vintage thirties, or so Fran had told me. Now in seedy decline, George's was run by the original owners, two bald, ancient-looking brothers who quarreled constantly. Today they weren't speaking, taking care to avoid each other as they moved behind the counter toasting bread and serving up ice cream in cool metal scoops.

I had ordered a grilled cheese sandwich, sixty-five cents and melted to perfection. A little old woman sat beside me. None of the stools was taken, but she sat right next to me as if leaving a space between us might be wasteful. She was one of those odd little old women. Makeup formed rouged circles on her wrinkled cheeks. Bright red nail polish gleamed in spite of the brown liver spots that freckled her hands. A pert velvet pillbox hat sat neatly on her dyed black hair, the spidery veil came to just above her nostrils.

I tried not to look, but her image and mine were reflected in the huge mirror behind the counter. When her lunch arrived, slipped courteously over the smooth marble by one of the bald brothers, she sighed and slowly rolled the veil back over the hat.

She didn't eat as I'd expected her to, as anyone would have expected her to. She held the steaming hamburger in her freckled hand and dipped it, ever so slowly, into the coffee. Ketchup ran in thick hot streams down the side of her thumb.

Rain splattered against the sidewalk outside. A musty smell seeped beneath the open door. The two ancient brothers moved in a seamless dance among the patrons. No one seemed to notice the woman beside me.

I wanted to look away, but I was trapped. Concentrating on the yellow ooze that had become my sandwich, I wondered if this was how it would always be for me. Seeing things that remained more or less invisible to everyone else.

When I glanced up. I inadvertently caught the reflection — mine and hers, in the mirror. It was then that the woman smiled at me, revealing large teeth spotted with lipstick and bits of hamburger. Her smile was neither desperate nor pleading. It was a smile of complicity. We're odd, she seemed to say. That's why I chose you.

I reached into my purse for change and, once again, caught myself looking in the mirror, only this time someone was looking back. Duane. He was standing just to my left wearing a long khaki raincoat. And he smiled. Without saying any of the usual polite greetings, he slid into the empty counter seat beside me. He smelled of rain and the streets. I leaned my head in the direction of the old woman. Had he seen her?

"Did she dunk?" he asked.

I would be lying if I didn't admit I was surprised. I never would have thought that Duane would notice something like that. I'd already typecast him in my mind as some sort of primitive working-class type.

"How did you know?"

"I seen her before. I seen lots of things."

"Like my friend dressed as a man?" I couldn't help that. It still bothered me.

"Yeah," he said. "And other things too."

I waited patiently, not sure I wanted to hear what Duane was going to say. Then he surprised me again.

"When I was a kid and I lived on the reservation they had this swimming pool they let us use on the weekends. One time I'm swimming underwater and I look down and I see this eye looking back at me. No face, no body, just an eye. I came up to the surface fast and started screaming things like 'There's this eye down there.' The old people who sat around watching us thought I was having some kind of dream, some Indian hallucination. Like no one would believe me. They wouldn't let me back in the water to get the eye. To prove I seen it. Then this old guy name Pete Longboat, actually some relative on my mother's side, dives in where I said I seen the eye. He comes up and standing right in front of me holds the thing in his hand and slips it into the empty socket where he'd lost an eye in the war. Just like that. The old people all looked away. But not me.''

I was dumbfounded. It was a great story and it was the most I'd ever heard Duane talk. No doubt he was trying to tell me something. I wasn't sure what exactly, but it didn't matter. I had this warm cozy feeling sitting next to him, listening to the rain, watching him run his hand down his ponytail and trying to imagine the eye floating under the water.

We both ordered coffee and sat silently till the rain stopped. When the old lady got up to leave, Duane flashed me a conspiratorial smile. Now I got it. In an inexplicable way we were sharing something.

The rain had turned into a fine mist. Duane and I walked along Allen Street. I wanted to ask him more about Fran and that night at the Aragon. I wanted to tell him about Ned and the phone call I'd received. But it was hard to say anything. Sex was on my mind. Something about Duane stirred me up, excited me despite my better judgment. This was the narcotic all those adolescent books on heavy petting had warned me about. This was what I'd been missing with Barry and Ned. Okay. So I was out of control, a puppy on a leash, a love slave. Everything that, in my more rational, political moments, I despised.

Duane seemed to be taking me someplace. I followed, trancelike, feeling myself wanting him, wishing we'd go back to his apartment.

The alley was dark and only partially sheltered from the street. Duane pulled me toward the farthest end. It was the alley between our apartment building and a smaller one, a dead end where I'd once seen Barry slip a stash of hash behind a loose brick. There were sounds: the Beatles droning through faraway speakers, a car horn honking in the distance.

Duane took off his raincoat and slipped it over my shoulders. He undid the snap on my jeans, pulled the zipper down and pushed until my pants were around my ankles. He tugged at my underpants, lifted my blouse and pulled me toward him. I felt his tongue on my nipples, then his mouth against my neck. His hand worked at the wetness between my legs.

The mist turned into a fine rain, warm and damp against my skin. I remember unzipping his fly, watching as his penis became erect in my hand. Then he lifted my legs and held me against him as he entered me. I slipped my hands beneath his shirt, running my fingers along the smoothness of his body.

He was hard inside me, filling me, pushing deeper. I closed my eyes and felt him thrust himself against me, felt the heat and the urgency. It took seconds, minutes and it was over. The scent of our sex, mixed with the rain.

Still wearing Duane's raincoat, I buttoned my pants and watched as he zipped his fly. This was the real thing. Sex — hard and fast.

Duane half smiled. He pushed his hand deep into the raincoat pocket. The flask was silver and shaped to the curve of a man's chest. Southern Comfort. I rarely drank, but the liquor felt warm and good in my throat. Duane lit a Marlboro and we passed it back and forth, tasting each other in the smoke and the whiskey.

I knew he was going to say something even before the

words left his mouth. I could feel it coming. He shifted his weight against the brick wall and inhaled, releasing a twist of smoke that disappeared into the gray.

"I seen Ned get hit."

"What do you mean? There were no witnesses?" My own voice sounded silly, innocent. Of course there was a witness. Duane. He would never talk to cops.

"It was misty, but I seen how it happened. Some guy chased him. Ned ran to the Saab. Then this guy, I think it was the same one, comes speeding through the park and slams him against the open door."

"What did he look like?"

"Couldn't tell. Like I said, it happened real fast."

"Well, what did you see, the car — something?"

"It was a white sedan, one of them compacts, a Corvair. And the plates were out of state."

"How could you tell that? You said it happened fast."

"Yeah, but as he pulled away that light on the corner, the streetlamp, shined against the plates and they weren't blue and orange. I couldn't see any numbers or anything. But the guy was definitely out of state."

"What did you do then?"

"I walked downstairs real slow. Made sure no one saw me. I took one look at him and I knew. He was all smashed up. No way he was even breathing."

I slumped down against the brick wall.

It hadn't been an accident, a reckless driver wild on booze or dope. It wasn't a mistake or a miscalculation. Someone had planned it. In the darkness of their mind, someone had had a fantasy. And they had made it real with their own hands.

It is a danger that won't go away. A danger that follows me.

Ned had been murdered.

Duane was standing over me. When I looked up I saw something I'd never noticed before. It was a scar, long and white, that ran from his left ear halfway across his throat.

"What's that?" I said, pointing to the scar.

"I once killed a guy," Duane said. "I got cut."

Great. I just had sex in an alley with a murderer who now confesses he was a witness to another murder. No cops. Now I knew why.

I was out of my depth, way out there in the middle of the lake with only a leaky tube and the dog paddle. Suddenly I wanted Leon. I longed for him. I watched as Duane pressed the silver flask to his lips. A thin stream of Southern Comfort trickled down his chin. How come I'd never seen that scar before?

Suddenly it occurred to me that Duane was frightened too. The sex and the whiskey were props. He'd just confessed.

"Did you tell this to anyone else?"

Duane shook his head.

"Not even Vitale?"

Duane laughed. "He's an asshole."

Funny, I'd always thought that Duane and Vitale were the best of friends. Obviously, I was missing a lot.

"There's some heavy shit going down here." I tried to sound tough.

Duane passed me the flask.

"You know about my — about Barry disappearing?" I still couldn't say the word *husband* to Duane.

"Yeah. You told me that."

"Well I guess you know I've been getting all sorts of little threats which I had thought were from him. But then he got into my place yesterday and he took his stuff and didn't leave any notes or anything. And then you told me you saw Fran dressed as a man in the Aragon and that just happened to be the night I got one of those calls, and someone had left a matchbook from the Aragon in a chair in my apartment." I realized that at this point the whiskey had begun to kick in. All the information was there, but not in any way that made much sense.

Duane just looked at me.

"Yeah? So?"

"I guess there's something I left out."

"Like what?"

"Like the fact that the night Ned was hit, someone called me and told me."

"They told you they were going to kill Ned?"

"No, the voice, the same one that called before, said something like: 'Someone will die tonight.' "

Duane slid down next to me. I inhaled his Marlboro. "He was definitely murdered," Duane said. "I seen it."

It was weird, but right then I remembered what he'd told me earlier about the eye in the bottom of the swimming pool.

I believed him.

I pulled the raincoat over my head. Suddenly I felt cold and wet. I felt the trembling in my wrists.

I am running. Running through the bushes. I can hear my own breath. The smell is on my skin. It is mingling with the falling leaves. Leon is chasing me. Renee. Come back. But I saw. I know. She will drown now. Drown in the madness. Purple. Purple. Death has a color.

"Duane," I whispered through an opening between the buttons. "Someone is definitely trying to kill me."

■

We sat silently in the alley, watching the rain splatter against the sidewalk. Duane was thinking. He ran his hand up and down his ponytail. I closed my eyes and fought against the remembering.

"You think that crazy chick has anything to do with this?"

"What crazy chick?"

"Your friend."

"Fran? What makes you think she's crazy?"

"Listen, I seen white chicks like her before. There's somethin' about 'em. Somethin' shrieky."

"Shrieky?" It was an adjective I'd never heard. Did Duane mean freaky? And what was this stuff about Fran being white? Exactly what did Duane think I was?

"You know what I mean, like they're always kinda shrieking instead of talking."

"You mean shrill?" and then I wanted to add; high-pitched, hysterical, fragile and neurotic. All adjectives that came close to shrieky and fit Fran to a tee.

"Yeah, maybe."

"I don't see how Fran would be involved in this. She may be nervous and a little eccentric, but she's not a killer. Besides, she's my friend."

Duane looked at me in an odd way. Sort of soft and almost romantic.

"Anyway," I added, still trying to make a case for Fran, "she really liked Ned." I conveniently left out just how much we had both liked him. It didn't feel right telling Duane all the strange details of our sexual adventures.

He looked off into the oblong of gray sky that floated between the two brick walls. I could tell he was trying to put the pieces together in his mind.

"Yeah, then what was she doing dressed up like a guy in the Aragon?"

"Look, maybe you made a mistake about that. Maybe it was someone who just looked like her."

"I know what I seen," Duane said. He was unwavering, insistent.

"Did you say anything to her? Did you hear her speak?"

"Nah. I told you, she's crazy. I just seen her come in. That's all."

As much as I was willing to trust Duane's powers of observation, I just couldn't accept the fact that Fran had done something so exciting without telling me. If there was a dark, ominous side of her personality, I'd never seen it. I thought I knew Fran pretty well, well enough to share most of my secrets with her. I had met her parents, her sister. I knew about everything from her sex life to her predilection for designer labels. I wanted to trust her.

Be careful, Renee. Don't make this mistake again.

"Listen," I said to Duane, who was lighting up another cigarette. "Why don't you take me with you to the Aragon. I'd like to see this for myself."

"I only seen her there once," he said, staring down at the puddles that had formed by our feet.

"Well, maybe so, but if I see her then maybe we can get to the bottom of this."

Duane passed me the cigarette. I hated smoking but somehow the Southern Comfort and the Marlboros suited the moment. I was beginning to feel like a character in an episode of *The Mod Squad*.

Duane exhaled. "What's the story with this guy Ned?"

"What do you mean?"

"Like why would someone want to bring him down?"

Duane had a quaint way of putting things. Knock him off would have been my choice.

"You've got something there. I really don't know. He was totally harmless."

But of course I *did* know. Ned had been sleeping with me. And Fran. There was a connection there. Anyone who wanted to terrorize me, and someone certainly did, would find Ned an easy target. I wasn't sure if I should tell Duane or not. It was a touchy area. If he knew about Ned and Fran and me he might just write the whole thing off, especially me. I guess I was depending on him for more than sex. I had this crazy fantasy that somehow we were in this together and that he was going to protect me.

"I gotta go," Duane said. I handed him his raincoat. The drizzle had ended and a sliver of sunlight formed a shadow on the alley wall.

That's when Duane did something that surprised me. It

was a sign of some kind. He took my hands and looked down at my thumbs.

"I like them," he said. Just like that. Not many people noticed my hands. Then he took my thumbs and pressed them in a silent kiss against his lips.

"I seen thumbs like this before. A guy I knew on the reservation."

"Really?" I said feeling woozy and out of focus. "Did he ever murder anyone?" I was thinking of Leon and the way he had taunted me about murderer's thumbs.

Duane didn't think the question strange at all. At least he didn't react as if he did.

"Nah," he said, slipping his raincoat over his shoulder. "We always thought them thumbs were a sign of good luck."

■

Much later, when I was back in my apartment, when the effects of the sex and the whiskey and Duane's revelations had worn off enough for me to think clearly, I remembered those words. I don't think I could ever forget them. But then I remembered all the questions I *hadn't* asked Duane. Important questions like: Who was the guy he said he'd killed? What had he done after he saw Ned crumpled against the car door, and if it had really happened as quickly as he said, then how could he have known that the person who hit Ned was a guy?

SEVENTEEN

When Leon and I used to live together in the house with the yellow kitchen, I had a recurring dream. Although at the time I thought it was very unusual, I've since discovered that it was not only common, but practically a classic. It went like this: Something upsetting would happen to me during the day, then I'd go to sleep and dream that I was eating a bagel. I'd get the unsettling sensation that my teeth were pulling loose from my gums. Eventually, one by one, like square white chiclets, the teeth would fall out. I'd wake up in a sweat and immediately run my fingers along my gums. Everything was in its place. It was only a dream after all.

That's exactly what happened the night Duane told me about Ned's death. Only in the morning it was as if all my teeth *had* fallen out, because nothing changed. The frightening thing didn't go away. It didn't fade like my childhood dreams.

*   *   *

After my encounter with Duane, life seemed inexplicably altered. It was as if the world had stopped for a few breathless seconds and I'd seen myself lost in a complicated pattern of secrets and betrayals. It was like glimpsing, if only for an instant, another dimension to life. A second layer. Something that throbbed just beneath the surface, that was the cause of every act, every longing. Something too powerful and too terrifying to expose.

I suspected everyone. Nothing was simple anymore. An anonymous midnight phone call had become a dire threat; an accident had turned into murder. I checked my teeth daily. It was the only way I could be sure I wasn't dreaming.

Finally, I decided to call Leon. I wasn't sure just how much I would tell him. It was more like a test than a call. I promised myself I wouldn't say anything about the girlfriend. I wanted to see if *he'd* tell *me*. I made a promise. The name Ruth would never pass my lips. Of course it didn't work that way. After we exchanged the usual pleasantries, I started crying. I couldn't help myself. I was terrified and Leon was my big brother. It was as if I'd never left home at all. I felt weak and sloppy and incapable of taking care of myself. No problem. Leon set me straight.

"In my opinion, you're involved with some very dangerous people. They might even be mentally unstable. My suggestion to you" (Leon seemed to have a box filled with endless suggestions to me) "is to find a new apartment, get a different phone number and avoid these people at all costs."

"Just like that? Pretend none of this happened? Just disappear and abandon my friends?"

Leon laughed. That awful know-it-all smirking laugh. I wanted to kill him.

"I'd hardly call people who threaten your life *friends!*"

That's when I broke my promise and started rambling about his girlfriend Ruth and how he never told me anything about his life and how he was always bossing me around and giving me advice.

Leon got very quiet. It was the sort of quiet I first experienced when I'd accidentally found condoms in his underwear drawer. His personal life was always something taboo, something he refused to discuss with me. Maybe that's how he maintained his power, maybe talking to me made him uncomfortable in ways I couldn't understand. I was never sure, and since there was no way to approach him, I guess I'd never find out.

"My private life is of no concern to you."

"You're my brother, for godsakes!" (I was screaming now.)

Leon was silent. When he spoke it was in those measured tones, the way nursery school teachers talk to toddlers.

"In my estimation, you've become hysterical. It's pointless to continue this discussion."

That *really* made me hysterical. I began sobbing uncontrollably. I begged him to come to Buffalo and rescue me. It was something I'd never done before, but then I'd never been involved in a murder before.

Leon remained logical. Irritatingly calm and logical.

"If you do the things I've suggested, you'll find that those crackpots you insist upon hanging around will lose interest in you and go back to their drugs and other sun-dry activities."

It amazed me how Leon talked. No one used expres-sions like that anymore. I wondered, silently of course, if Ruth talked the same way. No, it was impossible. Leon was one of a kind. I just couldn't imagine anyone loving him, except me. But that was different, after all we'd grown up together. I was used to him.

"So you won't help me?" I asked.

"Renee, you don't seem to understand. I *am* helping you. I'm telling you exactly what to do. What more do you want?"

I wanted a lot more. A big brother who would be warm and protective, someone who would dry my tears, fight my battles, who would come and rescue me, who would never abandon me for someone named Ruth. I knew my thinking was all muddled and confused, but that made it easier. It made it easier to say what I said next without thinking of the consequences.

"*You're* the one who's crazy," I shrieked. "You and your microscope and your secrets. How do I know you weren't the one who came here and killed my friend? You're the one who never tells me anything!"

I saw you, Leon. I know your secret.

That's when I heard the click. In all our years together, Leon had never, not once, hung up on me. I knew this time I'd gone too far.

When I called Leon back, to apologize, his line was busy. Typical. I knew he'd taken the phone off the hook. When we were kids, Leon had a way of blocking out anything he thought was unpleasant or painful. I remembered the time we'd gone to collect pond water samples. Leon had this thing about pond water. He liked to take droplets and peer at them beneath his microscope. As usual, I begged to come along.

It is a raw, gray day in November. Leon wears knee-high rubber boots and carries a little bag filled with delicate glass vials. He wades into the pond. Midway, he turns around. He shouts to me: Don't move, Renee. Wait right there on the shore. I don't completely understand these instructions, but I remain, frozen, unable to move. I watch my brother, watch how his jet black hair shines almost blue in the light, how his eyeglasses reflect tiny squares of murky brown water. He bends over the tall reeds, meticulously filling the vials and placing them ever so gently into the canvas bag. A real scientist, I think.

When we are back in the yellow kitchen, we see that my mother is having a good day. She is baking a seven-layer chocolate cake. She stares at us as we walk through the doorway.

Then she screams.

A long reed, about four inches' worth, is protruding from Leon's left nostril. He isn't sure about the scream and for a moment I see him falter. He is confused. Then he feels the reed. He tugs at it. The bottom breaks off in his hand. The blood begins streaming from his nose. The reed has gone all the way up into his skull. It is lodged there so firmly, he is rushed to the hospital.

The doctors conduct some sort of minor surgery to remove the reed. They are amazed Leon has not passed out

from the pain. He answers their questions calmly, nod-
ding, while he holds a gauze pad to his nose. I am not
surprised. I have seen this before, this way Leon has of
sealing off his feelings. He never admits to pain, physical
or emotional. Not since the day he stood by the fish tank,
the day the curtain moved behind his eyes. The day he
told me: This never happened, Renee. This never hap-
pened.

I was Leon's sister. We *had* to be alike in some way.
True, there was some slight physical resemblance, but our
dispositions were always so opposite. I knew if I reached
deep inside myself, I could find a little of the Leon stuff,
enough to numb me just temporarily. Enough to help me
sort things through.

By the time Fran knocked on my door, I had already completed the list. It was a short one, but it made me feel more
in control.

It was a list of murder suspects, and Fran's name was at
the top.

She didn't notice I'd been crying, which was surprising
because even a few tears left my eyes red and puffy. There
was something on her mind.
    "You won't believe this!"
    "Try me."
    "This is totally incredible, almost unbelievable."
    I was Leon. Calm. Rational. Unshakable.
    "I'm ready. Shoot."

"Look at this hexagram. It's uncanny."

Fran was at it again. The I Ching. It amazed me how she could really believe in that stuff. She threw these three coins, looked up some mumbo jumbo in a thick, yellow paperback called *The Book of Changes*, and proceeded to make wild predictions about future events. She knew I was a doubter, but that never discouraged her.

"I'm going to read this word for word. This third line, undivided, shows the younger sister who is to be married off, in a mean position. And are you ready for this? The fourth line shows someone blind of one eye and yet able to see. And then this last line, the broken one, shows a stranger acting in a way that is contrary to what is proper. Then it says, clearly, there will be evil."

I expected Fran to go on. She didn't. She continued to sit cross-legged on the floor, staring at the coins.

"You can't imagine how positively eerie this is. I've been thinking about Anna and that weird Polish mortician all day. Then I throw the coins and I get the answer."

"What answer?"

"Can't you see? If we don't rescue my sister, something evil is going to happen."

It was already clear that plenty of evil things had been happening, none of them even slightly related to Anna's upcoming nuptials. I tried, in a halfhearted way, to explain that to Fran. I wasn't quite ready to tell her all that I knew. She was, after all, first on my list of suspects.

"It doesn't say that," I said, staring vacantly at the coins.

"It says what you want it to say. If you trust your subconscious, the meaning is always clear."

Fran was excited now. She had a mission, something to focus on. What I couldn't figure was where I fit in.

"You're coming with me. You're the stranger. You can be objective."

"Coming where?"

"Listen, we're going to see my parents. They're unbearable, but you'll be able to see what's going on, why they're encouraging Anna to marry this creep. I'm just too involved."

"So I'm the stranger with one blind eye and I'm going to do something improper?"

"Isn't that great? It's all in the coins."

At that point I was tempted to blurt out a list of improper things I'd just completed: making love with Duane in an alley, withholding possible information about a murder, my brother hanging up on me after I'd made some wild accusations. There were probably more things lurking in the depths of my subconscious, but that was enough for starters.

Fran looked up from her coins.

"Hey what's with you?"

For a second there, I was afraid she could actually read my mind.

"Your eyes. You've been crying, either that or you've got some kind of allergy."

"Very funny."

Fran knew what happened to me when I cried. There was no way to deny it. I decided to edit my confession.

"I just had a fight with Leon over the phone. You know how he gets to me. He's so straight."

"Hmmm." Fran was thinking. She had an insatiable curiosity about Leon. Of course, they'd never met. I never told her, but I knew, without a doubt, that Leon would hate her. As Duane so aptly put it, she was "shrieky." Leon would find that characteristic extremely distasteful. Probably, the exact reason why I was so attracted to it.

Lucky for me, the topic of Leon wasn't pursued. Today, Fran had other interests. She was staring at herself. There was this old-fashioned full-length mirror on a stand in my living room, and she seemed engrossed in her reflection. Then she did something that really scared me. She asked me how I thought she'd look with a mustache.

"A thin blond one, sort of right here." She pressed her finger against her upper lip.

I started to get that fluttery sensation in my wrists, as if I was standing right on the edge of something.

We are in the purple room. She shows me the photograph. This is me, she says. And him. I had a brother once. We were almost twins. Thirteen months apart. And then I lost him. We were just like you and Leon. Her voice shakes. I think she is looking at me, but I cannot be sure. We are not Sylvia and Sidney I want to say. We are Renee and Leon. She does not hear me now. She looks past me at the photograph. I know she is going into that place. Her voice gets thick. I am scared. Mommy. Come back. She is drowning. Going deeper into the darkness. I can do nothing. For an instant I think I understand. For an instant, I feel the unbearable weight of her pain.

"I bet my brother has a mustache, maybe even a beard. Something very Van Gogh," Fran said.

She pressed her hands against her chest and stood sideways, eyeing her profile. I was sympathetic with her longing for a brother who might not even exist.

"My mother always bought me bras. I never fit into any of them. It was as if I could never measure up. My mother really fucked me up. She had this way of talking like I wasn't there, or was deaf or something. But it all just seeped inside. Right into the subconscious."

I knew what she was talking about. Grown-ups always did that to me too.

Fran rubbed the place over her lip where she'd imagined the mustache. There was something so sad about this gesture, something that brought back another, deeper sadness, that erased my uneasiness. I wanted to hug her, to hold her close and absorb her pain, but something stopped me, a warning, an intuition, a vague and nameless fear.

"You know the worst thing? They'd never admit saying any of the things I'd hear them say. That's why they still deny my brother's existence. But how else would I know? They'd close the dining room door and get into these terribly serious conversations. First they'd whisper, but then, as if I'd dematerialized or something, they'd start shouting. It always had to do with money and another woman and someone they called 'the boy.' After a while, I didn't even listen anymore. I just *knew*. I used to stand in front of my mirror and rearrange my hair, paint on sideburns and borrow my dad's tie. I figured that was what my brother probably looked like."

Fran's confession made me feel guilty. True, it wasn't an emotion I cultivated, but this time I allowed myself the luxury. After all, if Fran really did have a brother (which I doubted) she'd missed out on most of it: the silly games, the secrets, the weird combination of love and rage. I'd had more than my share with Leon. And what did I do? Turn around and tell him how terrific it had all been? No. I'd accused him of murder.

I was thinking about how to make up with him, when my mind drifted back to what Fran had said earlier. It occurred to me that we still weren't completely visible to the rest of the world. Maybe chronologically we were adults, but in other ways we still operated, largely unseen, in our own impenetrable universe. That's why Fran and I could walk into stores and steal anything we wanted. It was more than just being good thieves. We still had some of that little girl magic. We were untouchable. And that's when I realized something even more startling. As long as no one took us seriously, as long as we were still kids, we could get away with almost anything.

Even murder.

EIGHTEEN

Duane and I were taking a walk. It wasn't as though we'd planned it. We'd accidentally met on Allen Street. He was standing beneath the Allendale marquee. The featured selection was *Around the World in 30 Ways.* He smiled when I read it.

"Wanna catch the matinee?" he asked.

I'd only seen a porno movie once, we called them "stag films" then. It had been at my friend Robin's sweet sixteen party. She'd planned the celebration in the basement of her parents' split level. When they excused themselves to join the grown-ups, Robin flicked on the family movie projector and I got my first glimpse of coitus. The film was an amateur production: scratchy with jumpy black-and-white images that drifted in and out of focus. The lead actor had pimples on his buttocks. The heroine had chipped nail polish. I don't remember much. My eyes were closed during most of it. Robin later told me her father had a whole collection and invited me over for future screenings. Needless to say, I never took her up on it. Now that Duane had asked, I was reluctant to relive that particular moment of my girlhood.

"Are you serious?"

He smiled, not the least bit embarrassed. "Nah, this one wasn't so hot. Now that *next* one," then he laughed. He pointed to a poster of the coming attraction. A Technicolor production featuring an overly made up woman with a blond wig and tremendous breasts. *Beauty and the Breast.*

Then Duane just slipped his hand down my blouse. Not in a pushy way, like the boys in high school, but in an exciting, erotic way. My nipples got hard and I ached between my legs. Right there on Allen Street. In broad daylight. I was reaching new heights in sexual ecstasy.

"You've got great tits," Duane whispered in my ear.

Now I'd heard *that* before. Those exact words. Most of the time they'd been shouted from a moving convertible, or hissed (with accompanying sucking sounds) from a dingy street corner. But for some reason this was different. It was as if Duane had pushed a magic button and whispered the words I'd been waiting to hear all my life. For a split second I thought about Fran. Her poor flat chest. The bras she would never fill. But now Duane was steering me toward 72 Days Park. We would have made it too, probably consummating our afternoon passion on the kitchen table, in the hallway or God knows where, if we hadn't seen Barry.

This time I was *absolutely positive.* There he was walking down the alley between the buildings holding a small plastic bag in his left hand. He saw me. I know he did. Because all of a sudden he started to run. Barry had this weird way of running, like a lame jack rabbit. Believe me, it was unmistakable. It was one of those moments you anticipate for a long time, but never expect will actually happen. I guess I never thought I'd see him again. Barry had become a ghost for me, someone from a stale, forgotten dream.

Maybe it just happened too fast and too unexpectedly. I really have no explanation for it, but I pointed to Barry's retreating figure and screamed at the top of my lungs, "Help!"

The next thing I heard was this metallic click. I looked at Duane. He had an open switchblade in his hand. We both started running. Barry was way ahead of us. But we followed him anyway. If there was such a thing as adrenaline pumping, this was it.

We chased Barry through the alley and across Allen Street. When I saw the pink Rambler parked on the corner with the engine humming, I knew we'd lost him. It was as if he'd anticipated seeing me. There he was with his own getaway car.

I couldn't be positive about this, but I think I saw someone sitting in the passenger seat.

I was gasping for air. Duane closed the switchblade and slipped it back into one of his pockets. He smoothed his ponytail.

"What was that all about?" he asked.

"That was Barry."

"Yeah, so?"

"It's a long story. Let's go up to my apartment and check things out."

"What sort of things?"

Duane was definitely the suspicious type. While we walked up the stairs to my apartment, I filled him in on the messages, the threats, the notes in blood. He seemed interested. Who wouldn't be? I liked sounding so mysterious and hard-boiled. It was an entirely new image for me.

Duane and I checked everything carefully. If he had been there, Barry hadn't left a trace. Then Duane got an idea.

"Let's check with Sherman. Maybe he stopped by his place."

Barry and Marshal had been friends since their freshman year. They'd both pledged the same fraternity, both grown their hair long and started smoking grass. When they left the frat house, they shared an apartment downtown. I'd asked Sherman if he knew anything about Barry's disappearance, but he'd always seemed as puzzled as everyone else.

When we knocked on the door, he opened it right away, as if he'd been standing there expecting us. But then his face got sort of loose in the jaw. He was surprised, but was trying not to show it.

We walked inside and sat down on the couch.

"What's up?" he asked.

"I just saw Barry."

"Really?"

"I'm sure it was him. He was running through the back alley, toward Allen Street. And his pink Rambler was parked on the corner with the engine going." I decided not to mention the person I thought I'd seen in the passenger seat.

"No kidding? Want a toke?" Always the perfect host, Sherman offered me a joint. I declined.

Duane looked around the room. His eyes got real small. He was almost squinting.

"You know anything about this?"

"Me? Shit, no. Barry's been gone for months now."

I stared past Sherman. A plastic bag of grass lay open on the table in the far corner of the room. A brown jacket with a purple button pinned on the collar was slung carelessly over an old metal bridge chair.

"Let's go," I said to Duane.

Wordlessly, he stood up and walked to the door. Duane was tall, about 6'2". Sherman, who was standing beside him, looked pale and sweaty. I could tell he was afraid.

"See you guys soon."

"Sure thing," Duane said. He touched the pocket where he kept the switchblade. It was a subtle gesture. I wondered if Sherman picked it up.

Later, when we were sitting in George's Ice Cream Parlor, eating grilled cheese sandwiches on white bread, I told Duane that Sherman had been lying.

"Yeah, I figured that. But I couldn't be sure."

"I'm positive," I said.

"How come?"

"Remember the room? There was this card table with metal bridge chairs in the corner. And there was a plastic bag of grass on top. When we saw Barry he was carrying the same kind of bag. He probably stopped off to get some dope."

"Yeah, maybe. Or maybe he had that shit stashed in the alley."

I paused dramatically. I knew that what I was going to say next would blow Duane away.

"There was something else. I don't know if you noticed, but there was this brown jacket slung over one of the chairs."

Duane pushed a crumb along the rim of his dish. He didn't look directly at me, but I knew I had his interest.

"Yeah, so?"

"Well, did you happen to notice a purple pin on the collar?"

Duane shook his head.

"I did. I even know what it said."

Then I pulled an identical pin from my purse.

" 'Love.' See it written there in the squiggles? I had bought one for myself and one for Barry a few weeks before he disappeared."

Duane smiled. "Good work. You a detective or something?" Then he laughed. Duane had this great laugh. It sort of bordered on a snicker but then midway it changed direction and moved down deep into his belly.

"With all this stuff happening I just don't know who to trust anymore." I felt my voice begin to quiver, I knew my tough image was about to bite the dust.

"I thought Sherman was a nice guy. My friend. Someone harmless. Then he looks me straight in the face and lies."

"He's Barry's friend too."

"I can't figure any of this out. Why is Barry running away from me? Why is he hiding out, slinking around back alleys? It's not like we had a fight or anything. We never even argued. One day he just split. It doesn't make sense."

Then I couldn't help myself. I started to cry.

Duane handed me a napkin. He moved his chair next to mine and slung his arm around my shoulder. We sat and watched ourselves in the big mirror behind the soda fountain. There was nothing else to say. Duane ate his cheese sandwich and I dabbed at my eyes, hoping they wouldn't wind up swollen and puffy the next morning.

We decided to spend the night together in my apartment. I wanted to be around if there were any weird messages from Barry or anyone else. Duane didn't think I should be alone. It was touching in a way. I liked feeling protected. I even liked the idea that Duane had a knife. It was very blue collar. Very (as I knew Fran would say) quintessentially Indian.

While we sat around drinking red wine and listening to Dylan, Duane told me about the guy he said he'd murdered. It had happened years ago when he'd been in his second year at Grover Cleveland High School. This big Italian kid named Vinny Palladino had pushed him against the wall of the men's room. There had been words and threats; Duane said he couldn't remember what it was about. Vinny cut him with a knife. Duane punched him in the groin. Vinny groaned, doubled up and dropped his weapon. Duane thought it was all over. But Vinny had a gun. Something small. Duane wasn't sure if it was loaded. He didn't wait to find out. It was only the two of them. When Vinny turned to point his gun, Duane caught him off balance, flicked out his switchblade and drove it deep into Vinny's stomach.

"It felt soft, like I was stabbing a pillow," Duane said. "Maybe I didn't kill him."

Duane never found out. That night his uncle drove him north to a reservation in Canada. He stayed there for three years. No one ever came after him and he never heard anything about Vinny Palladino.

"Don't you wonder about it sometimes?" I asked.

"Nah, not anymore. It was a long time ago."

"Well, what happened next? Did you finish high school on the reservation?"

Duane laughed. I guess that had been a very bourgeois question, considering what he had just told me.

"Sure, I finished high school, went on to college and got me a good job at the steel mill."

I assumed from his tone, half bitter, half sarcastic, that his education had come to an untimely end in the men's room of Grover Cleveland High School.

"Can I feel the scar?"

He took my hand and ran it down the side of his cheek. A thin seam of skin. Tissue slit open with the point of a blade and then left to heal, closing in on itself, freezing a moment, a memory in human flesh.

"Does that turn you on?"

There was something wild about Duane, something hot and alive.

When we made love it was slow and complicated. Not hard and fast like the other times. We had all night. Duane made me keep my clothes on. Then he took things off: my blouse, my jeans, my bra. The light was dim, casting shadows along the bedroom wall. It was then I realized how beautiful Duane was. How his body moved with an energy, a danger that made me want to swallow him, to lose myself in the smell of him.

Duane knew things about sex. He touched me, slowly, gently, then rough and hard until I begged him to come inside me. I was different with him. Transformed. Before, sex had always been a silent, predictable dance. Casual and cool. With Duane it was all sweat and juice, crazy and out of control.

"I love the way you taste," he said as he pressed his fingers to his lips then kissed me, open, wet.

He ran his hands over my buttocks, pulling me up until I enveloped him and we were moving slowly, almost painfully, toward orgasm. Then he stopped. He stroked my hair, I felt his breath, moist and burning against my cheek.

"Say my name when you come."

Two seconds later I was shouting his name as he pushed deep inside me.

■

When I awoke it was 4 A.M. Duane was asleep in a tangle of sheets. The lamp we had left on threw a yellowish light over the room. I glanced down at the jumble of clothes beside the bed: my jeans, Duane's plaid shirt, his worn boots, the knife folded neatly in its case. I touched it, sure I could feel it vibrating in my hand. There was a tiny button on the side. When I pressed, the knife shot out. Razor sharp. Ready. I remembered firing the gun that day in the field. I remembered the thrill. But now that I knew about the knife, it seemed more violent. I saw how the blade disappeared back into the case. Fast, clean. Deadly.

I was careful not to make a sound. When I glanced back over my shoulder I saw that Duane hadn't stirred. He slept while I slipped into a bathrobe and tiptoed into the moon-lit kitchen. I opened the drawer. My list of suspects was right where I'd left it. Using the red pencil I kept beside the telephone, I wrote two words. Marshal Sherman.

And while Duane continued to float in his own secret dreams, I silently crossed his name off the list.

NINETEEN

No sense kidding myself. Duane wasn't the type to leave a note. Still, when I awoke and found him gone, I felt that familiar morning-after sadness. Would he be back? Of course. He only lived two flights down. But then there was always the possibility that, like Barry, he might just vanish. Nothing surprised me anymore. And nothing was totally unexpected.

I silently reviewed yesterday's events. I was missing things. Like the fact that after I'd met him, Duane had just completed an afternoon viewing of *Around the World in 30 Ways*. It was probably silly, a feminine hang-up, but I felt just a tiny bit betrayed. Was his lovemaking original, or was it something he'd borrowed from the silver screen? I had to give credit where credit was due. He'd been so sweet and understanding. So protective. And he *had* told me about the scar.

I got a chilly feeling thinking about how he'd described stabbing Vinny Palladino. I can't say I wasn't titillated by the thought that the same man who had made love to me had also been capable of such violence. Duane was right. It *did* turn me on. And that surprised me. I was discovering another side of myself. And it was as if Duane knew all about it — that I had it in me all along.

Then I thought about Barry. There was something big, something just beneath the surface going on with him. There could be only two reasons why Barry was running from me: fear or shame. Fear seemed pretty ridiculous. It was obvious to everyone that I was more a target of violence than a perpetrator of it. Shame. Now that was a thought. It was a word from the past. Shame was something that brought back memories of scolding parents, repressive relatives, reactionary bureaucrats. This was the Summer of Love. Everything was cool. If there was anything to be ashamed of, it was shame itself. No, I just couldn't see Barry feeling anything as old-fashioned, as uncool as shame. And there was something else that bothered me. Had I imagined it, or had there been someone sitting in the passenger seat of the pink Rambler? Now if I could find out for certain who that someone was, I was sure all the pieces would fall neatly into place.

As I got up and walked over to the window, I made a mental note to ask Duane if he'd seen anyone in the car. I also thought I'd try and get more information from Sherman. It gave me a creepy feeling to think that he'd lied to me. But he'd obviously had contact with Barry. He *had* to know something.

I toyed with the idea of calling Leon. He was always such a master at figuring things out. But I knew that wasn't being realistic. Leon and I needed some breathing room from one another. It was like when we were kids and I'd get on his nerves. He'd lock his bedroom door and tell me not to talk to him until he opened it. That was that. When Leon was ready to return, he'd give a sign. That's the way it was with us. I wondered if it would ever change. I wondered about the precise moment when brothers and sisters could relax into a casual equality, when all the charged emotions, the boundaries, the private territory rigged with taboos like invisible electric wires could finally be abandoned. And then, just for a fleeting instant, I wondered if that would ever be an entirely safe thing to do.

There was no reason to get out of bed. I could have lolled around all day in the sheets that still smelled of Duane and the night before. It would have been glorious to have spent several more hours reviewing what had happened yesterday and making predictions about the days to come.

But Fran had other ideas.

She called my name from the hallway as she bounded up the stairs, knocking at my door like a drunk with a jackhammer.

I can't say I was overjoyed to see her.

She took one look at me, and sensed something.

"You look different."

"Really." I couldn't help smiling. "I just woke up."

Fran glanced into the bedroom. "Anybody here?"

"Just me."

"I mean," she said, *"was* anybody here?"

Then I did something I'd never done to Fran before. I lied.

"No. I had a rough night."

"How come?"

Maybe because I felt guilty, or maybe because I just felt sorry for her, I told Fran a creative version of the day before. I told her about seeing Barry, about the car and the passenger I might (or might not) have imagined, and even about how Sherman had lied. Just to cover myself, I mentioned bumping into Duane. Who could be sure? Sherman might mention seeing us together. I was amazed how easy it was to leave out essential details and still come up with a coherent story.

Fran devoured the information.

"This is all v-e-r-y intriguing. Barry vanishing only to reappear at the very scene of the crime. Sherman in on it too. Hmmm. What do you think this is all about?"

"That's just where I was when you knocked."

"I think we're on to something here. Something big."

Fran sounded like Agent 86 on *Get Smart*. I could tell she was enjoying the information I'd passed along. Ordinarily it wouldn't have been so easy to fool her. Fran was pretty sharp that way. If she'd persevered, I probably would have told her about Duane. In detail. But I'd thrown her a curve, and she was swinging at the ball. I was becoming adept at all sorts of sports.

"Smuggling. That's my bet. Sure. It makes sense. Sherman got fingered by the mob. He expanded the operation, only kept it going underground, using Barry as a runner."

"Fran, that's preposterous and you know it. Marshal Sherman is a good little boy from New Jersey. He smokes pot. He takes speed. Occasionally he sells some stuff to his friends. Smuggling? Come on. Just walk through Days Park. No one has to hide anything. Drugs. Sex. Guns. And even if that was true, why would Barry get involved? He has no use for money. And he certainly wouldn't have to run away from me. I'm not a narc for godsakes!''

"Listen," Fran said, narrowing her eyes to let me know she was absolutely serious now. "We're *all* nice kids from nice places. If our parents had any idea what we've been up to, if the straight world saw what we do in a normal day, they'd think we were criminals or freaks or crazies. Nothing's preposterous anymore. There are no rules we can't break. Renee, it's just like when we were little. They still don't see us."

I didn't need Fran to tell me this. I'd known it since I was a child. It was a lesson I'd learned in the green house. A lesson I would never forget.

No one believes that she is different, that she is not the same Sylvia who once played Chopin on the piano and painted bright pictures. The aunt does not notice the thick voice and the empty eyes. My father is packing his suitcase when I tell him. Mommy cuts herself. She leaves blood in the bathroom and on the walls. He shakes his head. Don't exaggerate, Renee, he says. It's a stage. She's just high-strung, artistic. But he does not look at me when he talks. And we both know he is running away. Daddy, I want to say. Daddy, help me. But I know he does not want to hear. I only have Leon. And sometimes he frightens me.

I thought I heard a door slam in the hallway. Footsteps, fast and deliberate, moving through the narrow corridor. I glanced at Fran. Her mouth was twisted to one side. That was her thoughtful expression, the one she wore when she talked about her childhood, her first sexual experiences, her missing brother.

"Well then let's just go in there and ask Marshal to tell us the truth. Let's demand to know what's going on."

"Renee, you already did that."

She had me there. Duane and I had asked Sherman about Barry and he'd lied.

"So what do you suggest?"

"I suggest we proceed cautiously."

"Sleuth it out?" I was half joking.

"Absolutely!" Fran was serious.

"Give me some time," she said. "I want to come up with a way we can keep an eye on Sherman without him knowing."

"Why don't we just drill a hole in the wall and peep through," I joked.

Fran wasn't smiling. "There are other ways. Let me work on it," she said.

"In the meantime how about breakfast?"

"I'm fasting today. Purification of the body. Remember?"

Fran had lots of nutty ideas about eating and fasting, astrology, the I Ching — spiritual stuff I just couldn't get into.

"How about watching me eat breakfast?"

"Uggh! I came here to remind you about our dinner date at my parents' house."

"To inform me. I was never asked."

"Formalities. Listen, I'll pick you up early. I want to stop off at the Parthenon and get my mom a china teapot."

The Parthenon was one of Fran's favorite haunts. An offensively cheerful gift shop on Delaware Avenue that was run by Junior Leaguers. It gave Fran a special thrill to steal from them.

"Tonight? But you're fasting."

"Exactly. I need all the psychic energy I can muster."

"But won't they want you to eat?"

"I'll pick. It's easy to fool them. I've told you a hundred times, they don't *see* me."

Before Fran left, she wanted to choose my outfit. Only she insisted upon calling it a costume. As she talked, I began to see her point.

"You've got to look absolutely *jejune*."

I had no idea where Fran got these expressions. Books. Movies. The aunt on her mother's side who lived in Paris.

"I take it that means innocent."

"Straight as an arrow. The bereft widow."

That was going too far.

"You don't expect me to pretend Barry's dead. That's too morbid." Besides, I knew I could never carry it off.

"Just let me do the talking. You don't know Mel and Evelyn. Give them a little melodrama and they're all ears. If you can picture it, my mother still reads *Modern Screen*."

An image of Evelyn curled up on the naugahyde sofa, a tensor lamp concentrating a neat globe of light on the pages of *Modern Screen*, while Mel propped his feet up on the La-Z-Boy and watched Ed Sullivan, flashed before me. I *could* picture it.

"Are you actually going to say Barry's dead?"

Fran waved her hand in concentric circles. She was wearing a purple and red tie-dyed T-shirt that seemed to vibrate with a life of its own.

"Not *necessaire*. I'll just let them see how he irresponsibly vanished, tearing your heart in two. Let them fret about Anna winding up in similar circumstances."

"And if that doesn't work?"

"Then at least we tried. It's a *fait accompli*. I fulfilled my karmic obligation."

I wanted to believe Fran was being totally selfless, that she had no ulterior motives, that one roll of the I Ching was enough to convince her of the importance of her mission. But I had this feeling. This creepy suspicion that Fran, all decked out in her tie-dye attempting to be light and airy, spouting French like a fountain in Versailles and flashing me toothsome grins, was hiding something. There was another reason we were going to visit her parents.

Then I heard those footsteps in the corridor. Purposeful, staccato. Almost as if someone was pacing.

"Do you hear that?"

But Fran wasn't listening; lost in her own reverie, she was busily sorting through my clothes, looking for just the right disguise.

"Here. This is just ideal. Not too straight, not too outrageous. Solid and believable. I'll pick you up at four-fifteen. Be ready."

Fran was holding her trademark cloche, the hat that made her look mysterious and elegant. I don't know what possessed me, maybe I just felt like a disguise, or maybe I thought it might be fun to be someone else — even Fran — so I asked her if I could borrow it. Wordlessly, she plunked it on my head. It covered most of my dark hair. From the back, if you squinted, I could pass for someone else entirely.

After Fran left I was desperate for a breath of fresh air. The atmosphere in my apartment reeked of betrayal. Outside, the first pale streaks of afternoon beckoned me. Days Park hummed with the chords of steel-string guitars. Harmonicas vibrated in the sunstruck breeze. I dressed quickly and ran down the stairs. My Dr. Scholl's sandals clattered in the now silent corridor.

It was a perfect day. From the doorway, I could see all the way across to the far end of the park. There was Wesley, his hair in long, flowing braids, wearing a T-shirt that read "Off Pigs," and passing a corncob pipe to a thin blond girl beside him. He waved when he saw me. Waving back, I walked blindly toward the music. I was thinking of something else. I was working on forgetting — on killing time, on pushing the old, haunted memories of those last years in the green house back down into the darkness.

I honestly didn't see it.

The car came from behind, flashing by in a suck of air, missing me not by inches but by something immeasurable. An instant. A hairsbreadth. I fell against the curb, reeling from the sting of sidewalk against my knees; the bloody scrape of flesh on cement.

I saw my own skin, the wound that was fresh and red, and the past rushed out from the darkness.

We are driving in the car. There is a cement truck in front of us. Your brother is in that truck, she says. They are taking him away. They are going to bury him under the dirt. They are going to fill his ears and his mouth, his eyes and his nose with dirt. Her voice is heavy and distant. I know she is talking about Sidney. Leon is my brother, I say. I am Renee. But it is too late. There is a sound. Crushed steel. A windshield shattered like a spider's web. Glass and blood. I hold my hand against my arm. I look for her. Her hair is matted with bits of cement and specks of blood. There is a purple bruise on her cheek. It spreads beneath the skin like some hideous flower. My baby, she calls. Where is my baby? I move into her arms. I feel her heart beat with mine as we wait for the ambulance.

Wesley was pulling me to my feet. He smelled of garlic and tamari.

"Hey man, that was close."

When I looked past him into the dappled light, I saw the back of the car. A white square receding into the landscape. A white square with an out-of-state license plate.

TWENTY

It was no big thing. That's what Wesley and his girls said. The only eyewitnesses. Just some guy in a white car who was probably stoned. Maybe they were right. Maybe I was so freaked out I'd mistaken a stoned driver for a deliberate murderer. I needed to cool down, to take the edge off. The tension was becoming unbearable. So when Wesley offered me the pipe I didn't turn him down. I sat in the park taking a hit of this and a hit of that until the blood on my knee dried to brown crust.

Reality didn't seem so shocking anymore. If anyone had told me only months — weeks — before, that my husband would have disappeared, that someone I knew intimately would have been murdered, that I would become the target of a deranged madman, take on an Indian lover, accuse my brother of all sorts of heinous acts and lie to my best friend (also my prime suspect), I would have thought they were nuts. But now reality, such as it was, seemed to have developed a rhythm all its own. The shock value had dimmed, replaced by an unexplained need to move forward, to unravel the mystery in which I had become increasingly enmeshed.

Wesley and the pipe helped to numb the fear. The sun and the music eased me into a new level of acceptance. So the car had been white? So it had headed straight for me? Circumstantial. Coincidental. Not even a slight flutter in my wrists.

By the time Fran knocked at my door, I was pretty strung out. Sprawled gracelessly on the stolen purple bedspread, I had been trying to piece all the disparate elements of my life into some coherent, if not believable, whole. It almost felt good to have a pounding headache, a tight jaw, a swollen, fuzzy tongue. I was becoming a character in a Belmondo movie.

"What? You're not dressed yet?"

Fran's voice immediately took on that high-pitched, irritating timbre. Shrieky. I smiled when I thought of Duane's innovative adjective.

I allowed Fran to lead me to the closet, where I obediently took the striped jersey minidress she handed me. Slipping it over my head, I noticed how easy it was to transform myself, to push one reality into the background and another, entirely different one, into the foreground. This revived pleasant memories of the quick scenery changes I had learned to perfect during summer plays at Camp Winoway.

Fran was tugging my hair back into one of those covered ponytail elastics.

"It's never going to work," I said. "It won't last." A substantial amount of my childhood had been spent dealing with creeping hair. It crept out from elastics, barrettes, headbands and pink, spongy rollers.

Fran sighed. It was a sigh of resignation. "Let's just pin up the front so at least you look acceptable."

When I was finally ready, outfitted in the striped mini and my newly invented hair, Fran stood back and admired her creation.

"Okay," she said. "Just remember the I Ching."

My pupils had shrunk to specks, there was a nonstop hammering in a spot just over my left eyebrow. Vaguely, I recalled an attempt on my life, a speeding white car and endless tokes from Wesley's magic pipe. The I Ching. I was thinking something like a friendly dinner out in flat, suburban Kenmore. A friendly nonthreatening meal with someone else's completely normal parents.

"You mean all that stuff about strangers with one blind eye and doing something improper."

"Right. And don't forget the younger sister being in a bad way."

We both conveniently forgot to mention the last line. "There will be evil."

Fran flicked on the radio in the red Saab. WKBW was playing the Lovin' Spoonful's "What a Day for a Daydream," when she reminded me about our first stop. The Parthenon. The china teapot.

It was an easy cop. Even in my semi-nauseous condition, I carried off my part without a hitch. Tall, blond Althea Walters, whom Fran described as "Miss Junior Leaguer Par Excellence," greeted us at the door. We chatted. Or at least I chatted, watching the way Althea's face remained motionless while her bright red lips parted to reveal a yellowish film over her long teeth. That was my job. Chatting. My nasal, Long Island accent was an exotic attraction to Althea, so much so that she completely ignored Fran, who moved deftly behind the china counter in the rear of the store.

I wasn't wearing a watch, but it couldn't have taken more than five minutes. I was in the middle of one of my tedious New York mugging raps, Althea was mesmerized by stories of crime and violence (ironic since Fran was ripping her off as I spoke), when I saw that Fran had already slipped the teapot under her nondescript London Fog. Holding it there with one hand, she made a point to stop and smile warmly at Althea before we both walked slowly from between the two white columns with the words "Parthenon. A gift shop of distinction" printed on them. Walking slowly was our trademark. Running, Fran said, was a sure sign of an amateur. "Walk slowly, Renee. Be confident. Confidence and a slow walk are absolutely de rigueur."

As we inched our way back to the Saab, I felt as if I was moving underwater, the sound of the ocean roared reassuringly in my ears.

Fran had the gift box, already covered with blue and white wrapping paper, in the back seat of the car.

"Pop this in there, will you?" she asked.

I placed the teapot in the box, marveling at the perfect fit. Fran thought of everything. She was neat to the point of being annoying. A real stickler for details.

*   *   *

"Any final instructions?" I asked as we pulled up in front of the square house with the plastic bricks glued around the screen door.

"Just check out my father. He's got plenty of skeletons in his closet."

I pictured a rubbery skeleton falling out of the Johnstens' coat closet, the one in the front hall with the little pine deodorizer trees.

Fran's mother greeted us at the door. She was wearing a pink apron adorned with the words *Kissin' Don't Last, Good Cookin' Do.* There were tiny red lips and hearts embedded in the curves of the S's. Her hair was tucked adroitly into a French twist, her nails filed into mean points. She wore her Red Cross shoes with ventilation holes in the front and fanned herself with the sports section of the *Buffalo Evening News.* In the background I could hear the last strains of "Summer in the City."

Evelyn gave me a thin-lipped smile.

"Hello, dear." And then to Fran, "What took you so long?"

I thought to myself how it would be if I told Evelyn, in her apron and French twist, about the murder attempt in the morning, the endless tokes on the corncob pipe in the afternoon and, for a fitting finale, the bloodless crime in the gift store on the way over. Glancing at the chipped plaster deer beside the door, I understood what Fran meant by them not seeing us.

Fran answered her mother with an acceptable lie about traffic, and we were ushered into the paneled living room that reeked of ammonia and Air Wick.

While Evelyn unwrapped the teapot, Fran bent down beneath the early American breakfront to coax Arthur, her dog, out to meet me. I'd met Arthur once before, and I'd been unimpressed. An overfed beagle, he reminded me of a kosher hot dog about to split its skin.

I was just about to tell Fran not to bother, when it happened.

Evelyn, in a hurry to consign the new teapot to its proper place in the breakfront, opened the glass door. Unbeknownst to me, Arthur chose that exact moment to make his canine entrance. As he scurried over my feet, I jumped, crashing into a corner of the glass door.

My eye. Instantaneously, it swelled into a pink oozing lump. Fran and Evelyn became twin Dr. Kildares. They applied ice, compresses, towels and soothing words of consolation. The brandy helped. So did Fran's assurance that the swelling would go down in no time. Meanwhile, I blinked from my one good eye, while taking in only fragmented, teary images of the dinner.

It didn't occur to me until much later that the ominous prophecy of the I Ching was about to come true.

TWENTY-ONE

I didn't remember much about the dinner. There was my eye, swollen like a bruised Ping-Pong ball, and the measured sips of brandy that added up until I was slightly woozy. And there was something about the Johnsten home, something that made even a simple evening seem slightly surreal. I called it atmosphere. Fran called it ambience. We both settled on a perfectly descriptive term: the House of Kitsch.

Evelyn served bowls of meatballs and spaghetti while Fran talked endlessly about Anna and the risks of early marriage. No one seemed to listen to anyone else. The conversational ball was swatted expertly between mother and daughter. Mel stared thoughtfully at his plate, passing on his turn. Pressing a compress against my eye, I was mercifully excused from participating. It seemed to go on like that for hours.

After a while, Fran saw she wasn't getting anywhere with her mother. Evelyn was thrilled with the prospect of the upcoming wedding. So Fran changed her approach.

She told her parents about Barry and me. While Evelyn solicitously refilled my brandy glass, Fran unfolded a carefully edited version of Barry's disappearance. For the first time that evening Mel looked up from his meatballs. He seemed to be staring directly at me. I covered my face with the compress.

When he spoke, Mel's voice sounded rough, a creaking hinge that had grown rusty from lack of use, a wheel that needed oiling.

"What makes you think Barry's not coming back?" Under the table, I picked at the skin around my thumb. I was regressing, turning into the child in the yellow kitchen whose bloody cuticles were a sure sign of deceit.

What do you remember about the accident? the aunt asks me. Nothing, I say. My cuticles are picked raw. Well, how did it happen? she asks. I look at Leon. He shakes his head. She doesn't always tell the truth, my father whispers.

"Nothing really," I said, wondering if there was something I could eat or drink to make the room stop moving.

"A man just doesn't leave unless he's got a reason. There's got to be a reason."

Mel looked at me, waiting for an answer. I moved the ice around my eye, making wet circles over the lid. I could hear Arthur wheezing rhythmically beneath the breakfront. Evelyn sat at attention. A wrinkled flap of skin pulsated gently beneath her neck. She shot Mel what could only be called a knowing look. Fran pinched me under the table. When Mel spoke we were expecting something dramatic. Revealing.

"Sometimes a man needs to leave because he has a different life planned. Maybe with someone else."

Then, I thought of the pink Rambler. *Had* there been someone in the passenger seat? Impossible. Barry wasn't like that. Affairs. Adultery. Those were bourgeois concepts. We were beyond all that now. There was no way Mel could understand the world Barry and I inhabited. No one *had* to do anything anymore. Still, he *was* gone. Running. Hiding. There was no way to understand it.

Mel looked past me as if he just remembered something important. I felt myself arching forward, ready to receive some treasured secret. But he wasn't saying any more. He'd said enough.

Sometime between the Jell-O mold and the butter cookies, Fran disappeared and I excused myself and headed for the bathroom. Battered and slightly drunk, I steadied myself on the sink, trying to figure out why Fran had dragged me here in the first place. Ignoring the rhinestone-studded poodle that stared at me from the top of the toilet seat, I ran my fingers over my eye and felt the spot where the swelling was beginning to recede. Evelyn told me not to be shocked if there were some black-and-blue marks there in the morning. "A shiner" was what she called it. "Don't be upset, Renee, if you find you've got a shiner in the morning." I'd heard that word before. Once when Leon came home late from school, blood dried and crusty on his raincoat, he told me in a shaking voice about a kid named Harold who had tried to push him through a plate-glass window.

I punched him, Renee, he says. I try to picture Leon punching the boy. I try to picture his long, surgeon's fingers rolled into an angry fist.

That night the boy's mother calls the house. My mother is having a good day. The kitchen smells of chocolate. There are pink flowers in a vase. She offers soothing words and apologies. When she hangs up, everything is the same. But when I look at Leon, he is different. His hands are covered with tiny cuts. He is capable, I think, of hurting someone. I remember his palm against my back as we stood on the roof. He can do anything, I think. Even push.

I was thinking about that and wondering if my swollen eye would blacken and shine when Fran knocked on the bathroom door.

"You okay? I'm ready to leave."

It was a reprieve. A death sentence canceled by a last-minute pardon.

We scurried out the door, partaking in the ritual farewells and sentimental cheek-peckings. Outside, the sun still hadn't set, and I squinted like a mole with my one good eye.

Fran waited until we were in the car. She was breathing in short, gulping gasps. Wordlessly, she held out her hand. At first I had difficulty focusing. Then slowly the image gathered strength. Keys.

"I stole them from my father's jacket while you had dessert."

I thought for an instant about the Jell-O mold and the cookies, and how Fran had been rifling through her father's pockets at that precise moment. Maybe this was what the dinner had really been all about.

"What are they for?"

"They're the keys to his garage and all the file cabinets. This is my chance. I'm going to get to the bottom of all this hush-hush stuff they've been whispering about for years."

"What makes you think you'll find anything in the garage?"

"I've already been through all the drawers and the attic. There *have* to be letters, pictures, *something*."

"What if this is all in your mind?" I asked. What I thought was: What if all we find are some greasy wrenches and a lot of bills and just as we're getting ready to leave, a police car rolls up and we get busted? The idea of having to face Evelyn and Mel and admit our treachery was too much to bear.

"Listen, Renee. If I *do* have a brother, if there *is* some terrible family secret, I have a right to know." She started the car. "It's now or never."

There are secrets in the purple room. Secrets she hides in the bottoms of drawers and in the back of the closet. Leon knows about the secrets. He has been there. When we are alone in the house he searches. To understand, he says, to stay one step ahead. Leon does not tell me what he finds. I do not want to know. I am afraid of this darkness. I know it has to do with the dead boy. The brother. The uncle whose thumbs I have inherited. When he is finished he never talks. The house is silent. But there is that smell. Something bad. Something beyond terror.

Within minutes we were parked in front of the white stucco garage. I waited in the car while Fran tried the keys. It was at that moment I realized the second part of the I Ching prediction was coming true.

I was definitely doing something improper.

I experienced a discomforting mixture of dread, anxiety and inexplicable excitement as Fran tugged at the garage door. It was so easy for this silly game to turn suddenly dangerous. Without rules there were no boundaries, and without boundaries we had no way of knowing when the bad things — the frightening dark things — were coming. For an instant, when I looked at Fran, I wondered if what she might find would unite her with a brother who would fulfill her fantasies, or if, in some unexpected way, it might destroy them.

The door slid open with a smooth metallic *whoosh*. Fran reached inside and flicked on a light switch. Then she jumped back. Recoiled.

I felt myself getting out of the Saab, moving as if some force was beckoning me. I knew it was bad. There was something in the garage we had not anticipated. Something we were not meant to see.

Don't come in here, Renee. Stay away. But I come anyway. And this time I see everything.

Fran was moving now, in halting half circles, letting out a low whistle between clenched teeth. The blue vein on the side of her neck throbbed as it pushed closer to the surface.

"You'd better take a look at this, Renee."

I was expecting a body, a skeleton with shards of de-
composed flesh clinging to bleached bones. Maybe Fran's
brother. Maybe some other, even more horrible, family
secret.

What I saw was Barry's pink Rambler.

Fran and I circled the car, as if it were a corpse. Afraid to
touch it, I looked inside. Empty. The car had taken on a
mysterious, haunted feeling. Like the clothes of a dead
person, or the spot on the sidewalk after a hit and run.
Time vanished. Time returning.

The black vinyl seat still bore the imprint of Barry's
body. I thought for an instant that if I touched it, he would
spring to life. His feet would magically appear on the
pedals and his small hands would guide the steering
wheel until the car rolled slowly from the garage.

"It was all a joke, Renee," he'd say. Laughing and shaking his head. Then we'd drive. Back to Days Park. Back to
the Holiday Inn where we'd spent our honeymoon. We'd
carefully retrace all our steps until we found out just
where we'd slipped off the edge and into this cavernous,
terrifying joke.

I was afraid to open the door. It was almost as if the car
was a threshold to some other dimension. A forbidden
place.

Fran looked inside the trunk. She opened the glove
compartment and checked out the back seat. Absolutely
clean. Nothing. That wasn't like Barry.

"It's been vacuumed," she said. "My dad does that as a
courtesy. Then he tucks a little thank-you note in the visor."

While Fran flipped down the visor, I stood back, still

too frightened to touch the car. It looked pinker now. Like flesh.

"See?" Fran flashed the card. "My dad's done work on it, although I can't see exactly where. Looks pretty perfect."

I tried to imagine Mel meeting Barry at some prearranged spot, some dingy, greasy bar where mechanics and runaway husbands drank beers and traded jokes. I wondered if Mel had promised to keep Barry's secret, or if the two of them had simply exchanged silent, brooding looks and it was understood that the Rambler would be housed in the garage.

Fran was at the files now. Working furiously at the locks with the tiny gold keys, she opened all the drawers in no time.

"Here," she said, holding a pink-and-blue receipt with a carbon neatly sandwiched in between.

I took the receipt from her hand. Yesterday. Barry had brought the car in to have the starter fixed. There were some indecipherable notations about other things. But only the starter had been repaired. There was nothing about keeping the car hidden, no return address, no phone number. Just the name.

Fran peeked over my shoulder. "A special favor. Mel does that. Like he'll fix someone's brakes or transmission when business is slow. Mostly he just does body work."

"Is that an excuse?"

Fran looked startled. "You didn't expect him to tell, to call you up and tell you he'd seen Barry? It's part of the male thing. My father is an absolute cipher. He'll take his secrets to the grave."

Not if we can help it, I thought.

*   *   *

I sat looking at the car, trying to imagine Barry driving away, driving here, driving anywhere. It frightened me when I realized that his face was becoming a blur, an image floating in the muddy waters of my memory. A face that would soon be irretrievable.

"*Voilà.*" Fran was waving some canceled checks in the dank garage air.

She hunkered down beside me, spreading the yellow rectangles on the concrete floor.

"One hundred dollars. Every month. Made out to a Marianna Johnsten."

I was still trying to pull Barry's face out from the darkness.

"What does that mean?"

"Well. I don't know any Marianna Johnsten for one. And then, look here, there's an old envelope, empty of course, with a return address. Marianna Johnsten, Quarry, Ontario."

Fran was convinced she'd found something. The bruise over my eye throbbed and I was angry that her curiosity had brought me here. It was one thing to catch a glimpse of Barry, to imagine him. It was another to confront the reality of the pink Rambler. I wanted to go home, to brood in silence, to drink wine and eat Hershey bars. I was ready to admit I couldn't care less about Fran's missing brother. That's when I noticed the writing on the envelope Fran had placed on top of the canceled checks. It was the same cramped handwriting that had been on the garage receipt.

Carter's Birthday. November 29.

*   *   *

I flipped the envelope into Fran's lap, and watched her face. Her skin got pale. White. What had been, only moments before, a smirk of discovery, now drooped into a downward frown.

This was what she'd been looking for. The secret. The brother. We both knew it was true, even though the evidence was hardly convincing.

"This is his name." She was whispering, her voice wafting like smoke in the dim garage. "This is him."

In that moment, reality became, for both of us, a fragile, haunting illusion. Anything could happen. People could appear and disappear, be found and get lost. There was nothing we could be sure of. All the underpinnings of our world had loosened, become undone.

I wanted to ask Fran what she was thinking, how she felt now that she knew for sure, now that her suspicions had been borne out.

Fran looked distant. She looked old. I saw where, in a few years, she would begin to resemble Evelyn, where the flap of flesh would unfold beneath her neck. She didn't say anything for a long time. When she spoke it was in a high-pitched voice. Something false. I closed my eyes against the memory of that other voice. It was only Fran I heard forcing out the words, trying to sound as if it was all still a hilarious game:

"Shit. Can you believe it? My brother is a Sagittarius?"

TWENTY-TWO

It was all beginning to unpeel, like the thin, translucent layers of an onion. And I was terrified of what I'd find at the core.

Barry had disappeared; Carter (if that was his name) had appeared. Ned had been murdered, and if I wasn't totally hallucinating, someone had surely tried to kill me.

That night, after we'd broken into Fran's father's garage, I accepted the fact that reality was an illusion. It didn't much matter what I thought, what my reason told me. Maybe it was better to believe in karma, astrology, the I Ching. Leon's world of science and logic had come crashing down on me. I was becoming a heretic to the world of empirical knowledge. Everything the I Ching had predicted had come true.

Including the part that warned: there will be evil.

After Fran returned to her parents' house, under the guise of forgetting her purse, and slipped her father's keys back into his jacket pocket, we drove around Buffalo for hours, stopping at Held's bakery for a two-pound bag of sugar cookies and at Russell's Tastee Shoppe for a gallon of milk. The plan was to eat our troubles away. And for a couple of hours in Fran's apartment, while we listened to Dylan, the Doors and — as we began to wind down — Simon and Garfunkel, it worked. Fran admitted that finding out about Carter had been a shock, but she was over that. Now she was thinking up a plan. A caper. Some way to arrange a meeting between Carter and herself. Okay, so she wasn't being completely realistic. All she'd found were a couple of canceled checks and a scribbled note. Carter could be anyone. An employee. A friend. A dog. But Fran was convinced, and the way things were going I allowed myself to be swept along.

We didn't talk much about the Rambler. It was clear now, crystal clear, that Barry was alive and well. Maybe he had another car. Maybe he'd become a pedestrian runaway. In light of the evening's events, including Mel's cryptic remarks over dinner, it was obvious that Barry was up to something. Something more than smuggling. Even Fran was beginning to admit that now.

Another life, she said.

It struck me then about other lives. Mel and his secret son. Barry and his shadowy passenger. I'd heard of double lives. Double agents. Spies and counterspies. But that was all TV stuff. So, I reminded myself, was murder.

I went on like this, theorizing and second-guessing myself, until it was well past 2 A.M. Fran yawned. I glanced out the window. The night was still there. Tenacious. Black. Refusing to yield to morning. I fell asleep on Fran's couch.

■

In the dream it's hot. Parched. I'm on hard, dry ground. My bare feet feel the heat of the earth. Someone is with me. It looks like Fran, but when she turns to face me, her features blur into the faces of Mel and Evelyn. There's a thick black line around us. I want to touch the line but electricity is there. I can hear it humming and droning, warning me to keep away. The line is deadly. It forms a circle, moving closer, shrinking. I try to run. There doesn't seem to be any escape. Suddenly I see the pink Rambler. Only it's different somehow. It's lit from within. I can see inside. It's coming toward me, coming to save me, to re-lease me from the deadly circle. I can see Barry's face framed by gleaming black curls. There's someone beside him. But it's dark on the passenger's side. The car comes closer. Instead of slowing down, it picks up speed. It's coming toward me. I hear the shrieks; laughter mixed with something sinister. Howls. Barry and the passenger are holding hands, their eyes shine with evil — their mouths are twisted in mad grins. The car knocks me down. I feel a painful, shining blackness around my eye. But I can still see. I'm on all fours and the car is twisting crazily into the distance. The circle is closing behind it. When I look up, the car slows, moving in and out of focus. I see only the back of Barry's head. But now there's a light on the right side — the passenger's side. The person who sits there turns slowly. I know this is important. This person will give me the key — will save me or destroy me. I look up and stare into his face. Leon. He shouts something to me, but the words are incomprehensible. All I hear is the echo of his voice shrieking like a demon in the darkness.

TWENTY-THREE

Nothing seemed to happen during the day. It was as if the sunlight had some sort of healing power, a power that faded as night fell like an inky black pool. It was during the night that I got another call. The same rasping voice, the same labored breathing. This time there was something new. Music. I heard a click and a scratchy tape of "Walk Away, Renee" played through the receiver. I almost had to laugh. I'd heard that song so many times, heard it sung by well-meaning friends, by angry, rejected boyfriends, by just about anyone who heard my name for the first time. Leon, in particular, liked to whistle it under his breath, after tormenting me with stories of the dangers of drugs, the importance of graduate school and incomprehensible difficulties of advanced physics. "I don't take drugs," I'd shouted, "and I'll never take physics or go to graduate school."

The perfect time for him to accuse me of hedonistic escapism — the perfect time for a verse of "Walk Away, Renee."

*   *   *

The song was the only light moment I'd had with my mysterious caller. The message was heavy.

"Just a little warning. Next time I won't miss."

I was sure he was referring to the near fatality — mine — in front of Days Park.

For an instant, I had an impulse to call the police. But in the next instant I saw myself as they would see me; some hysterical hippie who had no proof of anything. Okay, so the cops were out and a bodyguard wasn't likely to volunteer. Still, I desperately needed protection. I found it in the most unexpected way.

Vitale asked me to dog-sit for Nickel Bag. He was going to the Haight to check things out and it was a hassle to bring a dog along. Besides, Nickel Bag was simply too much of a free spirit to be caged in one of those repressive airline carriers. No problem. A dog was just what I needed. Vitale gave me a lid of grass to keep Nickel Bag well stoned. "If you need more," he said, "stop by Rex's place on Delevan. You know, the white house overlooking Forestlawn Cemetery. If he's not home, the grass is in a plastic bag under a tombstone with the name Harry Grass." This was Vitale's idea of a joke. I'd been to Rex's place before. It was a lamentable two-story frame house, with a slanted roof that Rex called a porch. I remember standing on the roof with Barry, feeling that twittery sensation in my wrists, while inside, Rex played Donovan's "Mellow Yellow" and tried shaving, drying, rolling and eventually smoking the pulpy insides of two dozen banana peels. No one got high on the banana peels and instead Rex turned on a red light and offered everyone something called Lebanese Blond. Barry and I fell asleep on the floor along with the rest of the group. In the morning, I awoke just in time to watch a purple mist linger over Forestlawn Cemetery. It struck me then, for the first time, that the cemetery was probably the most scenic spot in Buffalo. Ironic that the living had to suffer in gray ugliness, while the dead soaked up the only pastoral beauty the city had to offer.

There was no way I was going to feed Nickel Bag marijuana, and no way I was going to furtively dig up the burial place of someone unfortunate enough to be named Harry Grass. As for Rex, there was something both secretive and overly friendly about him. Something I couldn't entirely trust. He didn't like women. That's what Fran said. Besides, he had recently been classified 1-A. It was only a matter of time until he disappeared into the Canadian underground, leaving his house, his banana scrapings and his terrific view of sculptured tombstones. It was a location we all coveted.

I was thinking about Rex's house and the slanted porch, when Fran stopped by. Daylight had just shriveled into an opaque orange dot that lowered itself gracefully into the horizon. Night was beginning, and with it all the weird and unpredictable events that had turned my life into a strange commingling of fantasy and reality.

Fran's revelation qualified as both.

"I slept with Sherman."

I was stunned. Were there no limits, no taboos? I tried to be cool. Unruffled.

"What was that like?"

"Weird. Like sleeping with your brother."

That's when the eerie, inexplicable humming began. Something electrical. Something from inside my head. The noise wouldn't go away. It moved along the surface of my skin, sending little shock waves into my wrists and ankles. I felt for a moment as if I was going to faint — to black out. There was an odd pressure on my chest, like a large, leaden finger prodding at my rib cage. I slumped onto the couch. Nickel Bag threw himself at my feet and whined. Fran stood back. Her face became a pale, faded moon.

"You okay?"

Actually, I was finding it increasingly difficult to breathe. I was remembering something. A dream maybe. When I closed my eyes, I saw thick black circles. The humming had faded, but it was still there, barely perceptible over Nickel Bag's furtive whines and Fran's solicitous questions.

"What's wrong? Is it something you ate?"

I was beginning to reconstitute. Like orange juice mixed in a blender, I was forming myself, moving back into a recognizable shape. The humming became a drone and the drone melted into the night. Nickel Bag nudged my hand until I petted his furry head with a reluctant, automatic motion.

"I'm okay. Really."

"Is it your eye?"

Fran was still guilty about my hapless encounter with her mother's breakfront. The fact that the next morning the swelling had disappeared and there was absolutely no sign of a bruise, no shiner, troubled her even more. Internal injury, she had muttered as she ran her cool fingers over my eye. She had wanted me to go to Millard Fillmore. We'd heard about a doctor there who wore his hair in a ponytail and gave out Demerol free for the asking, but I was feeling fine, and I had no need for downers.

"Maybe I'm just a little hungry," I said as I eased myself onto the rug. The swirls were motionless now. Everything was steady. I asked the obvious question.

"Why on earth did you sleep with Sherman?"

"Renee, I did it for you. Remember, I said I'd figure out a way to pry information from him? About Barry? Remember?"

I remembered. I guess I just didn't want to be reminded.

"So? What happened?"

"He was terrible in bed. All speedy, talking a mile a minute . . ."

I didn't want the carnal details. Marshal Sherman was someone I felt as though I'd grown up with. I didn't want to say the word that I knew would make the humming return. I didn't even want to think it. Marshal Sherman was like a brother. I interrupted Fran's erotic monologue.

"Did he tell you anything?"

"He never shut up. But about Barry, he was pretty close-mouthed. He did admit he'd seen him though. He sold him a lid of grass and some black beauties. All from his private stash. He's not dealing anymore. Those guys from the mob really spooked him. He showed me where he still keeps the gun. He's really freaked about all that."

I thought about the gun and how it had sounded that day in the field. The pop pop, shattering the air, splintering it into jagged planes of sky. Ned had been alive then. Everything had still been an innocent game.

"So he doesn't know where Barry is?" I asked.

Fran was hedging. Her lips were parted and a half-formed word seemed to linger on her tongue.

"Not exactly."

I waited. If Fran wasn't going to tell me, she wouldn't have bothered coming here in the first place. She just liked drawing things out. There was theater in that.

"Barry's been around. You know. Sleeping here one night, there the next. Crashing at Rex's place."

The house by the cemetery with the slanted roof. A perfect hideout for Barry.

"Where is he now?" I asked.

Fran looked down with disdain at Nickel Bag, who was licking his private parts.

"That's the thing. Sherman swore he didn't know. The day Barry came to see him he was all nervous, said he'd had a change of plans and was splitting. That's all Sherman knows. He sold him the grass as a special favor."

It surprised me to think that Barry had any plans at all, let alone the presence of mind to change them. I wanted to ask Fran if she'd found out anything else, if Barry was traveling alone, but something stopped me. Nickel Bag. He'd lifted his leg and was peeing on the corner of the couch.

"Uggh! that beast is positively disgusting," Fran hissed. "What ever possessed you to take care of him. He's completely uncivilized."

Not like Arthur, the wheezing, stuffed sausage that hid

beneath the breakfront, I wanted to say as I scurried into the kitchen to rustle up some paper towels.

When I got back, Nickel Bag was licking the rug and Fran had left. Another missed opportunity.

It occurred to me then that I really didn't want to know any more about Barry. I didn't want to know about his secret or his other life or his mysterious comings and goings. In all probability, Leon had been right. I should get an annulment. Move. Find new friends. Buckle down and get serious about my life.

But first things first. Someone was after me. I was no longer sure about Barry. As a matter of fact, as a suspect he had lost some credibility. For one thing, he was on the run, for another he seemed to have someone with him. All right, so my ego was bruised. There was someone my husband loved more than me. Of course he could have been kidnapped, held against his will by some sinister fiend who sat motionless in the shadowy passenger seat of the pink Rambler. It irked me to think that Barry, the boy I'd married practically on a dare, the not-quite-grown-up man, might actually have a past, one that was so compelling he'd practically become an outlaw to protect it.

I stared out the window, thinking of some way to understand.

I thought about our dinner at Fran's parents' house. I remembered what Mel had said.

"Sometimes a man has to leave because he has a different life planned."

Another life. A second life. I wondered if that was possible.

The white envelope is open on the kitchen table. It is a thick envelope. That means he's been accepted. There was never any doubt. Not really. But now I feel the panic. Leon is leaving. He is going to college. I will be all alone in the green house. All alone with her.

When I find Leon he is in the back yard, dissecting a frog. He has carefully peeled back its skin using implements made of tiny pins imbedded in slivers of wood. When are you leaving? I ask. He does not answer. The air is thick and hot. I feel a throbbing in my wrists. What will I do? My arm is still in a sling from the car accident. Leon squints. The sunlight bounces off his glasses. Don't worry, he says. I do not know what that means. I need to understand, to be prepared. Things are getting worse. Dangerous.

She will not be here, he says. What does that mean? I want to ask. But I know he will not answer. Leon, I say. Then I am suddenly silent. He stares at my arm, at the bruise on my leg that has already turned yellow. He frowns. There are wrinkles on his forehead I have never seen before.

She will not be here, Renee.

Using the pins, he deftly removes the frog's heart. A tiny purple fist the size of a dime. I shudder when I see that it continues to pulsate with life.

Like the thin transparent slides Leon placed beneath his microscope, I too had a second life, one that barely overlapped, existing side by side, almost simultaneously with the first.

My first life was the one I shared with Leon in the green house. And my second life began when I came here to try and forget.

■

I clipped a leash into the ring on Nickel Bag's collar. It was time for a walk. The air in my apartment had become heavy, leaden with sadness and a quiet, inescapable truth.

TWENTY-FOUR

It was my sixth time around the park. Nickel Bag was sniffing and I was thinking. I'd just had a cup of tea with Fran. Herbal tea. The kind she mixed in a little metal tea ball and immersed in a china mug; the kind that signaled she had hatched a new plan. Devised a caper. And this one was a doozie. I had to hand it to her, Fran was clever. She'd come up with a way to find out about her alleged brother, Carter. It wasn't complicated and she'd done most of the groundwork already. As a matter of fact it was diabolically simple. I just wasn't sure I could carry it off. Of course I was involved. Ever since the night when the I Ching prediction had come true, I was mystically intertwined with Fran's missing brother. At least that's how she put it. I couldn't argue. I felt something. A tug. A link. Call it karma. Call it fate. Call it a form of cosmic curiosity, but I really wanted to get to the bottom of this business with her brother. Almost as much as she did.

*　　*　　*

199

Fran had made an afternoon visit to the hall of records, the place where birth certificates and marriage licenses are kept. She'd discovered something surprising, something she'd always suspected but never had the nerve to actually confront. Her parents were married in January. She was born in March of the same year. That meant, according to Fran, that along with being a Pisces, she was also a love child.

"Can you believe it? Evelyn got knocked up? They *had* to get married."

It didn't seem like such a big thing to me, but to Fran it was earth-shattering, a childhood fantasy biting the dust.

"They've been lying to me for twenty years, telling me they got married a year *before* I was born. Manipulating time. Deceiving me. No wonder I'm so screwed up."

I intervened at this point, trying to sound Freudian, trying to sound like Leon, and posited the theory that being conceived out of wedlock was hardly traumatic, since Mel and Evelyn were legally married at the time of her birth. That's when Fran's mouth became a hard lipless line.

"You're forgetting one little thing, Miss Modern Library Freud." (I thought that was a low blow.) "You're forgetting that in all probability my father was already married, and already a father. Marianna Johnsten? Carter? He had a family. I," and she pronounced this pronoun with an equal measure of disdain and importance, "was no doubt an *in utero* homewrecker."

I thought that was a novel idea. If, as Fran insisted, mothers could transfer feelings to their babies as they floated blissfully in amniotic fluid, it was no wonder Fran was born with a case of colic that lasted for months. It was no wonder Fran was still high-strung, hysterical and shrieky.

But there was more. Fran believed her father had run off with Evelyn leaving Marianna and Carter stranded and penniless.

"They must hate me," she said. "Those negative vibrations were always there, following me since the day I was conceived."

I sipped my tea while Fran got overly dramatic about the evil karma that had to come to an end, the bad vibes that must be reversed, and waited patiently until she got to the nitty gritty. The caper.

It involved costumes. Personas, Fran called them. And accents, only slight ones. It was nothing we couldn't do. Nothing that would get us in any serious trouble. We were simply going to pose as Canadian census takers. Fran already had the forms. The fact that they were U.S. census questionnaires didn't faze her one bit. "We'll use a clipboard and slip the top line under the clip. They'll see the questions and the official document and that will be enough." By "they," Fran meant Marianna and Carter Johnsten, assuming of course they still lived at the address she had found on the envelope, and that they were who she thought they were.

Now it was one thing to slip anonymously through department stores wearing curly wigs and straight-looking raincoats, it was another to actually talk to another human being while pretending to be someone you're not. To be an impostor. A fake. A *poseur* (Fran's word).

"Don't be a drag, Renee," Fran said as soon as she saw I was showing the first signs of reluctance. "Think of it as a giant goof. A growth experience. A wild, spontaneous act of abandon. We have everything to gain and nothing to lose."

That's when I asked her a question. THE question. Just what did she hope to accomplish by visiting these people, by disguising herself as some official of the Canadian government?

"I just want to see them, Renee. I want to see my father's other life. I want to see my brother. I want to know the whole story. My *raison d'être*."

The fact that Fran was in no way related to Marianna Johnsten did not escape me. But the stuff about her brother, her half brother actually, made some sense. I couldn't imagine my life without Leon. I had practically internalized him. He was like a voice in my head, my flip side. My superego. I no longer needed to see Leon's face, or even to hear him speak. His existence and mine were connected in a way that only brothers and sisters can understand. So I was sympathetic to Fran's need. I just wasn't sure if I could go through with it. And I'd hate myself if I screwed up.

"You'll be fine," Fran assured me. "You did a great job at my parents' house the other night. The perfect foil. They never suspected."

"But that was because *I* never suspected," I said.

"Don't sweat the details. We'll rehearse. We'll try out the whole scene on someone else first, see how it goes. You'll be perfect. You underestimate yourself. You've got to stretch. Grow. Break out of that rigidity. We're part of the revolution, Renee. We're changing all the rules. It's a new world out there. We can do anything. Trust me."

*   *   *

By the time I left Fran's apartment, I was feeling pretty sure of myself. High, almost. I could do anything. Anything goes. Nothing is real. I am the master of my fate, I am the captain of my soul. I recited all these comforting words to Nickel Bag, who sniffed at tree trunks, chewed mounds of grass and lifted his leg every couple of steps. He seemed unimpressed.

On the way back into the apartment building, I was feeling so up, so ready for adventure, that I stopped by Duane's apartment. There was no bell and it seemed quiet inside. I was ready to knock, when I realized maybe that wasn't such a good idea. I was a mess for one thing, and Nickel Bag was an awkward encumbrance. I decided to go upstairs, shower, brush the knots out of my hair, feed the dog and then make my move. I was, after all, the master of my fate.

My apartment had been ransacked. The door was still open. Nothing, it seemed, had been taken, but my clothes were everywhere: strewn in the hallway, flung over the chairs, half flushed in the toilet bowl. It was like a crime scene, only there were no cops, no yellow ropes cordoning off the area and no body outlined in white chalk.

I walked through the rooms, Nickel Bag sniffing at my heels, surveying the damage. My bedroom had been destroyed; dresses, blouses, underwear, thrown every which way. Drawers completely overturned, their contents scattered like confetti throughout the apartment.

It was messy, but not ominous. No threatening notes. No messages in blood. The tub was clean. No knives. I considered myself lucky. Somehow, when I heard Nickel Bag whining and digging in the living room, I suspected the worst.

My good luck had just run out.

The dog had my best red nylon underpants in his mouth. He seemed to be chewing at the crotch.

"Get away from those, you disgusting mutt!" I couldn't help myself. Nickel Bag slunk pathetically beneath the couch. Then I smelled it. Something faintly ammonia-like, something primitively familiar. Semen. There was no way I could be mistaken. I'd know that smell anywhere. My underpants positively reeked of semen. And they were still wet.

I would have vomited right there, but Nickel Bag beat me to it, heaving great undigested lumps of dirt and twigs in irregular piles among the scattered clothing.

Great. All the confidence of only moments before melted away like the look of distress on Nickel Bag's face. The dog was licking my hand in a humiliating attempt at reconciliation. I collapsed in a heap beside him. There was dog puke on the rug, my apartment had been ransacked, and to top it off, someone had jerked off in my underpants.

TWENTY-FIVE

I did the only thing any normal female in my place would have done. I cried. Then I cleaned up. Then I cried again. Then I called Leon.

He didn't answer the phone. SHE did. Or at least I imagined that's who it was. Ruth. It was a woman's voice, throaty and full of sleep. I wanted to ask to speak to my brother. I wanted to sound confident and adult. Instead, after she said "Hello" for the third time, her voice rippling with annoyance, I hung up.

I wonder if he tells her. I wonder if he shares the secrets of the green house with her. Our secrets. Does he tell her about what he did in the purple room? And then what happened. After.

I was alone. It was just Nickel Bag and me.

This was no time to fall apart. So someone had broken in. Again. It had been happening for months. But this time, the maniac had gone too far. Had he fantasized about me,

I wondered, as he spent himself in my panties? Or was he just some random pervert who had a thing for red nylon?

There was no way I could laugh myself out of this one. Or smoke myself out.

I started the breathing. Slow and deliberate. I meditated on Leon. I conjured him into my conscious mind. If I couldn't reach him by phone I could reach him by telepathy. Help me, Leon. Tell me what to do now.

At first I saw a lot of clouds. Things you'd expect to see when you meditate. Then it was fingers. Long and graceful. Leon's hands. He was holding the vials while he waded into the pond. It was that cold day in November. Renee, wait right there, he had said. He had been trying to protect me. To watch over me. I never realized that before. Not until this very second. I felt warm inside. Safe.

When I opened my eyes I still wasn't sure what to do, but I *was* calm. Not quite in control. No longer the captain of my ship, but at least not a slave in the lower galley.

I walked into the kitchen and looked for my list. The list of possible suspects. It was right where I'd left it. My tormentor had no interest in my kitchen, that much was clear. I was sure no one had seen these names but me.

I thought over each one. Then I drew a line through Vitale. He was gone. Haight-Ashbury. Thousands of miles away, and he had trusted me with his best friend. Someone who wants to kill you wouldn't give you his dog. No, Vitale was no longer a suspect. That still left a pretty long list. Just about everyone I knew. There was no one left to eliminate, but I did have a name to add. Call it a crazy hunch, call it intuition. I knew it wouldn't make sense if I thought about it, but I wrote it anyway.

Mel Johnsten.

It wasn't as if Fran's father was completely innocent. He *had* seen Barry and he hadn't told me. He'd dropped all sorts of cryptic hints and never once did he let on that he just might know something. I didn't trust him. He'd left his wife for Evelyn. Possibly even left his son. He was a double agent. A man with a past. But, I asked myself, as I stared at his name, written neatly beneath Marshal Sherman and Wesley the warlock. Was he the type of man to write my name in blood, to murder Ned, to sideswipe me in broad daylight, to (and this was the clincher) masturbate in my underwear?

No, of course not. But then no one I knew could possibly be capable of all those things. Some of them, maybe. But all? There were only two solutions: First, I didn't really know people the way they were, the seamy, dark underside of people, or, second, whoever was doing all these things was a stranger. A complete and utter stranger with no motive whatsoever. That's because strangers don't have motives. They have impulses. Impulses can't be explained — they just *are*. Now that was no mystical mumbo jumbo. That was psychological. Scientific. Leon would have liked that.

I tried not to think about the fact that a stranger wouldn't know my name. That bothered me. Then I figured, well, maybe it was a stranger who'd dropped by 72 Days Park and had seen my name on the doorbell downstairs, the one Fran liked because McCullum, the landlord, had reversed our last names. Ned had found me that way, why not someone else? A perfect madman who was looking for someone to drive insane, saw my name on a doorbell and just took it from there. There was no way he could know about Barry having disappeared or any of the other coincidences that occurred at the same time. Like that stuff about Fran dressed as a man. That was either a mistake on Duane's part, or a curious coincidence. There. Had I left anything out? Didn't it all make perfect sense now? It did, except that I was more terrified than ever. I was dealing with a complete unknown. A masked man, a hit-and-run murderer, a sexual pervert.

How long I mulled this one over, I couldn't tell, but by the time I was finished I had an interminable pounding in my head and a horrible premonition that whoever had been here wasn't through with me yet.

There was only one place to go. Duane. Aside from Vitale, who was definitely out of reach, he was the only nonsuspect with whom I could safely spend the night. Assuming, of course, that he was home, and alone.

I left Nickel Bag with a generous portion of doggie chow and alerted him to patrol the premises. Somehow having a dog around made me feel better. How long did Vitale say he'd be gone?

Cool, composed and determined to remain so, I walked purposefully down the stairs. No lingering shadows. No furtive footsteps. No one making love alone in a dark corner.

I put an ear to Fran's door. Silence. She was either asleep or stoned, or out exploring what I was coming to suspect was her seamy, dark side.

There was no answer at Duane's door. I knocked. I called his name. I even put my eye against the keyhole. To no avail. It was dark and silent inside. Duane could be anywhere. As it happened, he was sitting on the front step of Days Park. Amazing. Maybe things were beginning to go my way.

It was getting dark. The pale sky was already thickening into something deep and black. Duane turned and smiled. I guess he could feel me approach, even from the back. An Indian thing. I sat down beside him, careful to maintain control of my face. Hysterical expressions, tears and involuntary trembling would be a sure giveaway. Then I told him. In carefully measured words I explained everything, beginning with the dinner at Mel and Evelyn's and ending with my underpants.

"No shit."

I was hoping for something more. It was coming.

"You said you got a dog up there."

"Nickel Bag."

Duane laughed. "I guess he's better than nothing. Maybe you better crash at my place tonight."

Prince Charming.

I asked Duane what he thought. He looked at the changing sky and ran his hand down his ponytail in that characteristic way of his. For an instant I wondered if guys felt more in touch with their feminine sides when they wore long hair. You could even say that from the back, sitting down, Duane looked like a girl. Something told me not to pursue this line of thought out loud.

"This whole thing is pretty fucked up. Someone is definitely flipping out."

"Exactly. But who and why?"

Duane smiled. That great smile that went with that great laugh. Only this time he wasn't laughing. Just smiling. At me.

"Renee, you're a wild chick."

I guess I was supposed to take that as a compliment. Although I knew that I hadn't done anything at all wild, unless you consider being an unwitting accessory to a garage break-in wild. It was more like wild things were being done *to* me. But I was so disarmed, so knocked off by Duane's smile, the way he said my name, that I just grinned and flicked my hair casually over my shoulder.

Then he asked me if I wanted to go for a drink. To the Aragon. It wasn't like me to tempt fate, one near collision with madness in an evening would normally have been enough, but I was under Duane's spell. I was also afraid to be alone and had nowhere else to go. Maybe, I thought as we walked together across the park, I was falling in love.

The Aragon vaguely reminded me of a scene from *On the Road*. Sweltering. Smoky. Thick with the stench of unwashed men. And there was no mistaking *that*. This was the real thing. Indians.

Despite their fleshy swollen faces and alcoholic pallor, I could still see the cheekbones, the noses, the faces that even bruised and puffy would make guys like Barry, Marshal Sherman, even Leon, quake in their boots. These guys were *mean*.

Duane was obviously in his element. He propped one elbow on the bar and muttered something to the bartender. A tattooed arm passed him two drafts.

Bodies pressed up against mine. It was hard to breathe. The first beer felt good. The second one was even better. Duane didn't talk much. He just leaned against a greasy wall and flung his arm around my shoulder. I guess that meant I belonged to him. Whatever, I was grateful. I certainly didn't want anyone here to think I was up for grabs.

By the third beer I had a little buzz. Enough to wobble to
the ladies' room. It was occupied. Funny, I hadn't noticed
any women. They were probably somewhere in the back
behind the curtain of smoke. There was no place to wait,
so I sat in the vacant phone booth, the old-fashioned kind,
all wood, like they used to have in the back of drugstores
and five and dimes. There were lots of things written —
carved — into the wall. Interesting things like "Rosa
sucks" and "Red power." There were hundreds of phone
numbers; a jumble of digits with dashes, lines and gouges
where the knives had slipped. Then, there it was, plain as
day. My phone number. Carved in a little circle next to
the initials R. J.

I was thinking that this couldn't be real, that it was the
atmosphere, the beer, Duane's smile, when a fat lady with
a serious scowl etched in her forehead banged on the door
and jerked her thumb toward the phone.

"Gotta make a call."

I was out in a flash, back at Duane's side with a full
bladder and an urgent request to leave quickly and quietly. Duane belched. "No problem. Nothing's happening
tonight." Plenty was happening. But there was no way I
was talking until we were safely out on the street, far from
the anonymous transvestite, pervert, madman with a knife
who was lurking somewhere in the smoky shadows of the
Aragon.

■

Nightfall in Days Park: strains of guitar music, wafting
clouds of marijuana smoke, trees, gnarled, thick, slowly
dying of Dutch elm disease, forlorn outcasts of the sub-

urbs slumped in narcotic dazes against tattered backpacks and greasy sleeping bags. I reached out to touch Duane, to reassure myself that my life hadn't become some dangerous, pathetic, psychedelic nightmare, when I turned and saw *HIM*. An apparition. A ghost.

A man with Fran's face moving stealthily through the darkness.

I began to jerk violently. I wanted to run, to scream, to explode into the night. I pulled at Duane's sleeve, my voice a throaty rasp.

"Did you see that?"

Duane, who was looking in another direction, trembled. His arm was drenched in sweat. He crumpled like an old paper bag. We steadied ourselves against a rotting elm.

"That was *HIM*," I said.

"Shit. It *WAS*."

The deadly apparition had vanished.

"I can't believe what I just saw. I just can't believe it."

Duane nodded. His eyes had gone strange. He pulled at his ponytail. His reaction seemed even more visceral, more intense than my own.

"Either can I," he said. "After all this time. I thought he was dead. Shit. It was *HIM*. Vinny Palladino."

TWENTY-SIX

Duane was naked. We both were. He passed me a joint. I inhaled, watching the smoke spiral toward the cracked plaster ceiling.

"But I felt the knife go through. Felt it go deep. Shit, I was sure I'd killed him."

I propped a pillow beneath my head. Inside, behind my eyes, it still felt like a nauseating carnival ride — the kind with the blinking lights and the announcer shrieking in a horrible, taunting voice. I hadn't exactly fainted in the park, but I had gotten sort of weak in the knees. I remember leaning on Duane as we both limped back to his place. Once safely behind the locked door, hidden away from the demons who had spooked us, we threw off our clothes and crawled into bed like crabs frantically burrowing into the wet sand.

It would have been fun if the demons had been imaginary, if they had been some mad ghosts conjured up from the primeval swamps of our unconscious minds. We

213

would have laughed then, rolled around in the worn sheets, made hot juicy love and felt exotic and thrilled to be alive.

Only what we saw was real.

Duane was positive he'd seen his former murder victim: the infamous Vinny Palladino — gun-toting gangster of the high school bathroom. But Vinny wasn't dead. There he was, lurking in the most unlikely of places. Days Park at midnight.

Duane traced the white line of the scar along the side of his face. He was thinking. Had Vinny seen him? Had he tracked him down, intent upon some hideous revenge?

"Either way, I'm a dead man," Duane said as he inhaled the pot, holding it for a long time in his lungs, holding it until he got a rush that would soften the edge.

I wasn't sure I understood. What had happened was a long time ago. Vinny had been the attacker, Duane had defended himself. It was over. Or was it?

"It ain't over. It's never over. Not with those guys and not with Uncle Sam."

Now he'd lost me. I was pretty shaky as it was. I'd just seen my best friend decked out like an awfully convincing male. A female transvestite. And now Duane was insinuating that he was a wanted man. What, I pondered, could Vinny Palladino and the United States government possibly have in common?

"They both want to kill me," Duane said as he reached under the bed for something. A switchblade? A gun? Wrong. A draft notice.

"Congratulations," Duane said, a smile nudging ironically at his mouth. "I've just been classified 1-A."

"Can't you get a deferment?"

"What, and become an elementary school teacher like all those little white boys? Pay off my rich uncle and get a C.O.? Pay off a shrink and get out on a psychological? Or maybe I should shoot off a couple of toes and get a 4-F?"

Duane certainly knew his stuff. There wasn't a male under the age of thirty who hadn't considered every one of those options.

"You're not going, are you?" Suddenly I felt panicky. I didn't want Duane vanishing into the night, leaving me for a jungle war halfway around the world.

"Shit no. This is one Indian who ain't bleeding to death in no rice paddy."

I was relieved to hear it. I took another toke. Vietnam. On top of everything else I didn't want to deal with that.

Duane stared up at the ceiling. I joined him. There was an irregular brown stain in the corner. If you looked at it long enough it began to resemble the continent of Africa. I looked long enough.

"So what are you planning to do?" Either way, I was beginning to see that Duane wouldn't be sticking around.

"I'm not sure. Toronto. The underground. Some relatives on a reservation in Alberta. There's no rush. Unless Vinny gets me first."

What was all this stuff about Vinny getting him?

"Maybe he's forgotten about the whole thing. Put it behind him. You were both just kids. Teenagers." I reminded myself of all the wounds that had been inflicted on me by snotty adolescent girls in high school. Cruel gossip in the cafeteria. Being left out of the right cliques. A splash of red paint on my gym locker. True, I hadn't been knifed. Maybe that made it easier for me to forgive and forget. Maybe Vinny *was* the vengeful type.

"Those guys are always teenagers. They walk around with hard-ons till they die. Palladino would love to cut me. This time for good."

Could someone really die with a hard-on? Some of Duane's metaphors were lost on me. But I was beginning to get the idea. Mafia. Omertà. Unfinished business. This was serious stuff. More or less equal to having your apartment ransacked by a madman.

That's when I decided to mention what I'd seen in the park. It was obvious by now that Duane hadn't seen Fran. He'd been looking in a different direction at a nightmare distinctly his own.

"I saw Fran dressed as a man."

"Did she see you?" Duane was moving his hand up my thigh.

"I don't think so. She sure looked like a guy. She was wearing this knitted fisherman's hat so I couldn't see her hair. It was a terrific disguise. Nobody could tell."

"I told you. She's a weird chick. Nuts if you ask me."

"I think she's complicated. Interesting."

Duane gave me one of those half smiles again.

"If her get-up was so terrific, how'd you know?"

That was a good question. "It just looked like her. Like a male version of her. I can't put my finger on it."

Actually, when I thought about it, staring up for a few more minutes at the continent of Africa, it occurred to me that the apparition in the park resembled one of those bad police drawings. A composite sketch of a murderer. The thought chilled me.

"Come'ere," Duane said. I was already there, but I knew what he meant. There was nothing left to do when facing death, but live life. To the fullest.

"Let's fuck," he whispered.

If there was one thing I could say about Duane it would be that he was an incredible lover. He was able to succeed where the beer and the pot had failed so miserably. He was able to transport me, to make me forget. His fear and his rage, his pent-up violence vibrated against my skin. Shook me from my own self-absorption, my frightened, timid, and now tormented, middle-class existence.

We made love, moving effortlessly from one position to another. His lips were hot against my neck, wet as he kissed me under my arms, behind my knees, between my legs. When I covered his penis with my mouth, he told me what to do. He spoke quietly, moving his hand down the small of my back, moaning as he swelled inside me.

■

I couldn't tell what time it was. There was no clock on the dresser beside Duane's bed. There was no dresser. There wasn't even a bed, just a mattress on the floor. The windowless room seemed sealed, filled with our heat. I rolled over and closed my eyes. I imagined time, a translucent liquid, something trapped in an amber glass, something without motion or energy — without power. We would never grow old. It was impossible. Death and danger, they were impossible too — visions floating in a tinted glass. Everything would vanish and we would be safe and young. Forever.

I watched Duane as he slept. There was a trembling beneath his eyelids; traces of dreams as they inched their way through the darkness. I outlined the scar with my little finger. He didn't stir. The skin pulsated where it had healed itself in a jagged line. The mark of time, moving forward, pulling us along.

We could grow old and we would. Death was real and danger had already found us, or we had sought it out.

I moved closer to Duane, pressing my body against his, sharing a warmth that I knew could never last. I wrapped my arms around him, determined to savor the moment, to watch it carefully as it crept away from me. Because after this, things would change. I would never be young in exactly the same way. Time would leave its scars on me as well. But for now, for this instant, I was still a child, still safe, untouched.

I slipped my hand in Duane's, curling my fingers into the empty spaces between his.

Please, I whispered to the windowless room. Please, I said in a voice I was sure no one could ever hear.

Please, let this last forever.

TWENTY-SEVEN

Nickel Bag had exhibited remarkable bladder control. He lost it, however, on the stairs going down to the park. I tugged at his collar. "Bad dog. Bad. Bad."

He whimpered apologetically. What could I expect? I'd left him alone all night. By the time I'd dressed and slipped quietly from Duane's bed it was almost 10 A.M.

When he saw the open door leading to the street, Nickel Bag lurched forward. Freedom. I remember smiling as he made his way toward a gnarled elm tree, but then the smile froze, hardening into a sickly smirk.

"Where the hell have you been?"

It was Fran. Her hands strategically placed on her hips, her face crimson with fury.

"Here boy!" I shouted running clumsily past Fran in a halfhearted and fruitless attempt to attach Nickel Bag to his leash.

"RENEE-E!" Fran was chasing me — screaming, her hair a yellow blaze billowing behind her like a sail.

I ran. She ran. Nickel Bag scrambled ahead, probably thinking all this was a terrific game. When I fell, tripping over a sleeping mass of rags and hair, a lump of human skin and bone, a runaway flower child who'd chosen Days Park as his temporary resting place, the chase came to a screeching halt. That's because now Fran was screeching. Actual high-frequency decibels were issuing from her mouth into the languid morning air. I was embarrassed. I was humiliated. And I was scared shitless.

She made an effort to compose her face, to calm her unfettered hysteria.

"I demand an explanation."

I'd never seen Fran like this before. Out of control. Off her rocker. Beyond the pale.

"An explanation for what?"

"Where the hell *have you been?* I called you. I knocked on your door. I thought you'd been kidnapped or murdered or slashed by some madman. Don't you remember about my plan? About going to Canada. Carter. My lost brother?"

Tiny pear-shaped tears had gathered in the corners of Fran's eyes. A bubble of spittle sprang from her lower lip. A muscle beneath her cheek twitched almost imperceptibly. I was trying desperately to figure all this out. Last night I was sure. No, positive, I'd seen her masquerading as a man, walking confidently through Days Park with the lumbering gait of an arrogant male. Now this outburst. This pleading angry voice telling me she'd been looking for me, worrying about me. Calling. Knocking. It didn't fit. Either Fran was a terrific actress (a genuine possibility) or I had been hallucinating last night (also possible).

Nickel Bag licked my face. I pushed him away. I needed time to think about this. There wasn't any.

"I'm waiting, Renee. I'm waiting."

Fran had quickly shifted from angry to testy, like some mean nursery school teacher demanding an apology for something you hadn't even done.

"I'm sorry," I mumbled. "I didn't know you planned to do this today. I thought we were going to prepare, to rehearse."

Fran watched Nickel Bag defecate behind a greasy backpack.

"So I guess you're just not going to tell me where you were. I guess that's just none of my business."

It wasn't, but I was too afraid to say that. I've always been bad at direct confrontations. Afraid of losing. Probably for a good reason. I always lost. So I did what came easiest in situations like this. I lied.

"I was out."

Fran tapped a foot against the hardened dirt.

"No kidding."

My mind churned with several possibilities. There was no way I was going to tell Fran about Duane. He was mine and mine alone. Then I figured I'd buy some more time. I told her about the break-in. The nylon underpants smeared with semen. Fran's face softened. She was all ears.

"That's unbelievable. Disgusting. What else did he do?"

"Nothing that I could find. I was so freaked out I took Nickel Bag and walked for hours. Then I used Vitale's key, he left it with me, and slept in his place." Quick thinking.

"Look, I'm sorry," I said. "I'm flipped out by all this weirdness. Maybe we should just give up and go to the cops."

I couldn't believe I'd sunk so low as to apologize to someone who, from what I could tell, had a dark, secret life she had no intention of sharing with me. Someone who had carved my phone number into the wall of a public telephone booth, leaving me prey to every pervert in Buffalo.

"No pigs!" Fran said. Then she went into a brief harangue on the evils of a police society, while I watched a slow drowse of light move promisingly through the trees. It was going to be a nice day. Weather-wise.

I followed Fran obediently back to our apartment building, Nickel Bag in tow. The tramp, hippie, derelict — whatever, over whose body our conversation took place, and behind whose backpack Nickel Bag left a fragrant deposit, never even stirred. Maybe he was dead. The thought fluttered through my mind like a dry leaf in a summer's breeze. As we walked into the building I glanced back over my shoulder. The pile of human flesh had stirred. A girl with long black hair parted down the middle was running toward him holding a container of orange juice. The sun glinted off the love beads wrapped around her wrists and ankles. She was shouting something. His name I guess. "VINNY. V-I-N-N-Y!"

"This park is getting disgusting," Fran whined as she opened the door for me. "It's becoming the mecca for every lowlife in western New York."

I thought about that and the visions of the night before.

Lowlives. Old lives. Secret lives. The park was a magnet all right.

Fran locked Nickel Bag in the bathroom. She refused to allow him free rein of her apartment. Besides, we had work to do. I guess she had forgiven me, because now she was talking quickly, her eyes shimmering with anticipation.

This was the plan:

We were going to drive up to Quarry that afternoon. Fran had checked her horoscope. All her stars were in their most promising positions. The proper planets were in conjunction. Her moon was in a house of some sort. It was all nonsense to me, but since my collision with the I Ching, I was less likely to scoff at her theories. She'd also done my astrological chart, and wonder of wonders — my stars were aligned, my planets were conjugated and my moon had found a room of its own.

That's why we didn't need a rehearsal. Our celestial destiny was preordained.

"I still want to practice." I was adamant.

Fran relented. She gave me a clipboard with the U.S. census questionnaire she'd copped from a table in the Student Union.

"Now just ask these simple questions: date of birth, occupation, dependents living at home. It's all there. And remember to sound Canadian. Say 'Eh?' a lot. I'll do the rest, the subtle stuff. Anyway, all we have to do is get a foot in the door. I only want to get a look at them. Check it out. See if they are who I think they are. Feel the vibes." She grabbed my hand, squeezing hard. "Renee, this is so thrilling. I'm at the crossroads. The turning point of my life."

I knew this was a crazy half-baked scheme, a wild nonsensical intrusion into the lives of innocent and probably ordinary people. But Fran had turned it into some sort of spiritual quest. It meant so much to her. And now, the images of the night before faded in my mind and older ones returned.

She is showing me the pictures of Uncle Sidney. My baby brother, she says. The purple room is warm and smells of her perfume. I lost him, she says. We were both sick, but he was the one to die. They buried him, Renee. In a wooden box under the dirt. I watched them shovel dirt on my baby brother. But this was so long ago, I want to say. Even the photograph of the two of them, adolescents dressed in somber winter coats, their arms intertwined as they smile at the huge mounds of snow, is yellowed and fuzzy. Can't she forget? Is it remembering that makes her go away? That makes her voice thick and her eyes haunted?

I turn the pages of the photo album until the years spin forward. Uncle Sidney is left behind. Now the photographs are colored and glossy. Suddenly, I am looking at an image of a boy and a girl. A brother and sister. They are wearing snowsuits and linking arms. The sun is bright. The snow is piled high on either side of the slate walk. Leon and me. But the other picture, the older one, keeps reappearing. Sylvia and Sidney. Renee and Leon. I look away. This is it. This is what she sees.

I have glimpsed her nightmare.

With a pain so sudden it left me breathless, I instantly understood the force that had been pulling me to Fran. It wasn't just the wildness, the curiosity, the adventure. It was the lost brothers: Carter, Sidney. And it was Fran and my mother. Somehow the past and the present had merged, intertwined like some crazy jigsaw puzzle. I had come to Buffalo to forget, but every day brought me closer to remembering. I still wasn't free. I wasn't doing this for myself or for Fran. I was doing it for her. For love. A love ancient — primitive. A love beyond words.

I agreed to go. Fran clasped me to her chest. I could feel the thump thump of her heart, the scent of her sweat.

"Listen, I've picked your costume. The blue skirt with the matching jacket. And a white shirt. It'll look almost like a uniform. I'm wearing the same thing in brown. Remember the day we ripped these outfits off from Jensens? That was the first time I used my lucky brown satchel. I'm bringing that too, stuffing it with paper so I'll look busy and bureaucratic. I've thought of everything. I was up all night."

Sure she was. Fran was speeding. I figured she must have swallowed at least two of Sherman's twenty-four-hour black beauties. That meant she'd be talking nonstop all the way over the Peace Bridge. The worst part was, she would be erratic. Maybe even a little out of control. Her behavior in the park had been a dead giveaway. This was beginning to look like a very bad idea.

"Fran, if you don't mind me saying so, I think you're a little speedy right now. Maybe you should come down, sort of level off before we leave."

Fran's voice was like a fingernail on a blackboard. "I'm

going to do some deep breathing, some heavy meditation, light a stick of incense and practice some Hatha Yoga. Did you know that real yogis can actually stop their own hearts at will?''

The only heart that was likely to stop here was mine. It was pounding uncontrollably. This was going to be more than an adventure, more than a caper. It was going to be a journey into someone else's nightmare — a journey that would expose the twisted, half-buried secrets of an entire family.

TWENTY-EIGHT

The car wouldn't start. I felt as though I'd been given a reprieve. Maybe my horoscope had been slightly off; the heavens had shifted, the moon had changed its mind, my stars had rearranged themselves.

Fran pressed on the gas pedal, she pumped at the clutch, she knocked her fist against the dashboard.

"Shit. This can't be happening."

I sat silently, hopefully, in the passenger seat, rubbing my legs together (Fran had insisted I wear pantyhose) and listening to the reassuring sound of nylon against nylon. Sort of like a synthetic cricket, I was thinking, when the engine made a sputter and almost kicked over.

"Come on, don't do this to me," Fran was practically praying.

Then as if in answer to her prayers, Wesley and the foul-smelling, skinny ragamuffin from the park came rambling over to help.

I was sure with the help of this dynamic duo, not only

would we never get started, Fran's car would be completely destroyed in a matter of minutes.

Boy was I wrong.

Wesley and his friend popped the hood and started mumbling things about spark plugs and electrical circuits and all sorts of arcane engine jargon. Huddled over the mass of wires and metal, they looked like two deranged faith healers as they turned this and twisted that. Before I knew it the car was humming like a swarm of wasps on a hot summer's day.

Fran pressed gleefully on the gas pedal. The engine responded with a resounding roar.

"I knew it," she said. "This was fated to be."

She popped out from the car to thank her saviors.

Reluctantly, I opened the door and joined her.

Wesley had his hair done up in a combination of scarves, beads and feathers. He was wearing a button that said, "LSD the only way to fly." Smelling faintly of incense and cheap wine, he gave Fran a power-to-the-people handshake.

"Thanks, Wesley," she said. "You'll never know how much this means to me."

Wesley nodded as if he knew *exactly* how much it meant. He pointed to his friend.

"This here's my spiritual master. Just returned from six months in India. He was with the Maharishi."

The reeking human beanpole nodded at Fran. He placed his hands together as if in prayer and bowed from the waist.

"You actually met him? The Maharishi?" Fran was awed.

The spiritual master said nothing. He smiled beneficently, wiping engine grease across the front of his nearly
threadbare shirt.

"You must be pretty heavy into this stuff to have gone
all the way to India. We have to talk sometime. But right
now my friend Renee and I are off on a sort of religious
quest of our own. Will you be in town for a while?"

The spiritual master held up his hand, palm outward.
He was either stopping traffic or parting some imaginary
waters. When he spoke his voice sounded as if he'd swallowed all the dust in India or maybe a substantial portion
of the dirt in Days Park.

"Peace."

Fran smiled. The spiritual master receded into the
background and Wesley wiped his brow.

"He's amazing. The Maharishi's right-hand man."

"Who is he?" Fran asked.

"His Indian name's Baswan Ghee. But he's actually a
Buffalo boy. Born and bred. Went to Grover Cleveland
High School. It's a trip, ain't it?"

Fran nodded.

Wesley watched as Baswan unzipped his fly and relieved himself against a tree in the corner of the park.

"The amazing thing is I knew him before he got The
Message. He was a real bad dude back then. We hung out
together."

"No kidding." Fran was interested in any sort of trans-
formations including spiritual ones.

"Yeah," Wesley said. "In the old days we used to call
him the V.P. That's short for Vinny Palladino."

■

We were moving and Fran was talking. That's all I remember about that moment. I could have been flying through space with the crew of *Star Trek*. Exploring new worlds. Boldly going where no man had gone before. Instead I was trapped in a speeding red Saab, dressed as a census taker, or at least Fran's interpretation of a census taker, heading for some hapless victim on the other side of the Peace Bridge.

"Wanna toke?" Fran handed me a joint.

Why not? Stoned or straight it seemed to make no difference. Life had become one psychedelic fantasy, one long episode of *The Twilight Zone*, where I had undoubtedly been beamed up into another dimension.

Vinny Palladino: the madman who haunted Duane's nightmares, the demon who'd forced him into exile, the gun-toting brute into whose stomach Duane had plunged his switchblade. The very same Vinny Palladino had now reached a satori of some kind; achieved nirvana in India, sat at the holy feet of none other than the Maharishi Mahesh Yogi. Could I believe it, or was it just another twist, another masquerade — a screaming shrieking punch line to a joke I still didn't understand?

■

Outside, the streets of Buffalo lingered in the uncertain light of early morning. Fran flicked on the radio. An eerie combination of male voices and electric vibrations. Cream. They were singing "Strange Brew."

Strange Brew
Kill what's inside of you.

It was during the rendition of that very line that Fran reached into her purse and showed me the gun she had brought along "Just for a goof. Just in case."

The music purred through the radio, smooth and seamless, warning about demons and witches and things that stick to you. Fran mouthed the lyrics, laughing as we came closer and closer to the Peace Bridge. There was no way I was crossing the border with a deadly weapon. I couldn't. Leon's voice was echoing inside my brain.

Be careful, Renee. Don't make this same mistake again.

I made Fran pull over while we discussed it.

"Just tell me what the point is?" I asked.

"Does everything have to have a point? Does everything have to follow some scientific line of reasoning?"

I had a horrible feeling Fran wanted to talk about the cosmos, karma and Vinny Palladino, a.k.a. Baswan Ghee, while I stared into the barrel of Marshal Sherman's stolen Smith and Wesson .38. She didn't say a thing. She just sat there, letting the wind blow her blond hair into free form kinetic sculptures, while I brooded. That's when I saw the irony of the moment. I'd always pictured myself as an outlaw, a rebel. Sort of a Natalie Wood type waiting for her Brando. But now that it was actually happening, now that I was on the brink of a great and dangerous adventure, I was scared. My self-image was in danger of reforming itself, becoming something horrifyingly close to a running dog in a pantsuit. Fran saw all that. Maybe she *was* a witch.

"This is our chance to really live an adventure, to invent ourselves. We can be anything we want to be. Renee, you're slipping into the bourgeois, you're giving in to fear."

It was the challenge that got me, I'm sure of it, because all at once I saw myself locked into the kind of life Fran and I loathed, the kind of life we swore we'd never live: nine to five jobs, mortgages and baby strollers, golf games and country club dances. It was as if all that was right around the corner, instant identity. If I made the wrong turn and backed out, my decision would be irreversible, it would put into motion a domino theory of destroyed possibilities. No more Natalie Wood. No more fantasies of life on the Left Bank, in the East Village, on a pig farm in California. I would immediately return to start, to a split-level in Long Island, to a premature, middle-aged hell.

"Just tell me the gun's not loaded," I whined.

Fran never had a chance to answer. She'd been inching closer and closer to our destination.

A man in a uniform was leaning toward us. His frowning face was pockmarked and scarred. He walked around the car, opened the trunk and asked us where we were born and why we wanted to cross the border.

Fran was unflappable.

"Denver, Colorado. Art galleries in Toronto." All lies, but very nicely done.

Crater Face pushed his head farther inside the car.

"What about you?"

"Long Island, New York. Art galleries." All right, so I was still intimidated by authority figures.

He let us pass. Just like that we'd crossed the bridge into another country. Fran had a .38 with no serial number in her purse and beneath my jacket were two clipboards with stolen United States census forms. I guess that counted for something. Maybe even a felony.

I knew, as Fran sped into the dust of Ontario, that I was hurtling headlong into the unknown and with each lurch forward, I was burning my trail behind me.

TWENTY-NINE

It looked like something out of an Andrew Wyeth painting. One of those eerie, rural landscapes where every blade of grass seemed to inhabit a separate and distinct world.

The barn was a washed-out red and there was a run-down farmhouse with roosters and chickens clicking and clucking every which way. There was no name plate on the door, no number and no bell. It bore the unmistakable earmark of a place people wanted to forget.

"Let's get out of here," I said.

Fran bit at the insides of her cheeks. She twisted her lips and ran her hands along the steering wheel. For a crazy, hopeful second, I thought that maybe she'd come to her senses, realized the insanity of it all and was ready to turn around and go home. But no. She surveyed the ramshackle surroundings, taking in everything from the barn to the free-range chickens. Then she turned off the engine and combed her hair.

"How do I look?"

What I wanted to say was: You look absolutely mad, like some unbalanced lunatic dressed in a pseudo-uniform, ready to invade the peaceful, rural tranquillity of two unsuspecting hayseeds.

What I said was: "Why don't we pull into the driveway alongside the house?"

Fran moved the car closer to the barn, where a make-shift driveway revealed a crude shed that housed a worn and mud-splattered late-model white Corvair.

They were probably home. Shit. It was the middle of the afternoon. I was hoping for emptiness. No answer. A house bereft of inhabitants.

Fran arranged her clipboard, her satchel and her blouse. She was the picture of calm, which surprised me. After all, she was about to confront a great, unsolved mystery — a secret that had been hidden from her all her life. She was acting as though she was just making a routine business call. Then it hit me. Fran was in character. She really believed in the persona. She was transformed, converted, reinvented. Even her voice sounded a little different.

"Bring the pencils," she said. Then as if that wasn't quite right she added: "Did we forget anything? Eh?"

I wanted to puke. Eh? That was Fran's idea of being Canadian.

She knocked on the door. No one answered. Through the patchwork screen we could see a kitchen. It was bare and plain. The ancient linoleum was scrubbed pattern-less. A simple table was set with coffee cups and plates. There was a napkin holder carved from wood and shaped like a cow.

Fran pushed her way inside.

"Hel-loo. Anyone home?"

*   *   *

After that things got fuzzy. They happened, but in a slow, jerky way, a disconnected, unsettling chain of events. I was prepared for something unusual, but nothing, not even my wildest imaginings, could have prepared me for Marianna Johnsten.

For one thing, she had no front teeth. When she smiled, which she did the moment she saw Fran, she revealed a black hole just beneath her upper lip. And she was old. Old as in wrinkled, worn, beaten down by life. Her hands were red and raw, the nails shriveled by some unknown fungus, the knuckles covered with scabs and bruises. She wore a shapeless house dress and her hair was covered with a faded bandanna. Fran was shocked when she saw her. Her reaction, imperceptible to Marianna, was evident to me. There was this slight quivery motion around her chin. And her fingers twitched like tiny insects. Something was getting in, slipping beneath the persona. Marianna Johnsten was a bad dream; a decaying, wretched, shell of a woman, a character from a gothic novel, a freak on the back page of a tabloid newspaper. She was certainly no one you'd ever expect to know, let alone be related to, sort of.

I think Fran was considering that when she cleared her throat and began asking her list of questions. I lurked in the shadows, trying to be unobtrusive, while I watched Fran's every move. There was no telling what she might do. Marianna was a shock all right, but the really mind-boggling thing about this was that Fran's father had been her husband. They had produced a son.

That's when my imagination took over and I pictured the obvious scenario: Mel locked in a conjugal embrace with this moldy beast, her fungus-encrusted hands moving along his skin, the two of them laughing as they commingled on a dilapidated bed in this godforsaken farmhouse; Marianna flashing toothless grins as Mel whispered sweet nothings in her ear.

Of course that's not how it happened. Not according to Marianna, who despite her discomforting appearance was not only articulate, but almost eloquent. She never even noticed me. It was Fran who caught her attention, who riveted her gaze, and who I was sure she identified almost immediately. But she never let on. She answered Fran's questions, allowing her own tragic story to take shape between the lines.

She was forty-two years old. Impossible as it appeared, she swore to it, never once hesitating on the month and year of her birth. She had married at sixteen and produced a son, Carter, nine months later. She had been a beauty then, long and lean with blond hair that hung to her waist. Her husband was a simple man, a farmer. The way she told it, it was an American love story, an agrarian dream. The three of them: living on the land, sleeping in a big feather bed that had been passed down from her great-great-grandmother, dreaming their dreams and planning for the future. Then disaster struck. One afternoon as she came in from the fields, Carter trotting happily behind her, she noticed the battered blue pickup truck was gone. Eight months pregnant at the time, she tried not to panic. But panic she did, because as soon as she entered the farmhouse, she knew something was horribly, terribly wrong. Clothes were flung everywhere, furniture was upended, cupboards were open and even the great feather bed had been overturned.

Her husband was nowhere to be seen.

Her first thought was that the place had been robbed and her husband had fled for his life. Five days later, when he hadn't returned, and she realized the only things that had been taken were his clothes, his tools and their life savings, which had been tucked beneath the feather bed, she came to her own desperate conclusion.

Her husband had left her.

Abandoned and grief-stricken, she had a bloody and painful miscarriage, which Carter watched in horror. He was never the same after that. Silent and moody, he withdrew into himself, refusing to speak and turning his face to the wall when spoken to.

Weeks passed and Marianna heard nothing from her husband. It was almost as if he'd disappeared into thin air. She tortured herself, asked question after question, but came up with no clue, no reason why he'd left. Until a distant relative, on her husband's side, told her something that made it all fall into place. A little girl, only fifteen years old, had run away from home the same day Marianna's husband had disappeared. The girl had left a note. She was in love and leaving with the man whose baby she was carrying. They were going east to start a new life. The girl's name was unimportant, it didn't matter. What did matter was the fact that she'd been spotted on the interstate heading east in a blue pickup truck piled high with belongings. And that wasn't the end of it, nor the worst of it. Marianna knew the girl, had known her all along. She was no stranger, no mysterious homewrecker. She had been Carter's babysitter; she'd helped Marianna shell peas and pick corn. She was more than a neighbor, less than a friend. She was her husband's second cousin.

*   *   *

Things got weird after that. Fran started shaking. Her lips trembled and her hands flew in every direction. She talked a mile a minute, but nothing she said made much sense. Marianna ignored her. Spitting through the black space between her teeth, she finished her story.

Less than a year later, penniless and plagued by complications from her miscarriage, Marianna traced her husband to Buffalo. Searching for a cheap place to live, she crossed the border to Canada and found a run-down farm the owner let her rent for a song. She filed for divorce, insisting on some recompense for her misery. Dutifully, Mel sent the checks, one hundred dollars a month, barely enough to keep her and Carter alive. She'd worked as a maid and a waitress, a dishwasher and a short-order cook. Carter had quit school at fifteen to help eke out a living from the farm. He mopped floors in the local K mart five nights a week.

Marianna stopped talking when Fran, now white as a ghost, and covered with an odd, prickly sweat, pushed her chair away from the table and shrieked that she had to go. Something about urgent government business. I held her elbow as we walked out the door.

The bright sunlight was an assault, a smack in the face. In the dingy, unlit kitchen Marianna's tale of misery had seemed like a gothic yarn, someone else's bad dream. Outside, with the chickens clucking and the roosters pecking, it became something else: a surreal tale of betrayal and brutality, an impossible and eerie chain of events that destroyed three lives while it gave birth to a fourth. Fran's spiritual quest had come to a screeching, gut-wrenching halt. She had gone too far this time, pushed herself to the edge — maybe even over it.

I was watching her face for some indication, some reaction, when I saw movement behind the makeshift garage. An arm, a leg, a shock of blond hair. I couldn't be sure. It all happened so fast, but I believe for an instant I saw him. Carter. A tall, silent apparition, an angry and palpable presence lurking in the tapering shadows.

Fran was walking rapidly toward the car. Her heels made little indentations in the bare ground. She was uncharacteristically silent, which worried me. Signs of shock, I thought. My mind was racing. Maybe she'd become catatonic. I'd have to get her to the nearest hospital, call her parents, tell them how it had happened, how she'd insisted. They'd hate me. How could I ever explain? Why hadn't I stopped her?

Fran was sitting behind the wheel of the Saab. She was moving almost normally, but the skin under her face was quivering like one of Leon's amoebas. Everything was very still. Even the chickens seemed frozen in time. Shit. I just wanted to hear her say something: open up, cry, vomit, shout, whatever she needed to do to exorcise the demons. The silence was unnerving, but my own voice failed me. I decided to wait it out, which was a mistake, because in that short space of time, it occurred to me that in some way Marianna and Fran were related, and that Carter wasn't only Fran's brother he was probably her cousin. It was a sickening turn of events, a lurid and miserable climax to an innocent search for truth. I wouldn't blame Fran if she never spoke another word, if she rolled herself up into a hard little ball and refused to communicate with the outside world ever again. Of course that would leave me with a few problems. Getting home, for one. I could barely drive an automatic, but the Saab was a stick shift. I could just picture myself explaining all this to a grinning, toothless Marianna, while Carter lurked ominously behind the garage, planning revenge. My mind was clicking off one fatal, demented scenario after another, when Fran finally turned to me. Her face had calmed down. Her hands seemed steady. She put the key in the ignition and cleared her throat. Here it comes, I thought, she's finally found the words. Grief, guilt, remorse, agony: I was ready for anything. I was steadfast, a rock. My eyes were riveted to her lips. I didn't want to miss a syllable.

She pressed on the gas and revved the engine.

"Renee," she said, pausing dramatically, "are you as hungry as I am?"

THIRTY

Fran gunned the Saab, leaving a strip of burned rubber in Marianna Johnsten's driveway. She drove as if we were being chased, flying along the one-lane highway in excess of 80 mph. There wasn't a restaurant in sight. Finally, low on gas, and claiming starvation, she stopped at a small roadside gas station/convenience store. Fran still hadn't uttered a word about our encounter with Marianna and I was reluctant to press. She was functioning. We were headed back toward the Peace Bridge. There would be plenty of time to chew things over in the U.S.A.

Fran asked me what I wanted. I wasn't particularly hungry, but I agreed to come along and see if anything tickled my appetite.

The store was one of those typical, dusty little places, well stocked with soda, milk, and all sorts of pretzels and roadside munchies. A fat, middle-aged man wrapped in a white apron leaned wordlessly over the cash register. I surveyed the potato chips and cream-filled cookies. Fran checked out the refrigerator section. I was considering a bright blue bag of cheese twizzles when I just happened to look up and catch Fran from the corner of my eye. She was slipping a container of prune whip yogurt into her satchel.

It was a sloppy move. Amateur night in Dixie. She was breaking all the rules. Our rules. I was pissed. I'd never seen Fran actually cop anything before and it was fascinating, like catching her making funny faces in a mirror. I wanted to look away, but I found myself staring, transfixed. I wasn't alone. The clerk, catching Fran's image in one of those round reflectors mounted in the corner, suddenly sprang into action. He moved quickly, rushing between the rows of cellophane bags, his ungainly form brushing against packages, knocking everything from gum balls to dog food from the shelves onto the hardwood floor. Like Moby Dick in a white apron, he crashed through an ocean of carbohydrates, heading straight for his prey. Fran remained oblivious. She was in a daze. Latent shock. She continued to pile cartons of prune whip into her purse. I screamed. She ran. We both flew for the door, Moby Dick in hot pursuit. We got to the car in time. Almost. The great white whale had me by the arm. Fran was already behind the wheel and ready to roll. For a horrible instant, I thought she might just pull away, leaving me to suffer for her crime. I was wrong. *W-H-A-P-P!* I was hit across the face with a container of prune whip. Moby Dick loosened his grasp, I slipped into the car. We were ready to leave. Not quite. Now the furious fat man had his hand clenched around the door handle. Fran flung

another container of prune whip. The street was beginning to look like a bad case of diarrhea. The clerk was
stunned but not deterred. That's when Fran got mean.

"Get your fuckin' hands off my car," she was screaming now, a hard, criminal scream.

No one moved. The whale held fast, frozen to the car
door. Fran reached into her bag. More prune whip? No. Bullets. She flashed the gun. I had no idea it was loaded. I'm
not sure what Fran was thinking, but thank God she fired
into the air. Moby Dick shrank into a tadpole and ran for his
life. We pulled away, leaving streaks of shit-colored yogurt
and smoking bullets in our wake. Fran fired off the rest of
the barrel, shrieking some incomprehensible jibberish
about Bonnie and Clyde, McKinley and the anarchist's
handkerchief, as we disappeared into the dust.

I was stunned into silence. Fran was energized. Her face
was flushed with excitement. She talked nonstop, a speed-
induced rap about outlaws and justice and living on the
edge. I longed to be free of her, to be back in my own life.
Leon was right. Once again I promised myself I would
move, change my phone number, disappear into the
brooding masses of academic life. Never again would I
make a move without my brother's consent. I had rebelled,
denounced him. Now I was a fugitive, speeding toward
the border with an armed madwoman. The border. I had
forgotten that. I grabbed Fran's free arm. My fingers left
marks in her flesh. She flinched.

"How're we gonna get over the Peace Bridge?"

"Drive, how else?"

"Are you totally crazy? That guy must have reported us

by now. We'll be in the slammer in two seconds." I was on the verge of tears.

Fran swerved, pulled over to the side of the road and cut the engine. She stared at me.

"Renee, are you all right?"

"Am *I* all right? You almost killed someone."

"Pul-ease. It was nothing. A harmless *pas de deux*. He never saw the back of the car. For all we know, he thinks we're two wild Canadian teenagers out for kicks. I'm sure it happens all the time."

"*All the time?*" There was no use answering her. She was in another world, another universe, an alien galaxy. That she could think that getting bombed with yogurt, shot at and robbed by two women dressed in suits was all within the concept of ordinary proved she had completely lost her mind. I should have known better. Her confrontation with her father's past had overloaded her mind. Her chromosomes had been singed. Brain damage. Leon, Leon. You were so right.

I searched furiously for a way out. I would tell them I'd had no choice. I was an unwitting captive kidnapped by a brain-damaged crazy woman speeding through Canada, her sordid past nipping at her heels. That would be my alibi. I was a hostage, not a guilty accomplice. Leon would testify to my weak will and easily deluded mind.

As it turned out, Fran was right. We glided over the Peace Bridge as smoothly as butter slipping into a hot skillet. The border guards didn't even pull us over to check the trunk. They waved us through.

"What did I tell you?" Fran smirked.

I was too numb, too frozen with rage and fear to answer.

When we drove up to Days Park, Wesley and his friend Bagwan/Vinny were seated on the curb. I rubbed frantically at the last traces of prune whip that clung stubbornly to my blouse and matted unattractively in my hair. Fran waved flirtatiously. The nerve! And I had actually been worried about her, concerned about the trauma she'd experienced.

"Want a toke?" Wesley asked as he approached the car.

Fran threw her head back and laughed. It wasn't a normal laugh. It bordered on the hysterical. No one seemed to notice. But I could see what was happening — how Fran was changing.

Look for the signs, Leon tells me. Her smile is fake. Her voice is different. And what she says, the way she acts. Lies. All lies.

While Fran leaned over the side of the car, gleefully filling her lungs with marijuana, I took care of business.

Silently, and invisibly, I reached into her bag, slipped the .38 and a round of bullets into my purse and disappeared into the dusk. It was perfect. She never saw a thing.

I had to do it. It was a matter of self-preservation. A way to stay one step ahead.

Leon would have approved.

THIRTY-ONE

Nickel Bag was overjoyed to see me. Jumping up on his hind legs, he covered my face with sloppy dog kisses. Sherman left a note that he'd walked him at 6 P.M. It was now 8:15. I figured I had some time to take a shower and relax.

I slipped the stolen .38 and the bullets under my mattress, threw off my clothes, which still reeked of prune whip, and walked purposefully toward the shower. I wasn't going to think about anything but the cool water, the relaxing tingle, the soft foam of soap and the heavenly isolation of the tiled bathroom. I was alone at last — except for Nickel Bag who followed me loyally into the bathroom.

About midway through my rinse cycle, the dog started to bark. Not harmless woofs, but loud threatening growls. I turned the water off and listened. Nickel Bag grred and arrfed, grred and arrfed. If there was a canine Morse code, this was definitely it. I shook the water from my ears. That's when I heard it. Footsteps, running sounds. Someone was in my apartment.

*   *   *

I grabbed a towel. "Who's there?"

No answer.

The doorknob turned. This was about to become a sequel to *Psycho*, when Nickel Bag leaped at the door, growling and barking like nobody's business. I retreated into the shower. The footsteps grew louder, then disappeared. Nickel Bag flung himself at the door one last time for good measure.

When I was sure whoever it was had gone, I made a beeline for the bedroom. The gun was right where I'd left it. Nothing had been touched.

At this point in the movie that had become my life, I had lost the ability to conjecture. It could have been anyone: Fran, Sherman, Duane, Barry, the mailman. I was too confused, too lost in a swirling muddle of suspects, car chases, petty crimes and lurid family secrets to care. I wanted out.

Grabbing Nickel Bag by the neck, I attached his leash, threw on a pair of jeans and a shirt and made for the door. I had no destination in mind. Then I had second thoughts, turned around and stuck the .38 in my pants. I counted out five bullets and put them in my breast pocket. I wasn't completely mad, just scared shitless.

I held my breath as I passed Fran's apartment. Lucky for me, the door was closed. I didn't hear any music or noise. Maybe Fran had fallen into a deep and, I hoped for her sake, dreamless sleep.

When I reached the landing I saw a familiar-looking girl sitting on the stoop. Then she turned around. It was Duane. His long hair was freshly washed and hanging loose in the breeze.

"Where you been?" he asked.

"Were you just in my apartment?"

Duane reached out and gave Nickel Bag a friendly pet.

"No way. Someone get in there again?"

In lieu of an answer, I lifted my shirt, exposed my midriff and pointed to the pistol.

"Wanna tell me what's going on?"

I didn't, but there was no one else to turn to. What I gave Duane was a condensed version of the day's activities, a sort of Monarch Notes of my trip to Canada with Fran. Duane just shook his head.

"I told you that chick was nuts."

Why, I asked myself, did everyone see this but me? Was it some sort of sisterly blindness? A fatal character flaw? I was in no mood for self-analysis. Someone was stalking me and I had a stolen .38 stuffed into my waistband. I was nervous and the bulge made me uncomfortable. I was beginning to cramp.

"Give me the gun," Duane said. "You go to the store, get some wine and I'll wait for you upstairs."

"In my place?"

"Yeah. Whoever broke in may just come back. I'd like to be there."

"Maybe you should take the dog and I should take the gun."

Duane laughed.

"Don't be so sure. This dog saved my life."

"Good. Then you take him."

I ran my hand through Nickel Bag's matted orange fur and handed the gun to Duane. He slipped it into his pants like a real pro, gave me the peace sign and walked upstairs. He never looked back. I wish he had, because halfway through the park, I realized the bullets were still in my shirt pocket. But it was too late, Nickel Bag was already crouched into position beneath a dying elm. What the hell, I thought. Duane had a knife. Besides, whoever it was had probably given up terrorizing me for the night.

On the way back from the liquor store, I spotted the local guru. Not Wesley, but his spiritual master, Bagwan Ghee. He'd already drawn a crowd of mesmerized disciples. I made a mental note to tell Duane that his former nemesis, none other than the villainous Vinny Palladino, had been transformed by peace and love and a six-month sojourn to India.

Keeping that happy thought in mind, I took the front stairs in two giant steps. Nickel Bag, catching my good mood, leaped onto the stoop as if he were still a pup. Things were looking up. Until I reached the second floor.

Something was definitely wrong. The door to my apartment was open. There were no sounds coming from the living room. No music, no conversation. I bent down on one knee and whispered in Nickel Bag's ear: "You go in first." It was ridiculous. As if a dog could understand. What kind of command was that? Nickel Bag scratched his balls. "Go!" I hissed. "Tell me what's going on." He licked my face and sat down. I pushed his rear end toward the open door. "GIT!" It was something I'd once heard Kitty say to Matt Dillon on *Gunsmoke*. Nickel Bag must have seen the same episode in reruns, because he sprang into action.

I waited in the darkness, listening for the familiar sound of Duane's voice, for the great belly laugh that would tell me it was all a big joke, everything was all right. All I heard was whimpering. Nickel Bag's idea of sending me a message. I prayed I was right. The dog had saved my life once, why would he fool me now?

I touched the bullets in my shirt pocket. No dog, no gun. I walked in totally unarmed. At first I didn't see anything. Only the kitchen light at the very end of the hall was on. Duane had been sitting in the dark. Probably watching the sunset. A purple glow filtered in across the living room. Duane was positioned in the big armchair facing the window. His back was toward the door. His long hair, which only moments before had been freshly washed and nearly dry, glistened in the moonlight. I walked toward him, reached out and touched his hair. Blood. Nickel Bag licked it off the floor, Duane's hands, the arm of the chair. Then I saw the knife. It was imbedded in a space between Duane's shoulder and his neck.

He was still alive. His eyes were open. I could see his chest rise and fall. He was breathing. The gun was jammed into his waistband. He'd never had a chance. I touched his face.

"Duane. It's me. Renee."

He made odd, bubbling sounds. Spittle gathered on his lower lip.

"Vinny," he said. I knew that was impossible. I'd just seen Vinny. Duane had been stabbed from behind. He probably never saw his attacker.

I grabbed the phone and dialed the hospital. I wasn't sure what I said, exactly how coherent I was, but a female voice asked me for the address. An ambulance would be by.

I waited. Duane sat motionless. His skin was cold and clammy. Five minutes passed. The street was silent. I dialed the hospital again. There was a busy signal. Then I

did something I thought might save Duane's life, something that came naturally, that made perfect sense at the
time. I called Leon. The phone rang once. No roommate.
No Ruth. This time it was Leon himself.

"Leon, I'm in trouble." There was silence on the other
end. I could sense the lemon-look, feel it through the
phone. "Don't hang up," I said. Then I told him Duane
had been stabbed. Leon's voice was strong and clear, no
sarcasm, no lectures.

"Call the hospital. Get an ambulance."

"I already did that. Twice. They haven't come yet.
What can I do?"

"Is he in shock?"

"How can I tell?"

Like a textbook, Leon listed the signs: cold clammy
hands, dilated pupils, shallow breathing. He was right on
target.

"Yes," I said.

"Okay. Get him out of the chair. Elevate his legs."

I placed the receiver on the floor while I carefully
slipped Duane from the armchair. A trail of blood ran
from the wound onto my hands, my clothes, the floor.

"He's bleeding pretty bad."

Leon cleared his throat. "I think you should pull the
knife out."

It was too much to consider. "I can't do that, Leon."

"Well if your friend is losing as much blood as you say,
you could help him by putting pressure on the wound. Go
get a towel."

I ran to the bathroom, praying the ambulance would be
there when I returned. No luck. While Leon gave me in-

structions, I put my hand on the knife. It was a big one. Not a switchblade, more like a kitchen knife, like people use to carve turkeys. Duane stared at me, a glazed, helpless stare. I pulled. The knife came out easily. "Soft tissue," Leon said. Then he explained how to put pressure on the wound. Where the hell was the ambulance? More than ten minutes had passed. Duane could bleed to death.

"Renee." Leon was shouting into the receiver. "I want you to get out of there as soon as the ambulance comes. I want you to get some protection."

"I have a dog."

"What does that mean?"

I wasn't sure myself, so I told Leon what else I had. A gun.

"Do you have bullets?"

I felt the small lumps in my shirt pocket.

"Yes."

"Do you know how to load it?"

"I'm not sure." The truth was, I was confused, shaken. The bullets slipped through my fingers, spilling onto the floor.

"Renee, Renee!" Leon was screaming now. "What kind of gun is it?"

What kind of gun? All of a sudden Leon was a weapons expert.

"A Smith and Wesson .38." I fumbled with the bullets, forgetting how to open the barrel and load the gun. I was doomed. Then Leon began to talk. His voice was softer now, calm and steady.

"Is there a little button on the side?"

"Yeah."

"Okay. That's the cylinder release. Push it. When the barrel swings out, put the bullets in those empty slots, then snap it shut."

Amazing. Leon was right. His range of knowledge was surprising. Either that, or he knew more about all this than he let on. I was about to ask him, when the ambulance pulled up. Red lights whirled, three medics raced up the stairs, a stretcher crashed through the door. Duane was lifted up and carried away.

"Leon, they're here. I have to go."

He shouted something about catching the first plane out of Chicago, about coming to get me.

"Don't worry. It's all over. Really. I'll call you as soon as I can."

I reached the ambulance as it was ready to leave. The medics had already hooked Duane up to an I.V. They said he was breathing. He'd lost blood but his vital signs were strong.

"Let me ride with him to the hospital."

"You next of kin?" The medic looked annoyed, as if I was some ghoul attracted by the sight of blood. I should have lied.

"No, I'm his friend."

"Drive to the hospital!" With that he slammed the door.

The ambulance pulled away with Duane inside. I had a horrible sinking feeling it would be the last time I'd see him.

Nickel Bag had followed me out to the street. He nuzzled up against my leg. As I bent down to hug him, I saw a splotch of Duane's blood on the pavement. That's when I realized what had probably happened. Whoever had been in my apartment had returned. They'd seen Duane from the back. In the unlit room with his long hair hanging loose, they'd mistaken him for me.

It wasn't Duane's old enemy. It was mine. But who? My midnight caller? The nut case who'd written my name in his own blood? The freak who jerked off in my underwear?

I was considering the possibilities, when Nickel Bag curled back his lip and began growling. Someone was there. The park was almost dark now. Amazingly, the ambulance hadn't drawn a single spectator. I pulled the gun from my jeans and brandished it in the uncertain light.

"See," I screamed. "See this!"

A figure moved in the far corner of the park.

Nickel Bag was off and running. Without thinking, I followed breathlessly behind him. Chasing a potential murderer was not a good idea. But I was fresh out of good ideas. Besides, the action helped me forget, the running gave me a purpose, pumped me with courage and adrenaline. Halfway down Allen Street, I ran out of steam. Nickel Bag had disappeared into the night. I was alone with my gun, my bloodstained clothes and a vague feeling — an indescribable sensation of a circle tightening slowly around me.

THIRTY-TWO

Although I wanted to, I knew visiting Duane in the hospital wouldn't be a terrific idea. He'd been stabbed. There would be questions, police, an investigation — everything I wanted to avoid. I figured I'd wait awhile, then call.

I walked around Allentown for what seemed like hours. Aimless, hopeless, dogless: I was a sitting duck, a tragedy waiting to unfold.

Nothing happened. No knives flashed at me from the shadows, no footsteps followed mine, no bony clasp locked me in a deadly embrace. If I didn't check the bloodstains on my blouse and jeans from time to time, I might have convinced myself that the last twenty-four hours had been one long life-like hallucination. No such luck. The blood was real, and if ever for a minute I doubted anything, I had only to run my fingers over the loaded barrel of the revolver.

How did I get myself into this mess?

*   *   *

Light was seeping through the thick cover of clouds. Allentown looked like some run-down honky tonk, a forlorn collection of clapboard and rotting brick. A few filthy hippies snored on the hard ground of Days Park. I stood in front of my apartment building. The first thing I noticed was Fran's car. It was gone. The second thing was a heap of orange fur rolled into a muddy ball beside the front door. Nickel Bag returned. So much for the good news. The bad news was fatigue. I was exhausted, drained, my nerves were frayed and I desperately had to go to the bathroom. There was no other choice. Grabbing Nickel Bag by the collar, I returned to the scene of the crime. This time the corridor wasn't empty. Sherman was pacing in front of my apartment. His door was wide open. Cream was singing "Strange Brew." It was the second time I'd heard that song recently. I took it as an omen.

"Fran was here. She left you this note."

I pushed Sherman aside. I was through with Fran's madness.

"Get out of my way. I'm tired."

"I think you'd better read it."

My eyes were bloodshot, my bladder burned, there was a dry, bitter taste in the back of my mouth.

"Why don't you read it to me?"

Sherman cleared his throat: "Renee, Have found Barry. Come quickly. I'm at Rex's place on Delevan. Will wait for you."

If I'd had the strength, I would have laughed. So Fran was at it again. Sleuthing. Digging up old memories. Would nothing stop her?

I was about to tell Sherman to drop dead, when he did

something so out of character, so totally unexpected, I, who by now should have been beyond shock, was shocked. He cried. Big, flat, comic-book tears welled up in his dilated eyes.

"Please, Renee. Here, take my car. You have a right to know."

Nickel Bag crouched down and began to whimper. A whining dog and a sobbing man. What an unexpected turn of events.

Sherman was bawling now. It was embarrassing. Obviously, something was eating away at him, had been for some time. He pushed the keys into my hand. Wordlessly, I took them and headed for the street.

Sherman's car, a 1965 black Dodge Charger, was gassed up and ready to go. Lucky for me, it was an automatic. Of course he refused to come along. This was my nightmare. I led Nickel Bag into the front seat, while I figured out how to turn on the ignition. A simple task for most people, but for someone who'd failed Driver's Ed. in high school and had never passed her road test, driving at night without a license was more of a challenge than a mundane exercise in simple eye-hand coordination.

The car lurched forward, crashing into the rear bumper of the vehicle unlucky enough to be parked in front of me. Nickel Bag careened off the front seat, falling with a thump onto the floor. A little less gas this time.

I turned the wheel, pressed ever-so-lightly on the gas pedal and found that it was just like driving a bumper car in an amusement park. Steer and drive. Steer and drive. I was doing just that, moving at my own unique and ad-

mittedly jerky pace toward Rex's place when a powder
blue Mustang started flashing its lights. It was a convertible. Brand new. Probably some wise-ass fraternity boy —
a bourgeois rich kid left over from the fifties. I ignored
him. But he was relentless, tailgating me and blowing his
horn. The streets were pretty much empty. Why didn't he
just pass me? I would have pulled over, but I'd finally
gotten into the mesmerizing rhythm of steer, drive and
was reluctant to stop. Besides, bloodstreaked and exhausted, I was in no mood to fend off some wise-ass potential pickup.

I stopped at the light on Elmwood. There was no
choice. It was red. The blue Mustang was right behind me,
honking and blinking and causing a racket. Then in the
midst of all that blaring and glaring, I was sure — no,
positive — I heard someone call my name. I glanced at the
dimly lit streets. A few long-haired students, an old man
walking a beagle. No one waving, no one I could remotely
identify. Then it hit me. The asshole in the Mustang. He
smashed into my — or should I say Sherman's — rear end.

Instantaneously, he hopped from the front seat and
came toward me. No way was I going to get involved in an
accident now. Not without a driver's license and not with
a stolen, loaded revolver in my jeans. I gunned the engine,
yanked on the steering wheel, and went directly up onto
the sidewalk, crashing into a fire hydrant. Nickel Bag
leaped from the car. I followed. I was already at Bidwell
Parkway. I figured I could make it to Rex's house in a few
minutes. But the guy in the Mustang wasn't letting up. He
sped after me, his car making serious grinding sounds. I
snaked onto the sidewalk, checked out back alleys and

was just about to try some clever and desperate diversionary tactic, when I heard him call my name. I froze. In the dim lamplight of Elmwood Avenue, my pursuer emerged from his powder blue vehicle. I fingered the trigger of the .38. So here I was face-to-face with my tormentor — the madman who had stabbed Duane and who had been threatening me for months.

This was it. The final showdown. I was Gary Cooper, Marlon Brando, Annie Oakley. I pulled the loaded gun from my jeans. Nickel Bag growled on cue.

"Hold it right there!"

Something was wrong. For a minute I was sure I knew this guy. He threw his hands into the air. "Renee, Renee, it's me." He wore pressed chinos, a pastel polo shirt and wing-tip shoes. He had white walls around his ears. Impossible. I hadn't known anyone who dressed like that since high school.

So now I had him. I was finally in control, finally the perpetrator instead of the hapless victim, the do-er rather than the do-ee.

That's when he started whimpering. Like a trapped animal, like the pathetic jerk that he was. I put down my gun. Now I recognized him. He was my brother-in-law. Noel Willinger. I hadn't forgotten how he'd left me stranded on the dance floor at Carole's wedding, how he'd humiliated me in front of hundreds of people. Suddenly Noel became more than a caricature, a laughable cartoon, a ridiculous stereotype. He was a symbol. Noel Willinger became all the TV people, all the perfect kids from perfect families who'd always made me feel like a misfit and an outlaw. His very presence was a sneering taunt — a reminder that

I would always be different, that everything in my life had preordained the weirdness of this moment.

I faced him.

"What the hell are you doing here?"

"Same as you. I'm looking for Barry."

I had a feeling there was more to this than Noel was letting on. So he was looking for Barry too. How odd. I think right then, as I stood, gun in hand, eyeing the snake who'd married Barry's sister, I began to get my first inkling of something very rotten — that sinister truth just beneath the surface.

When we got to the two-story boardinghouse overlooking the cemetery, I saw right away that Fran's car was parked beside some low-hanging trees. There was another car hidden in the shadows. It looked familiar, but by now my mind was racing. I was too pumped up with adrenaline, too crazed with power and fear to take in the small details.

Lights were on downstairs. Upstairs it seemed dark.

"Wait here," I ordered Noel. He was a sculpture frozen in a bucket seat.

Nickel Bag followed me as, bending low, I crept through the shrubs and planned to get close enough to peer into the curtainless windows. That's when I saw it. The pink Rambler. It was parked way up on the other side of the house facing the cemetery. Barry was in there, all right. I felt a not unfamiliar constriction in my chest. Suddenly, it was difficult to breathe. I could hear the sounds of the ocean in my ears. My body seemed out of control. I didn't want to faint. Not now.

But the smell was everywhere. The smell of something dead coming to life. The smell of horror.

This time it came from the ground. Vibrating. Pulsating upward. Rushing from beneath the trees. The night air thickened with an inexplicable darkness.

And I remembered.

It is late afternoon when I walk by the purple room. The house is strangely silent. I have learned to be wary of the silence. So I tiptoe. The purple room is bathed in a dreamy summer light. Iridescent. I am transfixed. I am not sure if what I see is real.

They are standing in the silence and the light. He is facing her. She is unmoving. A statue. Her face is twisted in a way I have never seen before. I look again.

His blue-black hair is combed back away from his face. His mouth is grim and expressionless. This is a moment I am not supposed to see. A darkness that was not meant for me. But I do not leave. I am beginning to understand. I know what secrets Leon has found in the drawers and the closets. I know because when I look at him, I cannot breathe.

He is wearing the dead boy's clothes.

Uncle Sidney. Leon is standing in the purple room, dressed as the dead brother.

There are no words. Only the sound I imagine in my head. Something high-pitched. An electric hum. And then I feel the burning. I remember Leon's palm against my back. This time he has done it. Pushed.

I look at her and I imagine a body falling, crashing from a high place.

In the morning we find her. I awake from the fog of a thousand nightmares. I stumble toward the living room, following the invisible odor.

Don't come in here, Renee. Stay away.

But I come anyway. And I see everything.

At first, I only notice the planter, tipped over, dirt and leaves scattered everywhere. Then I look down. She is still in her nightgown. Soft summer flannel with tiny pink flowers and pastel leaves. The leaves snake around her half-naked body, the flowers are flecked with dirt. And blood.

Don't look, Renee. Call an ambulance.

But I do look. This is worse than the fish tank. Worse than the accident.

Her body is smeared with dirt. She has stuffed it inside her ears and her nostrils. It bubbles up in a brown crust around her bloodstained lips. The razor is beside her on the rug. The cuts are deep this time. Too deep. One wrist is nearly severed from her arm.

I rush toward her. We are all dying now. Drowning in her madness. But he stops me. Leon. He grabs my arm. His fingers dig deep into my skin. Afterward, there will be bruises. Purplish marks I cannot explain. I will remember nothing.

Call the ambulance, Renee. Now.

While I dial the numbers, I watch him. He bends down beside her. He wipes the dirt from her nostrils and wraps the bloody wrist. And he is saying something. Whispering words in her ear. Her lips are moving. She is alive.

I strain forward. But their voices disappear in the hum.

I was still there, standing beneath the window, when I emerged from my memory. I rocked back and forth in the darkness, waiting for the trembling to subside.

Sitting down on the soft earth, I watched the past recede, watched it shrivel into a tiny black dot that hung suspended in the starless night. Then I waited to hear Leon's voice, waited for instructions. But there was only silence. The silence where nothing moves and nothing changes.

The ocean subsided. My breathing was steady and strong. I was alone this time. I could do this. I had to.

Balancing on tiptoes, I peered into the window. It was the kitchen. A pizza box lay ripped open on the chipped enamel table. Double cheese and mushrooms. Barry's favorite. It was half eaten. Then, bending low and scarcely breathing, I came to the next window. The bedroom. It only took one glance, one quick look, to recognize the shock of wild curls, the olive skin, the nose with the downward slope. Barry was stretched out, naked on the rumpled sheets. He was smoking a joint and he wasn't alone. There was someone beside him. A naked woman. She had the same hair, the same sloping nose and the same swarthy skin tone. It was a moment that flickered unconvincingly in the dim light. Something out of a dream. It was as if I had stepped through an imaginary force field. I was buzzing with electricity. Blazing. Burning. But this time I wasn't going to forget. There would be no vague, half-buried memories to haunt me. I was going to look — and to remember.

Reaching upward, the yellow light casting shapeless shadows on the ground beside me, I turned my back to the fathomless night and faced something primeval. Something loathsome. Something eternally forbidden.

Barry was in bed with his sister.

My mind ticked off all the evidence: our wedding night, Barry's odd, erratic behavior, his midnight phone calls, his unexplained absences, Carole's hasty marriage, the two of them dancing cheek to cheek. Clutching at my stomach, I vomited. A streak of green bile spewed across the side of the house.

When I stood up I was staring into the smug face of Noel Willinger. He looked at me with contempt. Bloodstained and reeking of vomit, I was pathetic, a wretched, crazed, marijuana-smoking hippie. He didn't say it. He didn't have to.

I could have spared him the trauma I'd just experienced, or I could have stepped aside and let him see for himself.

Suddenly, the decision was out of my hands.

As Noel shouldered his way past me, I heard a scream. Not just any scream, a bloodcurdling shriek. Fran. She was up on the roof. And she wasn't alone.

■

As I raced up to the roof, using the side entrance that bypassed the lower apartment, I felt as though I'd already penetrated the heart of darkness, seen all there was to see of the netherworld of human ugliness.

I was wrong.

* * *

When I got to the roof, I nearly lost all control. There, huddled in the corner, was Fran. And Fran.

Admittedly, it was semidark up there. The only light came from downstairs. A soft glowing arc seemed to hover over the cemetery, casting a purplish glow on the slanting roof. Nickel Bag nudged my leg. I walked closer.

"I'm going to kill you, Renee. You took everything."

There was silence. Then a scream, but it didn't come from my mouth.

What was happening here? Was this some sick joke? Some trick with mirrors? Some tilting, maniacal funhouse ride?

I squinted into the darkness, hoping to sort out form from shadow, nightmare from reality. Just then, I heard Fran's voice. She was pleading, begging, trying to cajole, convince. I moved toward her, compelled, hypnotized, the bizarre scene pulling me closer.

Through the irregular, ghostlike shadows, I located Fran. She was pinned against her own image. An arm encircled her neck. A knife flashed at her throat. A man was holding her. A slash of purple light illuminated the face. His face. Her face.

Identical.

"I'm not Renee." Fran was sobbing now.

Another voice growled in darkness. A male voice. "It's your turn to bleed."

Carter. The apparition behind the garage. The lunatic who'd run over Ned, stabbed Duane and tormented me for months.

The man with Fran's face.

I felt my fingers curl around the trigger of the .38.

Stepping into a rectangle of light, I confronted him. His hair was long and stringy, his forehead smudged with dirt and pimples.

"I'm Renee," I said.

For a moment I saw his doubt. I grasped the primitive, raw insanity of it all. Carter was Fran's brother. This had nothing to do with me. Nothing to do with Barry or Ned or Duane. It was all a grotesque, tragicomedy of errors, a drama that began when Fran's father abandoned his wife twenty years ago, when Marianna Johnsten, consumed with grief and rage, miscarried and was left to care for the half-mad, fatherless son Mel abandoned for the child his cousin was carrying. Fran.

Somehow, Carter had managed to track Fran down, had plotted her murder. But something had gone wrong. He'd confused us. It was me, not his sister, who'd become the object of his singleminded revenge.

"Renee, he thinks I'm you," Fran was shrieking now. "He read the names on the bell. Tell him. Tell him."

"She's right. *I'm* Renee. I'm the one you've been calling. I'm the one you thought you stabbed tonight."

Carter jerked away from Fran, sending her sprawling across the roof. I watched as he came toward me. Fran's flip side. The man I'd seen in the park that night with Duane. The one I'd thought was Fran in disguise.

I was calm. Sure. I was locked in the room with the spiders. I was looking down from the top of the apartment building. Now I understood. Leon had taught me well.

I was the master of the game.

I watched my own thumb as it rested against the trigger of the gun. My murderer's thumb. My good luck. I was born for this.

I fired all five bullets.

Carter careened over the slanted roof, falling through the soft top of Noel Willinger's powder blue Mustang.

Poetry in motion.

It was Fran who started screaming. I was strangely silent. I felt as though a piece of the universe had broken loose and I was floating — weightless — in some dark, alien light.

Fran took the gun from my hand. She held it close to her cheek, rubbing the barrel against her tears. I'll never know if she pulled the trigger. There were no more bullets; and if there had been a click I wouldn't have heard it over the sound of the ambulance and the squad car.

It must have been Noel Willinger who called. Fran and I were still frozen, caught in the bloody dénouement of our own creation.

They carried Carter's shattered body into the ambulance. Fran, the gun still dangling from her fingers, moved silently — willingly — into the squad car. I sat beside her. There were questions, answers, but I don't remember the words. They were just empty sounds, meaningless noise floating into the deadly night.

As we drove through the streets of Buffalo, the squad

car splitting the silence with its shrieking siren, I reached over and touched Fran's hand. She was cold. When she turned to look at me her face was somehow changed, an opaque mask with unreadable, haunted eyes.

■

I stared as the city flashed by in the glass square of the window. Everything was right where it had been before. The world hadn't been upended, ripped apart, shattered into thousands of pieces. But I saw it differently now. Everything was hard and real. The game was over. I had gone too far.

That's when I felt it dissolve. That last breathless moment of childhood. A moment that, for me, had become a dangerous commingling, a strange brew of magic — and terror.

I closed my eyes and whispered goodbye.

1974

I was on Fifty-third and Madison when I saw him. I'd just dropped Nickel Bag off at the groomer. I was racing to make an appointment at the prestigious ad agency where I was hoping to nail down a job as senior copywriter. Anyway, there he was. Barry. My ex-husband. Technically, I really shouldn't call him that since we got an annulment, which means the marriage never existed. But ex-husband sounds so much better than old boyfriend.

I didn't recognize him at first. His head was shaved and he was dressed in long robes. A tiny velvet purse was hanging from a rope around his waist. He was mumbling some sort of mantra.

"Barry, is that you?"

A line of white paint dribbled down his forehead. There was an unattractive yellowish cast to his skin.

He smiled.

"Renee."

I held out my hand in a gesture of friendship. He put his palm up in one of those holy salutes.

He'd become a disciple of a child guru, the fat one who loved chocolate ice cream.

I was afraid to ask him too much about his life — his family — his hopes for the future. We just sort of stood there, taking one another in.

Then he asked me for money. A contribution for his rotund master. When I thought about how he'd nearly ruined my life, how he'd lied and cheated, broken every rule, I felt enraged. There he was, Mr. Spiritual with what appeared to be pigeon shit dripping down his forehead, behaving as though a little loose change might release him from his past.

He smiled beneficently, like some lobotomized zombie. I looked him straight in the eyes, which seemed permanently dilated.

"Barry," I said, "I only believe in two things: sex and my credit card." With that, I turned on my heel and walked away.

■

Later, when I got back to my apartment, I wrote Fran and told her every detail. She loves letters. That's how we've been communicating for the last few years. I tell her everything, even about the one battered postcard I got from Duane, who disappeared into the Canadian underground.

I've actually seen Fran only four times in the past seven years. That's not counting the day I appeared as a voluntary witness before the grand jury that investigated "the incident." My lawyers were optimistic, even though the evidence for murder in self-defense had been overwhelming. Of course they still worried that at the last minute something might go wrong. I guess I was lucky. No indictment was handed down and I was free to go.

The hospital was the judge's idea. It was a condition of Fran's probation on the illegal weapons charge. But we all knew she would have had to go anyway. It was a nice place, really. Mel and Evelyn dipped into their savings to send her there. It wasn't one of those overbearing, Gothic-type institutions. The visiting area was plush: oriental rugs and salmon-colored roses in crystal vases. Fran stayed for almost twelve months. She was different when they released her. Toned down.

Now she's a librarian in Summit, New Jersey. She writes me long, amusing letters using a rapidograph pen on heavy bond paper. I've saved every one.

There was a time when I hoped she and Leon would finally get to meet. But it just never worked out. After Carter's death, things sort of went sour. The sixties ended for me then. I never even made it to Woodstock. Leon said it was all for the best. A hedonistic frenzy of drug-crazed adolescents, that was what he called it. For me the sixties was more complicated than that, more wonderful and more terrible. Sometimes I see those years as one wild psychedelic burst of innocence and passion. Other times I remember the sadness, the longing, the agonizing confusion. I don't think I'll ever put that part of my life, that part of history, in complete perspective. But I do know I've moved past the sixties, emerged from them. Survived.

Last month I flew down to Florida to visit Leon and Ruth. They still don't have a TV set or a good stereo, but they're both Ph.D.s now. Leon, in biophysics. Ruth, in marine biology. That's why they live in Florida, something about being close to the big fish.

When I was there, Leon seemed almost euphoric. Ruth, who's fat with their first child, planned a barbecue. While I mixed a pitcher of Bloody Marys, Leon flipped steaks. He wore a checkered apron that was printed with the words *Too Many Cooks Spoil the Broth*. He showed me around the small two-bedroom apartment. In the living room, on the piano, there was a photograph of me in my cap and gown. Beside it, in a simple metal frame, was a black-and-white snapshot of my mother and Leon. It was taken in front of the hospital, where she'd been institutionalized after she slashed her wrists. I hadn't been there, but the aunt, who came to live in the green house, had told me. It was the day of the diagnosis. The day when, finally, after endless scrutiny, my mother was explained: manic depressive with psychotic episodes.

That was the year I drifted into a half amnesia, remembering only bits and pieces of the incidents that had led to her suicide attempt. It was the year I stood on a roof in Buffalo and killed a man.

I watched Leon as he bent over the smoking grill. His blue-black hair was thinning, and there was a slight bulge around his middle. We never talked much about the past. It was something that made us both uncomfortable. But in the seven years since that fatal night in Buffalo, I'd thought about it, tried to piece the shattered fragments together, tried to understand.

When I look back into the nightmare of my childhood, I realize that Leon and I were helpless. As children we had been invisible. Leon had hardened himself against the pain. He desperately tried not to feel. He became master of the game. It was the only way for him — for both of us. Had it not been for Leon's determination, his control, the mask that he shaped to hide his own terror, I surely would not have endured.

I know now that Leon loved me. Fiercely. As brother and sister our pairing remains eternal, the depth of our attachment unspeakable. And I believe that that love — the love only a brother and sister can know — the longing for it and the devastating loss of it, was what drove my mother to madness, Fran to the brink of destruction, and Barry and Carole across a forbidden threshold from which there was no return.

Leon never knew I'd seen him that afternoon in the purple room. For the longest time, I'd repressed that day, not really sure why he'd done it. It was a memory that haunted me until I fired those five shots into Carter Johnsten. Then I learned something about desperation. I understood how Leon must have felt, knowing he was going away, knowing he had to leave me alone with my mother. There was no way he could have anticipated the outcome of his actions. But he had no choice. He risked everything for me.

After a while, I came to realize that that night in Buffalo when Leon had told me how to load a Smith and Wesson .38, that hellish night when I'd left my childhood painfully and irrevocably behind me, was the second time my brother had saved my life.

I was thinking about all that, when Leon called me into the living room. He had something to show me, a gift.

"What do you think of these, Renee?" he asked. It was

the first question Leon had asked me — besides "How are you?" — that I could remember. He was pointing to two small gray things in a glass bowl.

"Ruth found the eggs at the Marine Center. We waited for them to hatch. I thought you might like one."

They were turtles. Two tiny, just-born babies. I didn't say a word, just held out my hand. Leon carefully, lovingly picked up the smaller one. Our eyes met. There was a softness in his expression, a kindness I had never seen before.

I cupped my hand beneath the turtle, feeling its warmth in my palm. Leon stared at my fingers and smiled.

After everything I'd been through, after the shock and the violence, I wanted Leon to know that I was finally all right. I guess that's why I did it. That very day, for the first time in my life, I did something that, for me, had once been impossible — unthinkable.

I painted my nails bright red. All of them, even the thumbs.